Chapter One

Monsters Wanted!
Ogres, fel, and goblins welcome for poker game. Tonight only.
Dragon and Rose gastropub.
Ask for Monty.

DIGGER STARED AT THE crumpled bill in his hand in disbelief. The torn brown page had been posted on the market board between notices of workers needed and goods for sale. He squinted as he reread it.

What was Monty thinking? He stifled a curse. His brother was going to get himself killed.

He grabbed his two-wheeled cart and pushed it across the gravel lot as fast as he could. The wheels crunched as he maneuvered it towards the wide avenue that would take him from the slums to the Temperance District.

A card game? Really?

The more he thought about it, the angrier he became.

He and Monty had been safe for so long. What was Monty doing sticking his head up now?

He wasn't thinking, that was certain, Digger decided. Not thinking had gotten them into trouble in the first place and had cost them everything.

The shovel in the cart bounced and rattled beneath the white tarp. The street transitioned to gray cobblestone damp with moisture from the thick fog that clung to the upper levels of the tenements.

1

Diregloom. The city lived up to its nickname, from its rooftops down to its sewers. On which level did its soul reside? All of them. None of them. The onetime haven was now a prison for his kind.

Voices up ahead. The five guards weren't quiet as they headed towards him. They held lanterns and their faces were concealed by scarves or bandanas worn around their mouths. Their metal helmets and brooches for their cloaks shone orange in the light.

The first guard, a short man, raised a hand. "Halt. Where are you going with the cart? At this hour?"

A second guard who had his black bandana pulled down to his neck leaned in close. "Hey, you're no pureblood. He's fel."

Another man of the watch was coughing and he spat before peering at Digger. "You're right. Jawline. Brow. Show us your teeth."

Digger sighed and opened his mouth.

"Are you sure?" the short guard asked.

The coughing guard circled Digger once before holding his lantern up. "Look at those lower teeth. And then the orange cast to eyes like a cat. Dead giveaway. See the hint of green on the skin? Hard to notice in this light. But it looks like we have a fel out after curfew."

The guard with the black bandana prodded him in the chest. "It's after second watch. Care to explain yourself?"

"Careful," the short guard said with a snicker. "You're going to make him mad."

Digger stood dead still. "I'm on a job."

The short guard slugged him in the gut. The blow wasn't unexpected. He had been through the routine more times than he could count. He doubled over and groaned.

"You know how to address your betters."

"I'm on a job, *sir*. Body down at the Thirsty Seven Club. On Prudence Street. A notice was served to the graveyard."

Grunting, the guard threw back the tarp. "Grave duty?"

"That's what the cart's for. *Sir*."

The others chuckled.

Published by Lucas Ross Publishing.

Author website: gerhardgehrke.com

Edited by Brittany Dory at Blue Minerva Copyediting

Cover Design by Abbyanna.com

This is a work of fiction. Names, characters, places, brands, media, and incidents are either the product of the author's imagination or are used fictitiously. Any resemblance to similarly named places or to persons living or deceased is unintentional.

Midnight Monster Club

by

Gerhard Gehrke

Fallen Rogues Book One

The guard slapped him. Digger took the blow and met the guard's eyes for a moment before bowing his head. The guard wiped his gloved hand on the tarp before straightening his cloak.

"Mouthy wretch. Off with you. Next time identify yourself."

Digger kept his head low for a moment before rising. He pushed the cart away. The Dragon and Rose wasn't far from the Thirsty Seven. But the guards might follow. And having a body in his cart was an excellent way to avoid further harassment.

DIGGER CARRIED THE bundled corpse down the back stairway. The scrawny young man couldn't weigh more than a hundred pounds. Even with the heavy makeup, Digger could see the signs of hunger, drugs, and abuse.

A sharp-eyed crone watched him as he shuffled past with his burden. She followed him to his cart. A few other women were peering out the windows but turned their heads when he looked up at them.

The crone gave him a tencoin and made no comment as he covered the body with the tarp. What else was there to say? Another unknown body for the pauper's grave. If anyone would mourn, it would be in private. Few visited the place where Digger would take him. The poor soul was now invisible.

For the next few hours they would be invisible together.

The crone disappeared up the back steps. A distant bell tolled twelve.

He turned his cart and started to hurry. The job had taken too long. The Dragon and Rose was twenty minutes away if he hurried.

He had a card game to shut down.

Chapter Two

THE TAVERN SIGN DISPLAYED a dragon sniffing a rose. The two-story establishment was sandwiched between the burned skeleton of a house and a boarded-up bakery. The nearest streetlight either wasn't lit or was broken. A piece of wood had been hammered beside the entryway which read CLOSED FOR REMODELING.

Digger threw open the door.

A long wooden bar dominated the room, upon which was spread an assortment of food with rich aromas of spices, garlic, and bacon. A scrawny greenskin fel wearing a vest and cravat was picking stuffed olives off a plate and popping them into his mouth. Two others sat at a table with cards and chips in a carousel case. They held glasses of wine and had their own plates loaded with appetizers.

The vested man stuffing his face barely looked up as Digger approached.

Digger thrust his face down at him. "Place is closed. Get out."

"What are you talking about?" he asked through a full mouth.

Digger grabbed him by the coat and hauled him to the front door. The man was shouting indignities as Digger turned to face the other two.

"Both of you. Leave!"

They stared with mouths agape for a moment. When Digger took a step towards them, they both hurried out of their seats and ran past him.

Digger followed them to the door. "Diregloom guards are out in force. It's after second watch, so be careful."

The three stood outside, bewildered, before fleeing in different directions.

He let the door close behind him and walked along the bar. He was taken in by the colorful platters and the meticulous offerings on each. Clams wrapped in bacon with a cocktail sauce. Cucumber hummus canapés. Tiny quiches. Stuffed peppers. Sprigs of herbs and carved citrus rinds acted as garnish on all the plates.

While he hadn't eaten since his breakfast of cold day-old soup, the sight made his stomach uneasy. The last time he had seen food like this was at their parents' bistro before it had been closed by order of the duke. Both parents were now gone. And after what had happened, he and his brother were supposed to be in hiding.

A fel of slight build wearing a lavender frilled shirt with pinned-up sleeves emerged from the swinging door to the back, carrying a tray of brie tartines. The crusted cheese resting on slabs of bread let off a whiff of steam. He set the tray down on the edge of the bar, pausing to push the other dishes to make room. He then spent a moment turning each platter until he appeared satisfied with the arrangement.

"Monty."

Digger's brother looked up at him and then at the table with the missing card players.

"Digger? What are you doing here? Where is everyone?"

"I sent them home. Your game night is over. What are you even thinking, posting signs and inviting people here?"

"I was planning on having some fun and making friends."

"You'd risk your life for a card game?"

"I made food."

Digger let out a sigh. "That's what's going to get you in trouble. How many fel chefs are out there preparing palmiers and endive cups?"

Monty deflated. "The good ones were when there were more of us."

"Don't mumble. I hate that. If word gets out that you're still in the city..."

"I know." Monty flopped down on a chair and spread the stack of cards around. "But the same goes for you. Why haven't I seen you in so long?"

"Because I've been busy."

"Doing what? So busy you can't visit to let me know you're alive? I kept expecting to see you at the gallows on any given Saturday getting a noose around your head."

"I'm there every weekend. I just don't show up on time. I thought you just cleaned up here after the bar closed. What's going on?"

"The Dragon and Rose is out of business. Lady Sofia's starting to remodel and doesn't care what happens after hours. What do you think of the place?"

He hadn't taken the time to notice that while the walls were partially bare of paneling, the bar itself was new. A massive stained oak slab shone from a fine finish, as did the corner scrollwork. A brass foot bar ran along the bottom. The liquor shelves above the back of the bar had also been redone. The tables and furniture, which had once been nothing but benches and a few long tables of splintering wood, were now worthy of any of the new places Diregloom's pureblood tourists might patronize. A brass chandelier with a score of burning candles illuminated the bar.

Digger let out a frustrated sigh. "I think you advertising a card game and getting our people hurt is a bad plan."

The front door smashed open.

Digger turned. "We're closed. Game's off. Get out of here."

A woman with pale-green skin and wearing a dark blue cloak raced inside and vaulted the bar. Several plates spilled and shattered. She ducked down, her eyes wild with fear. She held a cloth package under an arm.

"You've got to hide me!"

Monty rushed behind the bar. "What are you doing?"

"You have a cellar?" She was yanking on a trapdoor with her one free arm but it wasn't budging.

"Stop it. It doesn't work like that. And you can't go down there."

"There's people after me. I can't let them catch me."

"Then go out the back."

Digger moved to bar or lock the front door, as a stiff breeze from outside was holding it open. As he reached for it, the door swung wide.

A man wearing leathers and a rapier on his hip stepped into the doorway. Not a soldier, Digger decided, but a mercenary or tourist pretending to be one. He gave Digger only brief consideration before pushing past him.

"We're closed," Monty said weakly.

"Where is she?"

The woman behind the counter didn't make a sound.

Monty bowed his head as he approached the man. "No girl in here, master."

The man backhanded Monty. Monty fell and held up his hands to ward off further punishment.

"She's here. I can smell her perfume. Felkind lying? Your lives are forfeit if you don't tell me where she is. Now!"

Digger went to the open door and scanned the street. There was no one else there. Only his cart waited.

He cleared his throat to get the man's attention. "Back entrance, master." He moved towards the door to the storeroom and held out an inviting arm.

The man strode towards him, his eyes narrowing.

"What did this woman do?" Digger asked.

"Not your concern, but she's a thief."

The back room had just enough light to reveal a few boxes of a food delivery along with a half-dozen wooden kegs of beer. Otherwise the shelves were mostly bare. The rear door had a steel bar across it and several latches.

The man stopped as he studied the door. "Is someone else here?"

"Just us."

"I was right on her tail. You couldn't have locked up after she left. I'll ask you one more time, fel. Where is she hiding?"

"I'm sorry, sir. She's hiding behind the bar."

The man gave Digger a hard shove, but not hard enough to knock him down. He feigned a stumble as the man returned to the common room. Digger followed on his heels.

Monty was crouching with fear in his eyes.

The man drew his rapier and rounded the bar. The fel woman was gone. But the trapdoor was in plain sight.

The swordsman pointed at Monty. "You. Open it."

Monty moved past Digger and opened the trapdoor, revealing the dark space of the bar's cellar.

"Girl, don't make me come down there. It'll go worse for you."

No one answered.

"Fetch a lantern. You fel are harboring a criminal. You'll be dancing on a rope on Saturday."

Monty was trembling. "We didn't mean to. She just barged in here. Please."

"You should have told me where she was in the first place. It would have gone well with you then. Bad enough we have to share the streets with you in this city. Share your air. But suffering with your lies? I say—"

Digger struck him across the head with a heavy pewter serving tray. The tray bent from the blow and the man sagged.

"You...dare?" he groaned.

Digger abandoned the tray and grabbed a cheese knife. He drove the short blade through the leather tunic and beneath the man's sternum. The man let out a wheeze. He looked at Digger in disbelief as if seeing him for the first time. His rapier clattered. He collapsed to his knees and keeled over.

Monty let out a whimper. "What did you do?"

"What I had to, brother. It's plus one for my cart tonight."

Chapter Three

"YOU CAN COME OUT."

Digger waited until the greenskin woman climbed up the cellar ladder. Her eyes went wide when she saw the dead man.

"You killed him."

"You brought him here."

"You know what this means for you."

"I know the law. All fel do. We're reminded of it every weekend."

She licked her lips and nodded. "I have to go. There's a back way?"

"Not so fast." He plucked the bundle from her arms.

"That belongs to me!"

Wrapped thick in a colorful scarf was another layer of plain paper wrapping. He unfolded it carefully and saw a large round watch made of gold. It had a shining face of pearly white and the numbers and arms were crusted with tiny sparkling gemstones. The second hand was turning and the watch appeared to be keeping time.

She held her hand out. "It's worth a lot."

"It's gaudy. Who'd you steal it from? Who is this guy?"

"What does it matter? It's mine now."

When she tried to take the watch from him, he shoved her aside. "This isn't any pocket piece from a nobleman's wardrobe. Where'd you find this?"

She didn't answer.

Monty had to lean on the bar to stand. He was staring at the body on the floor. "Digger? What are we going to do about him?"

"I'll bring my cart around back. I'll take care of it while the two of you clean up the mess."

The woman raised a finger to interject. "Excuse me? I need to get out of here. Give me my watch and I'll be on my way. I'll give you a cut of this once I fence it."

He wrapped the watch in the paper and shoved it into his cloak pocket. "As if we'd ever see you again. I'm holding on to this for now. You're going to help scrub the blood off the floor. You brought this down on us and you don't get to just disappear."

She went for the rapier on the floor. Digger stepped on the blade end.

"You wanted our help hiding you? This is the deal. Once our problem goes away, you get your watch. What's your name?"

"They call me Sprite."

"No handles. What's your real name?"

She sighed. "Isabel."

"Isabel? That's my brother Monty. I'm Digger."

"I thought we were sharing real names."

He ignored the comment. "We'll need an hour of your time, Isabel, and then you can run off and we can all pretend none of this ever happened."

Monty's face was pale. Then he threw up on the floor.

Digger sighed. "Make it two hours."

DIGGER WAS GRATEFUL to discover back alley access next to the burned building. He paused to listen and watch the alley. It was quiet and empty. He wheeled the cart to the back door of the tavern and uncovered the body he had taken from the brothel. The faster he could get the corpse of the tourist away the better.

Inside, Isabel had already wrapped the body up in a dusty rug taken from the center of the common room.

Monty was staring slack-jawed at the mess. Half the dishes were spilled behind the bar and now there was blood on the dark wood floor.

Digger snapped his fingers to get his attention. "Hey. Get soapy water and a stiff brush. We're going to need a lot of it. Grab every rag you can."

Monty nodded but then he hesitated, looking freshly horrified by the rolled-up body.

"Snap out of it. Get the water."

Isabel's honey-colored eyes narrowed. "Leave him alone. He's in shock."

"Fear and shock are different. If we want to avoid getting caught, he's going to have to do what I say."

She moved to pick up one side of the body. "Monty will be fine. He just needs a minute. Grab the other end."

They shuffled with the body through the back room and into the alley, where they flopped it into the cart. Digger replaced the tarp and tucked it in around the sides.

"The sword has to go too," he said.

As he followed her back inside, he saw she had the tourist's coin purse slipped into her belt.

"Really think having a dead man's purse on you is a good idea?"

"He won't need it. Now give me my watch."

Digger picked up the sword and pushed it into Monty's arms. "Put it in my cart under the tarp."

Sword in hand, Monty moved unsteadily out the back.

Isabel held her hand out. "That takes care of that. My watch?"

"We're not done. You're going to help clean first."

"You're just a bully, aren't you? Have you always treated your brother this way?"

"It's none of your business. We wouldn't be in this mess if it wasn't for you."

"I didn't kill anyone. I would have slipped away. But you had to stab him with a...what was that thing?"

"A cheese knife."

"Cheese knife. Right. Give me the watch and I'll start cleaning. But not before."

"Scrub first. Then you get your spoils." He removed the watch from his pocket and peeled the paper away. The poor lighting didn't do it justice. He imagined how much it would sparkle in sunlight. Imagined how much it must be worth. It was still gaudy, though.

"Don't get any ideas," she warned.

As a show of good faith, he set the watch on the counter. She pushed through the swinging kitchen door and then emerged with a bucket and water. With so much food on the floor, it would be impossible to mop until it was swept up.

Again, the front door banged open. Digger was expecting to see another fel ready for a card game who he'd have to shoo away, or perhaps Monty, having come around from the back.

His stomach gave a squeeze.

Standing in the doorway was a man he had seen every Saturday at the gallows but had avoided for many months.

"Apologies for slamming the door," the sheriff said, "but I saw this notice about a card game."

Chapter Four

"I THOUGHT YOU LOCKED the door," Isabel said softly.

Digger realized he hadn't. With all the excitement, he had forgotten and now he had a new problem to deal with.

The sheriff had dark hair and darker eyes beneath a broad-rimmed green felt hat. On his belt he wore a cudgel and a dagger, even though presumably he was noble-born and could have kept a sword on him. His piercing gaze took in the room as he stepped into the light. "With curfew, a game where your kind is invited at an hour like this is courting trouble."

Digger cleared his throat. "Yes sir, we know that now. The game's canceled. Everyone has gone home and we're cleaning up the establishment for the owner."

"And the owner of the place is...?"

"Lady Sofia. She's asleep."

"There's no problem here, sir," Isabel said and gave a curtsy.

"Oh, my, did I say there was?" The sheriff paused and closed his eyes. Smelled the air. "Is that bacon?"

He hovered over the bar and the remaining intact dishes. He sniffed before selecting one of the bacon-wrapped clams, which he dipped into the red sauce before popping it in his mouth.

"Delicious." He ate another. "My compliments to the chef."

Isabel was trying to mouth something to Digger but he ignored her.

"Fetch you something to drink, sir?" Digger asked.

The sheriff took a cloth napkin from a stack and dabbed his lips. "I thought this establishment was closed."

"Under renovation. The cook is new and wanted to try out some recipes."

Digger made a quick assessment of what was available. One shelf had a few bottles of spirits. On the back counter sat a small keg with a tap dripping foam.

"A glass of beer then? For you and your men?"

"I'm alone. And no, not while on duty. Have to keep a clear head. So what was the game tonight?"

"Dealer's choice."

The sheriff peered over the bar. "Looks like a waste of food on the floor. What happened here?"

Isabel kept her head low as she placed the bucket down on the worst of the bloodstains. "There was a mishap and a small disagreement. It was settled, but the mood was spoiled."

"Best thing, then. I'd hate to be the one who casts a shadow on your festivities by sending you all home. Shame, really. Your kind deserves to enjoy yourselves from time to time. A game night is better than a bacchanal, which will catch the ire of those more faithful pureblood neighbors. But not many neighbors here to offend, are there?"

"No, there aren't," Digger said. He watched the sheriff carefully. "We're cleaning up. We're not making noise. There's been no complaint."

"Yes, yes. 'So why is this lawman here,' you're thinking. Curfew is for the city watch to handle. As you may have heard, the duke has assigned me here to uphold his house's law on the island. Diregloom has become something of a prime focus of the duke, as his subjects and even his family enjoy the island's many temptations. But the law's the law and the duke can't be viewed as being lax."

"The Dragon and Rose isn't even open. When the renovation work is done, I'm sure Lady Sofia will file all the necessary paperwork."

"Again, not my purview. I've been here a few months and still feel unacquainted with the city, the island, and its people. In Bahia, your kind and mine don't intermingle much since the edict. But Diregloom has fel and pureblood shoulder to shoulder, in work and sometimes in play. The youth of Bahia speak of this place as an attraction. Is it the lure of strange flesh? Escaping parental oversights? The danger of the catacombs or the thrills of its blood sport? I honestly don't know."

Digger's jaw clenched. "Loom Island was ours."

"That's changed recently, hasn't it? Queen Claudia has finally succumbed to pressure. Curfews. Stricter laws. Must be a shame for you. Quite the adjustment."

"We're happy in our service," Isabel said, her eyes still on the floor.

"'The sleep of the laborer is sweet,' yes? I wish I could say that was true. I barely sleep anymore since being assigned here."

Monty emerged from the back room. He gave a bow but looked like a mouse caught in lantern light.

The sheriff smiled. "Well, I've taken enough of your time. This place has promise. Those appetizers are a keeper. Again, my compliments to the chef." He paused.

At first Digger thought he was reaching for him and backed away, his hands ready to ward off an attack. But the man picked up the watch from where it lay between two of the dishes.

"And what is this?"

The sheriff lifted it out of the paper to admire it.

"Someone left it here," Digger said quickly.

"Apparently. Such a treasure wouldn't come from a fel pocket. Unless, of course, that fel took it from a pureblood."

He turned it over and tapped its face before wrapping it again. Then he slid it into his pocket.

Isabel took a step towards him. "That's not yours."

"Obviously not. But whoever lost it will no doubt be heart-stricken until they find it again. Such a treasure isn't safe just lying about. I'm sure there's many an unsavory type who would make off with it. I'll make inquiries. If you come upon its owner, send word to the stockade. That way, the watch and whoever lost it will be reunited."

Digger motioned Isabel back as the sheriff headed to the door. She looked like she was ready to charge after him.

The sheriff paused. "Soap and hot water."

"What?" Digger asked.

"For your stain behind the bar. It looks like spilled cocktail sauce on the wood. Use plenty of soap and a little elbow grease. Gets out the most persistent spots."

He exited. Monty hurried past and slid a bolt across the door.

Isabel squared off with Digger, scowling. "He took it? You let him take it?"

"There was no 'letting' about it. We're lucky. He has it now and it's out of our hands. That's a bucket of trouble that we just avoided."

"But it's mine."

"You stole it fair and square, right? Brought trouble down on us. This solves it, once I get rid of the body."

"It doesn't solve anything. I needed that to sell. It would have set me up. I risked everything getting it, and you let it walk out of here."

"Maybe you should have killed him," Monty said.

Digger looked at his brother, not believing what he had heard.

"He'll remember where he got it when the watch's owner makes it known it's missing. We're still in trouble. So why not kill him?"

"Because it doesn't work like that," Digger said.

"It did when the first guy came in here."

"That was different. We didn't have a choice. You don't get to even suggest that."

"Monty's right," Isabel said. "Why not kill him? He's alone. I'd have my watch back. It eliminates the chance he returns to arrest both of you."

"And what if he was lying and had a squad of men waiting outside? What if the city guards know where he is? Get serious. At least right now we have time to figure out what to do."

Isabel moved towards the door.

"Where are you going?"

"To follow him."

"Don't. We have a mess here to clean and you're going to help."

"Are you stopping me from leaving?"

"Digger, let her go," Monty said.

He raised his hands as if surrendering.

Isabel went to the door and placed her fingers on the bolt. Hesitated. "If you help me get it back, you both might stay out of trouble."

"What are you suggesting?" Digger asked.

"We tidy up here like you want. Bury the body. And then we go find the sheriff and see if we can steal the watch back from him before he finds out who I stole it from."

Chapter Five

WHILE MONTY AND ISABEL cleaned, Digger began to scratch at a piece of paper.

Isabel paused to dab sweat from her brow. "What are you doing? We could use your help."

"Burying someone means paperwork. I need two forms for both the corpses in my cart."

"About that. I couldn't help but notice the other body. You move around the city with a corpse?"

"You think they just vanish on their own when a boy or girl in one of your brothels gets killed or overdoses?"

Her eyes flared. "You think I'm a prostitute?"

"Educated guess. You don't look like a factory worker with those painted nails."

"You don't know anything about me."

"I know you stole something no smart thief would lay their hands on in a hundred lifetimes."

She snatched his form away and squinted. "What does this even say? Is anyone expected to read this?"

"It's a burial order. It lists the name of the deceased along with where they were found and then what plot they're being placed in."

"Unknown has a 'k' in it."

He took the paper back. "I'm the only one who will actually read it, but the paper needs to be filled out for the cemetery keeper. Plus it gives me something to give to any guard who stops me." He tucked the page away into his shirt pocket. "I'm going. Finish up here. Monty, what about Lady Sofia?"

"She's never up before late morning. We have time. You're coming back?"

"Yeah. We're going to be okay. Just relax."

His brother nodded as he collected a stack of broken dishes.

Digger went out back. In the shadows of the alley his cart might have been filled with any number of goods. The hour would raise suspicions. Only those fel with legal dispensation could be out before the end of the third watch.

A large shadow moved at the opposite side of the cart.

"Who's there?"

The stranger reached into the cart and picked up the sword.

Digger began to approach but hesitated. The figure was almost two feet taller than he was, and twice as wide.

"Busy night tonight," a gruff voice said.

"This is gravedigger's work. Get out of here."

"Well, then you get the prize of a rather fine blade. One might assume the deceased's family would want it."

"This is none of your business. Put it in the cart."

"Or? Will you call the sheriff back? Go on then. I'll wait."

"What do you want?"

The large figure chuckled. He tucked the blade under a massive arm and fumbled in a pocket before producing a piece of paper. It was too dark to read, but Digger recognized the rough brown sheet. It was another bill advertising the poker game.

"Game's off."

"Yeah, I guessed. If this is what happens to the losers, what do the winners get?"

"I'll tell you what you get if you don't leave."

He hoped his threat would work. The large fel before him was an ogre, one of the rare giants who lived in the desert east of Duke Tito's lands. Most had been hunted down and murdered, but there were a few still living in the city.

"I don't think I'll go anywhere just yet, my friend. In fact, you're just the kind of people I was hoping to find at an after-hours poker game."

The ogre got closer. Digger adopted a fighting stance, feet spread with hands out and packed into fists.

"Whoa, hey! I was just going to accompany you inside for a moment so we can have a conversation that doesn't include two corpses staring up at us."

"Put the sword down now."

The ogre grunted and made a show of tucking the sword neatly away beneath the tarp. "I suppose it's a fair gratuity for your work. You get their boots too?"

"Say your piece."

"I've never been to a gastropub. Let's step inside and you can pour me a drink."

"No. We talk out here."

The ogre looked him over. "You even a fel? Figured you were because of the cart which smells of dirt, but now I'm not so sure."

"What does it matter? It's none of your business."

Before Digger could react, the ogre's hand shot out and clamped on his throat. He was slammed against a wall, his feet dangling. As the hand squeezed, Digger flailed to peel the iron fingers away. He couldn't breathe. The ogre was choking the life from him.

"You get to give orders during the day, pureblood," the ogre hissed, "but the night belongs to us."

Digger got a hand on the ogre's face. Tried to hook his thumb into his eye, but the ogre turned his head aside. He was growing weaker. The world faded.

"Halfblood," Digger gasped.

The ogre grunted as he studied Digger's face. "Oh yeah. I see it now. Those are fel eyes."

With the last of his strength, Digger slapped at the hand. The ogre released him. Digger collapsed to the floor of the alleyway, sucking in air as he coughed.

"Now about that beer you were going to get me."

Digger could only nod. He followed the ogre back into the bar.

Chapter Six

THE CHAIR PROTESTED beneath the ogre's weight. Dark tattoos ran up both tan arms. His mostly bare head retained wisps of fine dark hair. He wore a pleasant smile on his face as he surveyed the common room.

Digger sat across from him and scowled. Isabel leaned against the bar, her arms folded. Her expression was as sour as Digger's.

Monty set a mug of beer down before the ogre and took a step back.

The ogre sipped and smacked his lips. "This a small beer? Don't you have anything stronger?"

Digger massaged his sore neck. "You have your beer. Now tell us what you want."

"I'm Sprat Hellard. I saw your notice for poker players. Fel, ogres, and goblins welcome? I'm in. Although there's only a few of my kind and I've never seen a goblin. Maybe there's a few in the city I don't know about. Heard they're short."

"You're not here for a card game."

"Alright, fair enough. What I am doing is looking to recruit like-minded fel who are interested in improving their circumstances."

"What does that even mean?"

"It means we can strengthen our position in this city. All we have to do is decide we don't like living with a boot on our necks."

"You think anyone likes it?"

"I do. We've been broken to misery, and I've spoken with too many who won't have it any other way. I see it in the eyes. Our people have traded living for surviving one day to the next, grateful they didn't commit some infraction which gets them hauled to the gallows for Saturday's entertainment."

"I know you," Isabel said. "You were at the Black Rock Mission kitchen. You were thrown out. Your talk about rebellion is going to get people killed."

Hellard chuckled and drained the cup. "Oh, the Black Rock Mission. A bandage wrap for a severed limb. The place where a few purebloods soothe their consciences by throwing us their table scraps."

"We feed thousands. We help refugees fleeing the mainland."

"You're part of the problem."

"And we don't have time for this," Digger said. "You've had your beer. No one here is interested in joining any kind of resistance movement. Now see yourself out."

"My simple gravedigger, I'm not speaking of any kind of uprising. And the lady here must have misheard me at the soup kitchen. I come with a proposal which will fill your pockets with something besides Loom Island scrip. I'm talking silver. I can smell the soapy water and I saw what you have in the cart. You're not afraid of getting your hands dirty. There are other ways to fight our oppressors besides taking to the streets."

"Get to your point."

"You've made up your mind already. But your friends here look like they're interested in hearing more."

As if making his point, Isabel asked, "What kind of money are we talking about?"

Hellard grinned, revealing gnarled teeth. "I sense tension here. You have two out back who have an appointment with the ground. Why don't I wait here so I don't have to repeat myself. Besides, the guards are out in force and someone with my...stature doesn't have the easiest time moving unseen through certain neighborhoods."

"You can't stay here," Digger said.

Monty had been silent up until that moment. "I say he can. Sofia won't be up for hours. And I'm also interested in hearing what he has to say."

Digger shot his brother a look but Monty wouldn't meet his gaze.

Hellard scratched at the mug with his fingernail. "Unless of course you're turning me out. Be a shame if the city watch catches me and I have to tell them about this place and your idea of a fun game night. How well did you scrub that floor?"

Digger felt himself tensing. "You're blackmailing us?"

Hellard waved the comment off. "I'm saying I could use another beer. What's the harm in that?" He reached into a pouch and pulled out a silver coin. "See? Everything aboveboard with me. Go bury your bodies. I'll be here until the end of third watch. If you're back by then, we talk some more. If not, so be it and you won't see me again."

Digger took his brother by the elbow to the back room. Isabel followed.

"What are you saying, letting him stay?" Digger hissed. "We have a dead tourist out back and the sheriff's been by once. If this guy's been going around town talking about organizing fel, he's drawing attention we don't need."

Monty licked his lips. "More money might mean this place opens sooner."

"Are you serious?"

"Sofia's broke. I've been able to sell a few things to make enough so she has food and beer. Her remodel's stalled and she's been resisting lowball offers on buying the Dragon and Rose. I scraped up enough to host the poker game. I was hoping to get our kind in here to turn the place around. But then..."

"I showed up and ruined it all," Isabel said.

Monty blushed. "It's not your fault."

"You're going from a bad idea to a worse idea all in one night," Digger said.

"Hearing him out isn't going to hurt anybody."

The church bell's muffled clang declared the end of second watch.

Digger shook his head, disgusted. "I have bodies to bury. I guess I can't tell you what to do."

He opened the door to the alley.

Isabel pulled her blue hood over her head. "Let me go with you."

"That'll just complicate things."

"I'm not afraid of a little work. It's both of us who are risking our necks. And you still have to explain how we're going to get my watch back."

"Fine. Let's go. If we run into any guards, keep your head low and your mouth shut. Tonight's been a giant shambles, but don't believe that it can't get worse."

Chapter Seven

WITH TWO BODIES WEIGHING the cart down, both wheels kept catching in the gaps between the cobblestones. But when Isabel tried to help, he almost spilled the load. He pushed to free the right wheel from a particularly deep groove in the street that threatened to break the wheel pin connecting the axle.

"It wouldn't get stuck like this if you went slower," she said.

"Keep your voice down. It carries."

"You think the guards didn't hear you already?"

"There are people looking for you, not me."

He gave the cart a heave and got it moving until the left wheel abruptly hit a rut and stopped. He pushed, but it didn't budge.

Isabel lifted from the front and they were once again rolling. "You don't work well with others."

"I work alone."

"Yeah, I get the sense of that. You're also not very nice to your brother."

"That, like everything else in my and Monty's life, is none of your concern. Keep going."

"He might actually listen to you if you don't shove your choices down his throat."

"Stop pretending you know either of us. Everything I do is for him, including this job."

He immediately regretted saying anything. It wasn't a topic he had spoken of with other people. He had grown accustomed to his isolation. When he worked, people stood back and let him go about his business.

When he wasn't working and anyone found out what he did, they never asked for details.

Long swathes of shadow ran between the streetlights. The orange flames led from castle to harbor along the island, but there were few on the roads they walked. Most homes along the avenue were totally dark and shuttered. Few sounds competed with the clack and rattle of the cart. The fog carried a damp chill.

At any moment he expected to run into more guards, but no one stopped them as they exited the Temperance District on their way to East Hill where the cemetery waited.

A glowing greenish-yellow lantern hung at the top of the wooden gate. A spiked metal fence ran around the base of the hill.

Digger parked the cart and pushed the gate open. Xavier, the cemetery keeper, wouldn't be up, but his daughters might be, and they'd demand his paperwork and payment.

He went to an unlit cottage set behind a high hedge and knocked on the door.

A thin, pale girl appeared around the side wrapped in a thick blanket. She had large round froglike eyes and a broad mouth, which cracked into a smile. "Digger. What brings you out tonight?"

"Two for the communal grave."

A second girl appeared next to the first. She was identical except for a patch over one eye. "Two bodies. Two coins."

He paid her. Then he fumbled in a pocket and handed over the paperwork.

As he turned to return to the cart, the sister with the eyepatch seized his arm. "And who is that with you, Digger?"

"A helper."

The first sister stepped past him and strode towards Isabel. "A helper? A charmer, this one. Pretty things don't come here except under a tarp."

"Is this true?" the second sister asked. "Digger has a pretty thing now and has spurned us for...how long has it been?"

"Two years. Spurned us for two years despite our attempts to curry his favor. And now our Digger has a helper. Or is this one something more?"

"A charmer, sister. He has a charmer who might have captured our dear's brooding heart."

Digger tried to break away from the second sister. "I just want to make my hole and be done with the night."

She slid her hand along Digger's cheek and pressed against his chest. She smelled of hay and soil and her skin was dry as paper. "That's your problem, Digger. No time to taste what's good in life. Always in such a hurry."

"He's always in a rush, this one," the first sister said. "And so glum."

She crouched to peer under Isabel's hood. Isabel flinched when the girl took her hand and began to stroke it. "Such soft hands. Nice hands. Hands which don't belong on the handle of a shovel."

"It's my brother in the cart," Isabel said.

"So it's a funeral, then? Digger, Digger. You said just a burial. Funerals are extra."

"Extra indeed," agreed the second sister as she peered at Isabel with her one good eye.

"I don't have any more money," Isabel said. "I paid it all to him to perform the burial. I told him I'd help, as I was short a few coppers."

The first sister laughed. "So you found a soft-hearted gravedigger for your brother. Condolences for your loss. But a funeral is a funeral. Even on East Hill."

"Rules, dear Digger," the second sister purred. "We mustn't upset our father."

Digger dislodged her hand. "She can wait out here, then. You've been paid."

"Did you tell her about the extras? Flowers on the grave? A marker?"

The first sister chimed in. "Space in one of the crypts, even. We could even hire a trio of gelded boys to sing a dirge. They're well practiced."

"You heard her," Digger said. "She's broke. No extras. She'll wait here. Now let me grab my tools from the shed."

The second sister hissed in obvious disappointment. "Oh, Digger. It's no fun when you get mad. There's so little to smile about these days. Go on. Take her with you. No wailing, girl. And keep your prayers quiet. We'll tell Father you came with two bodies. And alone."

"And paid for both," the first sister said. "With papers signed and filed."

"No funeral was had. But we know Digger did have a helper. A soft-handed, sweet-smelling helper who went and dug her first grave."

THEY BROKE GROUND BEYOND a stunted forest of stone and planks marked with names. A pile of loose soil grew steadily beside them. The closest whitewashed board, planted upright, read *Luana – Died in Winter – Beloved Daughter of Ellen and Pablo.*

"We should have bribed them to not mention me," Isabel said.

Digger only paused for a moment. "Then they would have known there was something up worth protecting."

"This doesn't look like a communal grave."

"That would be quicker. But I don't want another grave worker finding who we're burying. Fortunately Xavier and his daughters don't check what I do as long as I hand in the paperwork. We have to work quick in case anyone else is here who might notice."

"What of the family of the girl who's already here?"

"It's a chance we'll have to take."

Digger expected her to quit after the first ten minutes. But Isabel kept digging even after it became obvious her hands were uncomfortable gripping the shovel. Neither of them wore gloves, but Digger had thick hands that had only grown more calluses since he'd adopted his current occupation.

"Take a break," he said.

"I'm fine."

"There's only room for one of us in the hole. Keep the soil from sliding back in."

She stepped out of their thigh-deep trench and scraped the soil pile away from the edge. Digger began to heave large shovelfuls of black dirt, his movements well practiced. Little rolled back in. The lantern borrowed from the graveyard toolshed barely cast enough light for him to see what he was doing. But soon it was deep enough. He braced himself on the shovel and pulled himself up to the lip of the grave.

Isabel was rubbing at a blister on her palm. "I could have helped more."

"I was faster doing it alone."

"Are you always like this?"

"I'm what I need to be."

"That's cryptic, pardon the pun. I didn't come out here to learn your trade. You said you'll help me find the sheriff."

He wiped his face down with a rag. "And that's what we'll do."

"Then let's get these bodies down and fill the hole. Unless there's words you say."

"I don't say anything."

"I figured."

Filling the grave went quick. Digger spent more than the usual amount of time tamping down the soil, but there would be no avoiding the obvious new dirt that had been turned up. The graveyard was free of weeds. He hoped for a rain shower. But few fel had the scrip to purchase more than a pauper's burial. The pureblood dead were no longer brought to East Hill.

"Good view of the castle from here," she said.

It was true. This high up on East Hill, Diregloom was hidden beneath the fog while the castle on the northwest side of the island loomed white in the starlight. Several lights were glowing in the windows. The night was quiet. The sound of breaking surf carried from the ocean.

From down the hill came voices. Lights.

If Xavier or his weird daughters were coming, they'd soon find them and the new grave dug on top of an old one. He didn't have enough funds to make that kind of trouble go away.

Digger placed the shovels and pick into the cart and hooked the lantern to a round bolt. They followed the path down between the rows of gravestones. The lights he had seen were heading towards the crypts, where souls were placed to rest by families who could afford all the extras.

It was another pair of gravediggers guiding a mule-drawn wagon.

At the cemetery entrance he put the loaner pick and spare shovel and lantern away into the shed near the cottage. His own shovel stayed in the cart beneath the tarp. The collection of tools had their place beside a barrel of quicklime. Inside the door he made a show of adding a note to a clipboard hanging next to a series of lot tags. All in case anyone was watching. He then closed the door as quietly as possible.

Mercifully, the sisters didn't come out.

Isabel kept checking over her shoulder as they exited through the cemetery gate.

"Relax, we did it."

"What if they see where we buried them? Any chance they'll find the body?"

"If it's just the sisters, they'll just gouge me for more coin."

"And Xavier? The cemetery keeper?"

Digger didn't comment. "Like I said, we're fine."

She let out a nervous laugh as they headed down the street. "You paid in silver coin. You must make good money."

"Looking for honest work?"

"I told you I'm not a prostitute. I just thought something like the graveyard would use city scrip."

"They do. But coins keep everyone happier. If you need to know, people pay me with what they have. The guards use scrip when it comes to a pickup no one cares about."

"Well, you're making extra from somewhere. Maybe Hellard was right. We should have kept the sword and boots to sell."

He gave her a look. "Why?"

"In case we have to come back and bribe those sisters all over again."

Chapter Eight

LORD ANGEL'S MORNING couldn't be any worse than his night.

He'd have to keep up the appearances of the attentive prince, smile, and bite his tongue lest his Aunt Claudia catch a whiff of what he had done. After all, the self-appointed queen of Diregloom would make him far wealthier than any of his brothers would ever be as they toiled away at his father's winery north of Bahia back on the mainland. All he had to do was stay on the witch's good side.

That would be impossible once she discovered what he had stolen. And then lost.

He followed Claudia as she strode into the castle's reception hall, careful not to step on the train of her sequined white gown.

A slight man in a frilly beige suit stood waiting with his hands clasped behind him. He sported a trimmed beard and mustache and had a narrow nose and face. His thinning hair was groomed back over his head. Around his neck hung a gaudy medallion of gold, which declared his rank as a representative of Bahia's Duke Tito.

Claudia beamed as she spread her arms. "Viscount Ilario. How pleasant it is to receive you."

The viscount gave a formal bow. "Lady Claudia."

"We hug on my island."

Claudia squeezed him. Angel thought the man might break. He took a moment to enjoy the viscount's obvious discomfort.

"Have you been accommodated? Your room has the best view the castle has to offer. The crashing waves. The eastern island. The sunset."

"Yes, quite," the viscount said, straightening his tunic. "Duke Tito has concerns which we should discuss."

"Straight to business with you? We receive so few guests worthy of the royal treatment. I have breakfast for us. Please, let us get acquainted first. And then we'll go over my brother's every concern, item by item. I promise. Come!"

She grabbed his arm and led him through giant doors held open by gloved fel manservants.

Angel trailed after.

He had known the viscount was coming at dawn, and his aunt had insisted Angel be involved. The viscount was one of the highest-ranking nobles serving in his Uncle Tito's court. Perhaps the man would temper his assessment of Claudia's activities if he saw the duke's dear nephew was being well cared for. The duke held long-standing misgivings over Diregloom and its influence on his subjects. More to the point, the city across the water from his dukedom of Bahia was becoming a bad influence. The fel had always had free rein on the island, up until his sweeping edict. But Diregloom was also luring royal youth into wickedness. The popularity of its entertainments and games had grown like a brushfire throughout not only his territory but all the neighboring dukedoms as well. And now his brother's second-oldest boy had gone off to stay with Claudia. Nobles were whispering. Duke Tito, according to the gossip, wasn't pleased.

So now the viscount was here for an audit of Diregloom's morals, and Angel was expected to help his aunt make a good showing to avoid trouble.

He massaged an aching arm as he kept up with his aunt and her guest.

Angel had only been on the island for a month. He had quickly discovered the game rooms and brothels, pleasures harder to come by in any of the mainland's counties, where such things were prohibited from operating out in the open. And while his own mother and father, a countess and count, had reluctantly sent their second son off with a full purse, his allowance hadn't lasted the first week.

Diregloom had club owners who would loan a young man silver until his luck changed. For a few nights, he thought it had. But then disaster. More loans. More busts. His cards never came up. And then the lenders sold his debts to Red Eye.

The arm-twisting that Red Eye's thug had given him was only a taste of what was to come if he didn't pay.

His entourage of companions who had accompanied him from home didn't have enough to come close to covering the debt. Aunt Claudia's gold watch would have squared everything. But then that damnable girl had taken it. They had been searching all night for her, and now his friend Victor was missing.

His head was pounding as he listened to his aunt give the viscount the grand tour of her castle, wending through chamber after chamber on their way to breakfast.

The silk room, the silver room, the gold room, the hall of armor, the sword collection, and the room with the stuffed animals, whatever that was called. Then they arrived in the clock room.

Aunt Claudia strode to a tall wall clock three times the height of a man. The massive timepiece was made of pewter and featured veins of inlaid fine silver and mother of pearl that ran up its panels in flowing floral lines. The long hands turned on a smooth round face of polished mirror set with blue gemstones. It must have weighed a ton.

An internal pendulum ticked off the seconds.

"This piece was designed by Florendo Freitas of Altea. It took his shop ten years to build it. It's said to be the most accurate timepiece in the world. I use it to make adjustments to our grand clock tower at the church."

The viscount nodded politely. Angel stifled a yawn.

"A trained attendant tends to it daily. I had a second clock of similar stature on order, but unfortunately, Florendo has perished. I await reports on which of his apprentices will assume the role of master. Such a loss!"

Dozens of resplendent clocks filled the walls. Their hands were in perfect synch with one another.

A long display case occupied the center of the room. There, under the glass, were Claudia's prize watches.

Angel's mouth was dry and it wasn't from the wine hangover. He had taken the jeweled watch from the case, judging it to be the largest of the bunch. There were enough other timepieces that he had hoped the gold watch wouldn't be immediately missed.

How was he to know it would be the featured trophy in his aunt's upcoming tournament?

Claudia's fel steward Rochus had almost caught him in the act. The greenskin had dared confront Angel and his companions as they had busted into the display case. Thinking quickly, Angel had wrapped the watch in a piece of paper from a nearby rolltop desk. He'd told the steward he was taking a broken watch to see if he could fix it as a gift to his aunt.

If only they had murdered the steward.

At least the display case glass hadn't broken. However, once she opened it Claudia would discover the lock was damaged.

"These are my cherished prizes," Claudia said. "The precision, the inner workings, each part having its place within the timepiece. I'm presenting my favorite as the grand prize for the upcoming tournament."

The viscount leaned over the display case but showed little interest. "Yes. Your blood sport, which has so many talking and brings the duke's subjects here by the droves. You believe encouraging such violent entertainments won't corrupt the spirits of those who dabble in them?"

"Why, no, I don't. I believe there's a certain catharsis to what we do here. In fact, the latest rounds of catacombs will be my largest spectacle. I've expanded the playing area and added new rooms. I've planned monsters and challenges which will test the skills of the contestants and provide an event that won't be forgotten."

"You cater to base desires which undermine the duke's law."

Claudia sighed. "The duke's law stops at the shores of Bahia. Come, viscount. Let me show you my centerpiece. Surely you can admire its beauty. Perhaps you will see what the possibilities are when our people set their sights on a prize which doesn't have to wait for their passage into heaven."

Angel stepped before them, hoping he was sufficiently blocking the view of the case. "If you'd allow me, Aunt Claudia? If I'm understanding the viscount's objection, his concerns should be allayed. On the surface, the games of Loom Island might seem frivolous. Gold prizes and sport of this nature do cater to a certain cupidity. But the hundreds of visitors aren't the serfs who work your farms. They're other nobles and highborn, most of whom have little to do with their accumulated wealth."

The viscount sniffed. "It's offensive."

"It's profitable. My uncle the duke controls the harbors. He also possesses the largest fleet. Imagine if the duke's own ships were given exclusive contract to ferry visitors to and from the island? I have drawn up figures for just such a proposal. Instead of sailing direct, it would require attendees from other dukedoms to travel to Bahia first before their voyage here. This would mean they'll be spending money on accommodations in Bahia while waiting for their boat."

"You'd have the duke take part in this endeavor?"

"I'd have you introduce a profitable business venture which will cost him next to nothing to implement. I've spent enough time at Bahia's docks to know most of the fleet remains in anchorage. There's been little pirate activity, we face no real threats. The boats and men are there, waiting. Keeping an idle fleet is a waste of funds. Imagine said fleet transformed into something lucrative. Perhaps Loom Island could also pay a fee for added patrols against potential raiders."

The viscount considered him with cold eyes. Angel recognized the look from his nights at poker whenever coins hit the table. There was interest there, veiled by stuffy priggishness.

"We could set a formal proposal to paper for you to present, viscount. Assuming my aunt agrees to this."

Claudia wrapped her hands around the viscount's arm. "My nephew is the shrewd one. He's been such a joy to have with me. You'll have to thank the duke for allowing him to stay."

"Duke Tito had no say in the matter," the viscount said stuffily. "We heard of Lord Angel's arrival here from a courtier. The duke was upset."

"Well, our castle tour is only beginning. Join me to the upper balconies. The views there are spectacular. And I hope you have an appetite."

Angel didn't follow. He dabbed sweat from his brow. Disaster had been averted for the moment.

His entourage was waiting in the grand hall. They stood armed and ready. They had been searching for the girl and then Victor all night.

It was time to leave the castle and resume the search. Wherever the girl had gone, the watch had vanished with her and Angel needed it back.

Chapter Nine

DIGGER STOPPED THE cart near a small crowd. The group of fel men and women shifted in place as they waited in silence. Breath clung white to the air. They clutched gloves, bundles of tools, and parcels of food.

The streets around them were lined with the cluttered apartments typical of where most fel lived.

A distant bell clanged, which was answered by another nearby. End of third watch. They could move freely about the city.

The crowd dispersed, most heading down Violet Avenue towards the factories. There they would toil until dusk. The hints of dawn shone in a deep red hue through the fog and rising smoke. The nearest factories' furnaces were already belching smoke. This, mixed with the charcoal cooking fires in the stoves of the apartment dwellers, turned the air into a gray haze.

No one paid Digger any mind. But more than a few gawked at Isabel.

"That bright blue cloak of yours will have to go."

"It's the only one I have."

"It's attracting attention. A little too nice for this neighborhood."

He led her up a narrow side street, taking a few turns down familiar alleyways until he came to a courtyard where he parked the cart. The tenements above them obscured the sky. Lines of laundry hung between windows. A group of fel wearing boots and long-sleeved shirts came down a nearby stairway and hurried off.

"What's here?" she asked. "Every moment we waste gives the sheriff time to report the stolen watch."

"Most of the cops down at the stockade won't show up until midmorning. The night shift won't bother filing a stolen property report. The sheriff's not technically part of Diregloom's guards, so he'll have to wait to start any formal paperwork. But I'm guessing that watch isn't going to leave his pocket."

She appeared antsy but followed as he began to climb the steps. "Is this where you live?"

"Thought it best if we wash up. Right now we look like gravediggers."

He led her to the fifth floor at the top of the tenement. The open corridor had apartments on one side. The railing sagged. A woman shepherded a pair of children out of the way and hurried to slam her door when she saw Digger coming.

"Welcome to the dirty nickel," he said.

"Why do you call it that?"

He chuckled. "Everyone does. The fifth floor has the cheapest places because of the stairs. And the factory smoke tends to cling to this level."

She hazarded a look over the railing. A crow landed near them. It bobbed its head and edged towards them until it was almost in reach. One of its feet was twisted and it limped as it moved. The front of its beak was missing. It cawed.

Isabel's eyes went wide. "Shoo!"

"It's okay. That's Stumpy."

"You have a crow?"

"No. But he drops by for scraps. Part of his beak is broken so he has a hard time of it."

"And you feed him?"

"Yeah, I do." He unlocked the door. "You coming in?"

"I'll wait out here, assuming Stumpy isn't going to bite or bring me bad luck."

"Suit yourself. I have something you can wear instead of that cloak. I'll be a few minutes while I wash up."

His small apartment had one shuttered window with no glass. His bedroll and a mound of clothes occupied most of the main room, along with a stringless mandolin he had rescued from a refuse pile a year prior but had never taken the time to see repaired. The bathroom featured a toilet and washbasin beneath a spigot in the center of a wall. He turned the tap. There was water that hour, for which he was glad. It only ran cold, but he was accustomed to it.

After washing up, he found leather pants, a wrinkled but clean shirt, and a thick black cloak. He would have to hire his neighbor to do a load of laundry and clean the place. She might not speak to him, but she'd take his money.

He opened the front door and handed Isabel a wool blanket. "Here."

"What am I supposed to do with that?"

"Use it as a wrap instead of your cloak. It's all I have."

She took it but looked at it suspiciously. Then she pulled her hood down and draped the blanket over her head and shoulder. "Want me to stoop and limp along behind you?"

"If it helps you look less like a princess visiting the favela, then yes."

He locked the door and they went down the stairs. He maneuvered the cart out of the courtyard.

"I thought you didn't want to look like a gravedigger."

"It could come in handy."

Groups of children were being led past, no doubt to workhouses where, if they were lucky, they might get more than one meal for the day. Residents were doing their wash in the running fountains. Even with the change of clothes, his neighbors avoided eye contact with him.

"It's like you don't exist."

"They don't know me, but they know the cart."

The broke-beak crow landed on a nearby overhang and cawed.

"No crumbs for you now. Shoo."

It considered him with a glassy marble eye before lighting off to a nearby balcony, where it watched them leave.

Violet Avenue took them away from the slums. He followed the route towards the main market square where his kind could freely buy, sell, and trade. The labyrinth of tents, stalls, and storefronts presented a colorful contrast to the gray squalor near his home. Merchants were opening for the day. The aromas of baking bread stirred his appetite. But no food seller would want him pulling up to their stall with his cart.

Better a tanner stinking of chemicals or a sewage system worker than a halfblood fel who handled the dead.

Fel worked and shopped side by side with pureblood. Some merchants would discriminate, but most wouldn't turn away scrip. With the growing number of tourists from Bahia and the other dukedoms, this was changing, but not in this market.

One street down was Stockade Square. Here were more upscale businesses. The stockade itself was a squat stone shoebox of a structure with no outside windows and an iron gate that led to an inner courtyard. The gallows out front were the prominent feature, with enough space in the open square for a large crowd. From there the main boulevard, Fountain Street, ran the length of the city up to the castle where Claudia the Second reigned.

More than a few sellers had set up ad hoc shops from their wagons. A cook with a fashioned metal grill arranged on the back of his buckboard was roasting skewers of meats.

"Char-coo-terie!" he bellowed.

A gang of bedraggled city guards marched past and entered the stockade.

"There goes the night shift," Digger whispered.

The meat seller made a sour face as Digger pushed his cart past. Digger led Isabel to an alley between a boot seller and a florist and parked the cart. From there they had a perfect view of the stockade.

A trio of fresh-faced youths with clean clothes and neat long locks paused at the meat seller. Two of the young men had rapiers on their hips. They didn't look too dissimilar from the man who had chased Isabel into the Dragon and Rose.

"Tourists," Isabel said.

"Yeah. Weekend's coming. Might be an announcement of upcoming catacomb games. Maybe a preview."

"It's the new spring season. Supposed to be bigger than last fall's."

"Oh? What have you heard?"

"Queen Claudia wants to run a game every weekend," she said. "And she's planning to open the new waterfront this summer."

"The construction's impossible to miss. Now keep your eyes peeled."

Stockade Square had its own growing tempo as the morning progressed. More vendors showed up. The square was a nexus of traffic heading every which way. Someone selling hot tea and cider set up next to the charcuterie.

The gate guards weren't the only ones in view. A few city watchmen wandered by in pairs, but they barely seemed to notice Digger and Isabel. A growing collection of tourists milled about.

Digger left the alleyway to purchase two cups of warm cider. "Quite the crowd today."

"Aye," the cider vendor said. "Tryouts here this morning." His brow furled as he looked up at Digger. Digger ignored the man's expression. He returned to Isabel and handed her a cup.

She sipped and made a face. "Too tart."

"Maybe instead of looking for the sheriff, we can walk the market and find something befitting your delicate palate."

"Don't be rude. It's just that the apples aren't in season and this has lemon in it."

"Go ask the vendor for a spoonful of honey. I'm sure a fussy fel like you will make his day."

Digger welcomed the warmth in his throat. The beverage staved off his fatigue.

All the guards in view were pureblood. That hadn't been the case a year before. Fel were still used for watch duty in fel neighborhoods, at least, and some during day hours. He had hoped to see at least one greenskin on patrol that morning, though.

Getting to the sheriff wasn't going to be easy. He questioned his own rationale for being there. If only he could get Monty out of the city, find a place, anyplace, where his brother would be safe. But he dismissed the thought. There was no such place for fel anymore. The sheriff would have to be dealt with. But he'd have to watch himself around this girl Isabel. She was more than an ordinary thief. No thief would risk their life going after a lawman like they were about to do.

The florist on one side of the alley received a delivery. The small woman then emerged from the shop and began setting up her displays. She looked surprised to see Digger and Isabel but said nothing.

"She'll complain," Isabel said.

"Yeah. Wait here."

The florist retreated inside and Digger followed. The woman stumbled over a crate of baby's breath as she backed up towards a rear curtain.

He paused to smell a yellow rose among a prominent bouquet of orange and pink. "I'm here to place an order."

"Get out."

He untied his coin purse and jingled it. "I know there's another shop over on Yellow Avenue. But my client prefers your arrangements."

The florist paused. "Your...client?"

"Lost her brother just last night. Wants a wreath for the burial. Surely you saw my cart. Who did you think I was?"

She took a moment to straighten her dress and apron. "It doesn't matter. I do funeral arrangements. Tell me what you want."

A silver tencoin lighter, he exited the shop.

Isabel was waiting at the corner. "How did it go?"

"I'll have flowers ready tomorrow. Let's hope I won't need them."

"Sheriff's here."

Digger spotted him immediately. The man stood in front of the stockade gate speaking with a group of tourists. His telltale green felt hat was impossible to miss. The armed purebloods around him were older than the ones Digger had seen earlier. They wore non-decorative rapiers, their clothes were less flashy, and they appeared to be alert to their surroundings. Their boots, their swords—it was all identical to the gear the man he'd killed had worn.

Not tourists, he decided. So who were they?

Isabel sank back into the shadows. "I know them. The blond man in front is Angel, Queen Claudia's nephew."

"So you know them. Do they know you?"

She nodded. "They're the ones chasing me."

Chapter Ten

DIGGER STUDIED THE group around the sheriff as he broke cover and walked closer. A few of them had departed, but Lord Angel and his entourage remained.

Isabel was right at Digger's elbow.

"Wait back in the alley," Digger murmured. "They'll spot you staring."

She lingered beside the cider wagon. "They'll see you too."

"No they won't. And we're going to have to talk about who exactly you took that watch from. But not right now. I'm going to try to listen in."

Lord Angel wasn't familiar to Digger. He was of average build, standing a head shorter than his tallest companion. He wore gaudy rings on his fingers and a red ribbon on his short blond ponytail. He was frowning as the sheriff spoke. Besides a rapier, he had a dagger on his left hip.

All their weapons had worn grips. These were the real deal. He would have to assume this band knew how to fight, a sharp contrast to a majority of the tourists who came as spectators. These purebloods were here for the catacomb games, which meant they had no qualms about murdering fel for sport.

Head bowed, Digger stepped close to the group and stopped at a respectful distance. Nearby, a pair of performers were setting up a puppet theater.

"What are you going to do about it, Sheriff?" Angel was asking.

"It will be investigated."

"That's what the city guard officer told me. But they can't find their privates without a map."

"It's the guard's duty to find missing persons. My assignment is broader and I have little legal power in the city."

Angel's voice rose. "Diregloom's part of the dukedom."

"The Isle of Loom is, technically. But your aunt has never relinquished her authority. My duke's own constitution guarantees—"

"Don't quote me law. The city guard will do what you tell them. This can't wait. I need to know what happened to Victor now. If you won't investigate a loyal subject of the duke vanishing, then your failure here will be reported."

The sheriff nodded gravely. "I've heard your request from the night guard captain. He said you had your companions on the street searching last night. But there were reports of them out even before Victor came up missing. What is it you're looking for? I'm sure that piece of information will expedite my search for your friend."

Angel shifted in place. Digger recognized a sudden case of nerves when he saw it.

"Perhaps there are two crimes which need my attention," the sheriff continued. "With so many visitors, the city watch has its hands full, and you've done well in bringing the matter to me. Your aunt, the queen, would no doubt appreciate my involvement in assisting her nephew, wouldn't she? That, in turn, would make my duke happy. But my inquiries will have to start with you, if you wish me to proceed."

"How much?"

The sheriff made a face and waved a finger as if admonishing an unruly child. "I serve at the pleasure of my duke. He compensates me with salary, so no bribe is needed for me to do my job. I extend my services to you, my prince, with all due consideration, and completely free of charge."

"I withdraw my request," Angel said. "I'm sure my friend Victor just tied one on and will turn up."

He motioned for his entourage to follow and they fell in. Digger drifted away towards the gallows and kept an eye on the sheriff. A guard who had also been waiting for the conversation to end approached the sheriff and the two conferred, walking to the stockade gate. Digger returned to the alley.

Isabel was nowhere in sight. His cart was still there, abandoned.

He saw motion in the shadows at the end of the alley. Three men in dark clothes had their attention on a balcony above them. Isabel was up there, working to open a sealed shutter.

"Come down now, Sprite," one of the men said. "I promise we won't hurt you."

Isabel ignored them and continued to pry at the window.

One of the three began climbing. He grabbed one fingerhold and swung himself higher to another. The crannies in the stucco were barely visible. The other two stood back and watched. One had a blade out, the other a metal pipe.

Digger grabbed his shovel from the cart. He walked on the balls of his feet. The alley was clean. Sneaking down it wasn't a challenge.

But the rogues were no amateurs. The one with the pipe turned in time to parry as Digger swung his shovel. Their makeshift weapons clanged. The man with the knife sidestepped and lunged. Digger twisted aside, grabbed the shovel by the neck, and swung the handle, catching the man across the back of the head.

The knife wielder reeled and stumbled away.

The rogue with the pipe didn't hesitate. He grabbed the hood of Digger's cloak and pulled it, tangling him in his own clothes. A blow struck Digger between his shoulder blades as he yanked the garment off and flung it at his attacker. The rogue swatted it aside and pulled a thin blade from a sheath with his left hand. He brandished both weapons and took a step forward.

Digger backed away. He clutched the shovel defensively.

The other man had recovered and stood next to his companion. The bandana he wore had slipped beneath his jaw. He was obviously fel, with green skin and a ridged brow.

Now Digger faced both of them, with the third still on the wall above. "Leave the lady alone."

"This is none of your business," the fel said.

"I'm making it mine."

"We don't have time for this," the pipe-wielding rogue hissed.

Above them, Isabel threw an empty flowerpot that struck the climber. He wavered, slipped, and thudded to the stone floor of the alley.

The rogue with the pipe did a half turn to look. Digger swung the shovel and caught the man's arm at the elbow. Bones and tendons cracked as the rogue howled and dropped the pipe. The fel slashed at Digger, launching a series of furious knife strikes. Digger fell back, swinging the shovel and warding off each blow. Digger managed a thrust of the shovel, which caused his opponent to pause.

They stared at each other. Digger waited. The man had black tattoos covering his forearms. One was a skull with starry eyes. The ogre Hellard wore similar ink.

Digger was almost caught by a feint followed by a low thrust. He parried in time, but just barely, and stumbled away as the rogue's blade swished the air near his face. The fel was quick and knew how to fight.

Any more lapses in attention would cost Digger his life.

Another flowerpot sailed through the air and impacted on the stone next to them. Isabel threw a third and a fourth. The rogue jerked back as the last one almost hit him.

Digger had regained his balance. He reaffirmed his grip on the shovel.

The fel rogue retreated and helped his companion with the injured arm. "We're not done here. You've made an enemy."

Winding up for a swing, Digger stepped towards him. But the fel hurried to check the third man who had fallen off the wall. That one wasn't getting up. The two rogues retreated along an interconnecting alley around the back of the flower shop and vanished.

Isabel peered down at him, another flowerpot in hand.

"We need to get out of here," he said.

She set the pot aside and swung over the railing. She dangled for a moment before dropping and rolling. He inspected the unconscious rogue, who groaned as Digger patted him down and grabbed his coin purse.

"Who were they?" he asked.

"They didn't introduce themselves. But they recognized me. What about the sheriff? And the watch?"

"It'll have to wait. Cover up. We need to get you off the street."

"Where are we going?"

"Back to the Dragon and Rose. One of those killers had the same tattoo as the ogre, Hellard. Which means Monty's in danger."

Someone from up the alleyway whistled. It was one of the younger tourists, and he had out a shining silver rapier with a ruby-hilted handle. He was waving someone on. A moment later four of his companions appeared, blocking the way back to the stockade courtyard. They wore broad grins as they moved towards them.

"Looks like the games have started early," the tourist said.

Digger cleared his throat and stepped towards his cart. "Nothing's started early. We're just working and these thieves tried to rob us."

The leader swished his blade before him. "This'll be a nice bit of warm-up, then. And it looks like that man at your feet is a pureblood. Last I remember, there's a law in effect. Bad for you."

"I'm a pureblood," Digger said.

"Not with those orange eyes you're not. We could call for the watch, but they're so, so busy." He motioned his companions on. "I told you boys this was going to be a fun week."

Digger shoved his cart over and ran. Isabel needed no prompting and was at his side as they raced along behind the shops, following in the footsteps of the retreating rogues. They dodged piles of rubbish and empty crates. The tourists behind them hooted and laughed as they charged after them.

There was little time to think as they came out onto a side street. One direction would lead back to the stockade where the city guards waited. There were several more alleys across the street. Any one of them might conceal an army of rogues lying in wait.

Digger made his best guess and picked one.

The catacomb games weren't waiting for the weekend. If they were caught, the purebloods would kill them and there was nothing any sheriff or city guard would do about it.

Chapter Eleven

THE PUREBLOODS WHISTLED and howled as they pursued Digger and Isabel. The sounds bounced off the walls of the buildings around them as they fled down the narrow lanes of the city.

They had been running for what felt like a half an hour. Digger's side ached with a cramp. The shovel kept getting heavier. They paused at an interconnecting series of steps leading between several apartment buildings.

Isabel was panting hard and shaking her head. "They're drunk. Let's stop and fight them."

"Doesn't matter. There's five of them and they have swords. Come on."

They picked a direction and were soon tromping through a muddy back lot that had been repurposed as a makeshift garden. They weaved around a dozen or so people who were working in the dirt.

"Look out!" Digger called as they ran past.

Someone was shouting from the alley ahead of them. It was one of the tourists. They had split up and at least one was now in front of them.

Digger readied his shovel with both hands. The tourist assumed a fighting stance and began to descend the steps to the lot.

Isabel tugged at his arm. "Now you want to fight them? There's too many people here who'll get hurt."

She pointed to a wooden fire escape leading up the side of one of the tenements. He followed her as she raced to the stairs.

The garden workers scattered as more of the tourists burst into the lot from behind them. Digger and Isabel headed up the creaking steps. The tourist leader shouted and pointed. Soon he and the others were coming after them.

The stairway shifted beneath Digger's weight. Isabel was well ahead of him and made the rooftop. A stair gave out behind her, almost sending Digger falling. He clutched the loose handrail and kept climbing.

She was waiting for him at the top. "We're in trouble."

"What?"

"There's no way down."

He took a moment to survey the building's rooftop. Someone had brought up a few planter boxes where lettuce and a small lemon tree grew. But there was little else. The neighboring buildings were too far away to jump to and he saw no access doors, skylights, or balconies.

The closest pursuer was on the last flight and coming quickly. He was laughing as he ascended towards them, with their leader and three others right behind him.

Digger planted his feet at the top of the steps, his shovel ready to swing. "You boys are making a mistake."

"Doesn't look like it to me," the closest tourist said. His hair was dyed a reddish color and light-brown roots were showing. His ruffled gold shirt had sparkling buttons and a starched high collar. He held his sword with a leather-gloved hand and swirled the blade as he mounted the final steps.

But the way the tourist held his blade like it was a fire poker, where he placed his feet—he was off-balance. The boy had never been in a real fight in his life.

Swinging, Digger struck the rapier near the guard and knocked it from the youth's hand. Without a pause he caught the tourist across the side of the head with his backstroke. Several teeth and a spray of blood exploded into the air as the man tumbled down the steps and landed at the feet of the others.

Digger towered over them. "Game's on. Who's next?"

The leader took a moment to look down at his companion. For a moment Digger almost believed the man would collect his friend and they would retreat. But the tourist just stepped over him. He held his sword poised before him, ready to thrust. When he was a few steps away he feinted, but Digger didn't fall for it, keeping his own weapon in front of him ready to ward off an attack.

It was clear this one was better trained than the man Digger had struck.

Digger saw no opening. Once on the rooftop the tourist would have all the advantages. The man's movements were deliberate as he climbed the final steps. He remained balanced, his eyes focused. Digger was about to lose this fight. One mistake and he would be cut to pieces.

"This way!" Isabel called.

She stood on the opposite side of a planter. A previously unseen trapdoor lay open.

Digger let out a shout and slammed his shovel down onto the top rail of the fire escape with a terrific *crack*.

The tourist jerked back, momentarily surprised, as Digger retreated and leaped down the opening in the roof onto wooden stairs. Isabel followed and swung it shut behind them. She wasted no time in sliding its metal bolt closed, sealing the door. She screamed and tumbled away as a blade came piercing through between the gaps in the trapdoor.

Digger pulled her up and they hurried down a dim stairway, taking two steps at a time.

They emerged in front of the building and hurried down a street Digger knew. It led towards Diregloom's manufacturing district. There were plenty of people on the street, but he and Isabel had to get out of sight.

The three factories dominated the skyline. Soon he and Isabel were hurrying past clustered two-level structures. Some were homes, but among them were the city's oldest textile and clothing manufacturers.

This was the neighborhood that gave Loom Island its actual name, from a time before any self-proclaimed queen began to rule. She had once been some minor duchess over the islands, an honorary title passed down among the pureblood nobility. This had been a fel-only city then, a haven for their kind.

No longer.

Past a material yard they approached what at first glance looked like a shuttered mansion. The drab domicile's roof was partially burned. A gable stood devoid of paneling or tiles. The visible beams and framing reminded

Digger of exposed bones. Weeds grew around all sides of the place and litter was strewn about everywhere.

"We're not going in there, are we?" Isabel asked, but she followed as Digger led the way to a side door.

He opened the door to a dark hallway. Curtains blacked out every window. Digger walked down the corridor and they emerged into a candlelit main room. The ceiling was gone, as was much of the wall paneling. A dozen men and women were drinking at several round tables. None were vacant.

The man behind the bar was reading a book. He looked up at Digger and arched an eyebrow. Digger escorted Isabel to an occupied table. The man sitting there with his head down didn't stir as they sat.

"Do they have a menu?" Isabel asked in a deadpan voice.

Digger placed his shovel at his feet and then raised two fingers. The barkeep brought two pitch-black beers.

She looked at her frothy mug suspiciously.

Digger sipped. The brew of the week was a silky brown stout. "It won't bite."

"Are you sure? What is this place?"

"It's where my kind can get a drink."

"You mean fel?"

"I mean gravediggers."

She looked around the room and back at him, confused. "A place just for gravediggers?"

"Not exactly. But it's a place where those who dig latrines, work the sewers, and do similar jobs can come."

"But the city needs all those people."

"Doesn't mean folks want them at their elbows when out for a pint."

She took a tentative taste and then drank. "Not bad."

"Hangman knows what he's doing."

"The bartender...?"

"Someone wears that hood."

"But he's fel."

Digger nodded. "And the job pays well."

She leaned forward to whisper. "He kills our kind?"

"Executes them. It's like every other law in the city. We either go along with it or we lose what little we have left."

She set her mug down. Digger swirled the foam in his before drinking more.

"We can't just hide here," she said.

"With everyone on the street recognizing you, we don't have a lot of options. I need to keep you out of sight for a little while. And then I'm going back to the Dragon and Rose and getting my brother somewhere safe."

"But you have to help me. The sheriff—"

"Doesn't matter. Once I find Monty a new place to hide, the sheriff won't be a problem."

"A new place? What do you mean?"

The word had slipped out. He was tired. Maybe it was the beer. He wasn't used to sharing his plans with anyone. "It means I take care of my brother first. I'm steering clear of this sheriff. If you want to survive, you're going to have to do the same. Let the watch go. There'll be other prizes for you to steal."

"Nothing that valuable."

"Why are you sticking your neck out like this? This jeweled watch is more than some score, isn't it?"

She hesitated before answering. "My work at the Black Rock Mission. I believe in it. And that watch will do a lot of good."

"I'm sure it would, if it could be easily fenced. But I don't buy it. Bringing the mission a piece of jewelry like that will cause problems for them, I'd imagine. And you won't help anyone if you're dead. You've got the law, a gang of thieves, and now a pack of well-armed tourists looking to kill you. So what aren't you telling me? Why is my brother's life in danger?"

Her voice grew soft. "Because stealing it from Lord Angel is payback for what he did to me."

He set his beer down and crossed his arms. "Explain."

The drunk sleeping at the table stirred for a moment to wipe drool off his mouth. He gave them both a dreary eye before stumbling away from the table, his legs miraculously staying beneath him as he tottered down the exit hallway.

Isabel waited until he was out of sight. "Like you, I can almost pass for pureblood. I was brought on as a house servant to Count Barca. His son Jamie was sick. I was helping him. We grew close. Jamie thought he could change his father's mind about us, but I convinced him not to. Count Barca found out anyway. He exploded. Jamie tried talking to him. But the count couldn't tolerate his son having a romantic dalliance with a fel. He tried to have me killed."

"How does Lord Angel and the watch fit in with this?"

"Lord Angel was the one who exposed our relationship. He's Jamie's younger brother. So I fled here to Loom Island."

"This place isn't safe for us either. Not in the last couple of years. Not since the edict."

"It's worse on the mainland. I'd worked before with the Black Rock Mission so I returned there. But then I saw Lord Angel was in the city. He didn't recognize me. When I was able to get close to him and learned about the watch, I knew I had a chance to hurt him. He's in debt. He stole the watch to pay off some gangster."

Digger saw something in her face that wasn't there before. Something dangerous. "You stole it so Angel would get hurt." It wasn't a question.

Isabel nodded. "Maybe this makes me sound crazy."

"A little, but I get it. That doesn't mean I want to risk our lives going after this thing. It's time to cut your losses."

She rose from the table.

"Where are you going?" he asked.

"Out to finish what I started. I'm sorry I brought trouble your way. I don't know how to explain it to you, but I'm not done with this."

"So you're going to charge out into the street and look for the sheriff again? He's not going to just hand the watch over."

"I'm going to do what I have to."

"Hold on. Sit. I said I was going to help. But I'm not committing suicide. We wait a few hours. The tourists will find someone else to bother. We go back to the Dragon and Rose. Find my brother and hide him. Then I'll join you and we get your treasure back."

She sat back down on her chair. "Why help me with this?"

"Because just now it sounded like you were being straight with me. And you weren't afraid to get your hands dirty tonight. So how far are you willing to go to get back at this pureblood?"

She picked up her beer and brooded silently.

After receiving no answer, he set his cup on the table. "There's a slim chance—slim—that we can pull this off. If we find an opening, we take it. With the sheriff out of the picture, my brother has a better chance of staying out of trouble. But if we discover this sheriff has handed the watch over, it means we walk away. Are you good with this?"

She nodded. Swirled her beer. Studied the white foam.

"You going to finish that?"

As if to spite him, she drank down the whole mug.

Chapter Twelve

ANGEL FOUND HIS AUNT Claudia in her waiting room just off the great hall. Early afternoon light streamed in through high windows. A few women were waiting their turn for her attention. Each bore bundles of colorful fabric, ribbons, and clothing.

Claudia inspected a bolt of satin. "I like the teals and orange. Will there be time to fashion uniforms for all the castle guards?"

One of the women curtseyed. "If we make haste, yes."

"Then off you go."

Angel waited for them to leave. "You sent for me?"

"I would have liked your presence this morning to have at least lasted until breakfast. The viscount still will need convincing."

"He sounded favorable to my suggestions."

"And what a suggestion it was. A brilliant idea, inviting the duke to handle transportation. But us paying a fee? I do wish you would have talked to me before even mentioning such a notion."

"He was being unyielding, and making a big gesture should soften him. And the numbers work. We can go over the figures together, Aunt Claudia. But I'm sorry if I overstepped."

She waved her hand. "No apologies. I'm impressed with you, Angel. But you have things to learn about making deals. He hadn't offered anything yet and we just handed him a generous prize. Once he tells us how much this will cost, the duke will find more to tack on. It's how these matters go."

"What would you have me do?"

"First, we don't give anything away for free. But you're perceptive in seeing the viscount will need careful handling. Let's find what makes him happy. Because when he's happy, he'll make the duke happy. And then you can guess what I'll be."

"Happy."

She gave a cheerful nod. "Yes! Now let's get you something to eat. You skipped breakfast but there's plenty left from lunch."

"I'm sorry, my stomach is a bit upset. I have some matters to attend to. Where is the viscount?"

"Retired to his room. Said he would pen a letter. The duke has requested daily reports. We're under close scrutiny, my dear. I *can* count on you, can't I?"

He kissed her cheek. "Of course, Aunt Claudia. My friends need me this afternoon. I'll return in time to speak with the viscount further. But my companions have expressed interest in the catacombs and I want to be sure they know what they're getting into."

Claudia giggled. "That would be lovely having them. I can't wait. I have such surprises in store. If we can convince the viscount to stay through the tournament, I'm sure we can make him a fan. Now tell what you think about this swatch."

One of Angel's companions, an illegitimate cousin, was waiting for him out in the hall. Her name was Marisol, and she was the fastest of his band with the rapier. On her left hand she wore a thick black fighting glove with which she could parry and even snatch a blade away from an opponent. Her bleached ash hair was in a long braid that dangled between her shoulders.

Even as his aunt was speaking, Marisol was trying to get his attention.

He set down a selection of scarves and neckties. "Aunt Claudia, please excuse me."

The queen frowned. "I was going to have you speak to the flower people while they're here."

"I know. But I'd like my friends to have the best chance of giving a good showing at the tourney. They've got a case of nerves and I'd be remiss if I neglected practice. After all, I was blessed with sword training from the finest instructors."

"Will you be in the castle courtyard? I'd love to watch!"

He shook his head. "Er, no. We'll go down to the inn's garden where we'll have some privacy. Plus, I'd hate to spoil the surprise."

"Oh, goody. I do love a surprise. I expect everyone to do their very best."

"Anything for you, Aunt Claudia."

He hurried Marisol away from the waiting room and into an alcove so none of the castle staff would be in hearing range.

"What have you learned?"

"We have a lead. We caught a wounded bandit who says he and his crew almost caught Sprite. What do you want to do?"

"Take me to him."

HIS COMPANIONS HAD taken over a small courtyard between four homes not far from the castle. A small fountain trickled water. Planter boxes stood replete with tiny red and orange peppers.

Sitting against a wall was a miserable-looking man in dark leathers who was cradling a swollen arm. The hand had turned purple. His face was beaded with sweat and he was gritting his teeth. A few fresh bruises were turning deep red on his cheeks, and his lip was split and bleeding.

Angel nudged the man with his boot. "Who's this rabble?"

"We stopped him and his friends coming out of an alleyway," Marisol said. "I thought there was something suspicious. His friends escaped. This one didn't want to talk at first."

"I'm no rat," the man said.

Marisol kicked him in the ribs. The man groaned but there was nowhere to escape.

"And I told you we're no city guard," she said. "We're just concerned citizens. We're not interested in you or your friends. Tell Lord Angel here who you were after."

"A girl. Isabel. Named Sprite by some."

Marisol nodded encouragingly. "Describe her."

"Pale-green skin, brown hair, dark eyes. Covers up that she's fel. Wearing a blue cloak, we were told, but she's changed clothes."

"That's our Sprite."

Angel sneered. "Yeah, I followed that. She beat the three of you?"

The rogue shook his head. "No. She had another with her. Some guy with a shovel and cart back in the alley by the florist. Right across from the stockade."

"Tell me what you wanted with her."

"We were supposed to catch her for the bounty."

"And who, pray tell, placed this bounty on her?"

The man didn't answer. Marisol delivered another kick.

He writhed and held up a hand. "All right! Red Eye hired us."

Angel crouched to get a closer look at the rogue. He pulled the man's good arm straight and turned it. The man winced but didn't cry out. On his arm were a selection of tattoos, but prominent under the forearm, in black ink, was a skull with stars in its eyes.

"You're Karanog? I thought you were all fel. You don't look even like a halfblood."

The men let out a laugh. "I'm no fel. Karanog's changed. Expanded."

"And you're here in Diregloom?"

"We're everywhere."

Angel released the arm and stood. "So Red Eye is working with you now. What kind of a purse was he offering?"

The man shook his head. "Lieutenant told us our orders. We obey."

"Had to be enough to get you involved."

Angel cursed under his breath. Marisol and his companions stood waiting on him. He had been desperate when appealing to Red Eye to give him enough time to pay his debt. He had been stupid to have mentioned the watch. Now Red Eye was after it. Had he learned what it was? The crime lord was going to find the watch first and keep Angel indebted, and wring every copper from him.

"This complicates things."

"What do you want us to do?" Marisol asked.

"Did his friends recognize you?"

"They were too busy running."

"Get rid of him. City watch will find a dead thief in a city full of armed catacomb contestants."

The man let out a cry as one of his companions ran him through with a rapier. The companion then cleaned the blade on the rogue's clothes before putting it away. Angel stepped out onto the street. No one was paying them any attention, but it was time to get out of there.

A murder, even of a thief, could still cause problems.

So where in the big city had little Sprite run off to? It had been such a surprise seeing his older brother's fel plaything at a party in the upper room of one of Diregloom's new clubs. He had heard the girl had come to the island, but he had no idea how she'd escaped his father's wrath. How his brother had raged after Angel had let it slip to their father that the new servant was not only a fel, but in love with his oldest son.

Angel had thought she'd make for a night of sport. A final chapter he could lavishly describe in detail in a letter to his brother. Knowing what had been done to his dear Sprite would send his older sibling not only back over the edge, but permanently down into the abyss of madness. Delicious. But Angel had overindulged, passed out, and woke the next morning with both Isabel and the purloined watch missing.

"Follow me," he said.

"Where to?"

"Our Karanog friend said they found her near a florist. So let's start there, shall we? Sprite has made a new acquaintance and it's time we found out who he is."

ANGEL'S COMPANIONS scoured the alley as he inspected the overturned cart. That and the broken flowerpots confirmed something had happened there. The rogue hadn't been lying.

What had the cart carried? There were traces of dirt. Made sense, if it belonged to the florist.

The flower shop was still open. Angel motioned for Marisol to follow as he left the alley and went inside. He made a show of perusing the dried arrangements as the small woman who ran the shop finished with a customer. Once the customer left, Marisol locked the door.

The woman looked confused, then angry. "Hey! Don't do that!"

Angel leaned on the counter. "You're closed for now. What happened out in the alleyway earlier today?"

The florist's lips trembled. "I don't want any trouble."

"Of course not. We're here to help. We understand there was a fight."

"I don't know...yes, there was. I didn't see it."

"Who was it out there? You must know something. Whose cart is that?"

"Some man. A fel. He placed an order."

"Name? Looks like he was delivering to you."

"He's not my delivery man. Not one of the greenhouse people either."

"Describe him."

Her description was next to useless. Large fel. Everyone was large to a squat woman like her. But as Angel studied her and pondered, the florist added, "He had a shovel in his cart. And orange eyes. A woman with him too. I don't know what they were up to in my alley, but I didn't like it."

"Yes, we know about her. These are both morally objectionable characters. I'll be sure to mention them to the watch. But tell me, what kind of order did he place?"

She pointed. A small wreath on the back counter bore a card that read *Beloved Brother*.

"He said it was for a client. It's ready for pickup."

Angel nodded. The woman knew nothing else. A cart with dirt, a shovel, and a wreath. The fel could hold any number of professions, but one obvious one came to mind. He exited the shop and crossed the courtyard towards the stockade, with Marisol following behind.

"What is it?"

"A hunch," Angel said. "I want to talk to the city watch. They'd be the ones who know the fel who collect the dead."

THE LETHARGIC OFFICER at the desk was mostly blind and his hearing wasn't much better. By the time he got out the clipboard of the previous night's incidents, Angel was ready to stab someone.

Angel snatched the clipboard away and paused to decipher the chicken scratch.

A few bar fights, the usual robberies, a drunk lighting a fruit stand on fire. One death.

A body needed pickup at the Thirsty Seven, a brothel and bar on Prudence Street. It was on the far side of the Temperance District. His man Victor had vanished near there.

Interesting...

Angel flipped the clipboard onto the guard's desk. "Our Sprite has gotten help from a gravedigger."

"Eh?" the guard said.

Marisol examined the clipboard but had nothing new to add. The officer stared at her, his hazy eyes settling on her breasts.

Angel snapped his fingers to get the man's attention. "Are there any reports of anything happening in the Temperance District after first watch?"

The officer sat with his mouth agape for a moment. Angel was about to repeat himself when the man motioned towards the clipboard.

"Just what you see here, son. Might want to ask the sheriff, though. He was out last night in that area according to the boys. But he doesn't report things to us."

"Oh? And why is that?"

The officer grunted. "Jurisdiction. Has his own investigation."

Angel felt the final shreds of his patience falling away. "Into what?"

"The missing lawmen from two years ago. That magister who vanished. Cold case. Nothing will turn up, if you ask me. Those men might have found a prize worth a career change. Of course, they might have tripped on something bigger than they were. It's why we double up patrols at night since then."

Angel stepped past the desk and marched down the corridor, passing the inner offices of the stockade. The officer protested, but Angel ignored him. The sheriff was sitting behind a desk in a small room at the end of the hall. The door was ajar.

The sheriff looked up from a notebook. "Lord Angel, how can I be of service?"

"You were in the Temperance District last night."

"I was many places."

"Is there a reason you're not being helpful? A noble is missing and not only will you not lift a finger, but now you're being obstinate."

The sheriff waved a hand. "Not my intention. I apologize for my poor manners. It's been a long day and night. Yes, I was in the Temperance District. No, I did not see your friend or anything else of interest. I'm still trying to get a feel for the city. The waterfront is where you and your friends should focus your efforts. It's well patrolled. The brothels there are clean, the bars full and safe, the fel are kept out of the district while your aunt the queen does her renovations. Your friend is probably holed up in a room with a whore."

"But that's not where you were, or where Victor vanished."

The sheriff sighed. "Temperance is old Diregloom. It hasn't been blessed with the traffic the businesses on the waterfront enjoy."

"A gravedigger picked up a body at the Thirsty Seven."

"I heard. The city guard responded. Nothing which required my attention."

"Was there anything else? Any fel out after curfew?"

"That's a city watch issue."

"Answer the question."

"It was a quiet night, Lord Angel. The only fel I saw were inside a bar under renovation. I did my duty and reminded them of curfew."

"What bar? We searched all the Temperance bars."

"This one is still closed. I believe it's called the Dragon and Rose."

Chapter Thirteen

ANGEL AND HIS COMPANIONS rode through the narrow streets. He led, urging his horse through the crowded bottlenecks. For some reason late afternoon brought everyone out. He shouted, cursed, and lost his riding crop trying to smack a pedestrian blocking his path. The good people of Diregloom moved when given encouragement. Still, carts and wagons choked the busy avenues at every major intersection, and merchant stands were set up in the most obstruent locations. The ride between Stockade Square and the Temperance District was taking too long.

His aunt would be looking for him, but he put her out of his mind.

The tip from the florist was the best lead Angel had heard since the hunt for Sprite had begun. The gravedigger matched the rogue's description. And now the sheriff had given them a location where the missing Victor might have gone.

Was the Dragon and Rose where Isabel had met this gravedigger?

They rode up Prudence Street. Compared to the waterfront, the district was broken-down. There were few businesses open. The street bore marks of a fire that had burned some time before his arrival. Many of the singed structures hadn't been torn down.

The bar lay ahead.

A woman stepped out of a doorway beneath an overhanging shingle bearing a dragon intertwined with a thorny rose vine. The creature in the sign was holding a faded red flower to its nose. The woman emptied a bucket of water before vanishing inside.

Angel must have ridden past the establishment several times and never noticed it. Compared to the bars on the waterfront, the Dragon and Rose was a decrepit place that should have been put to the torch like its next-door neighbor. Angel knew dive bars and tried to avoid them. He wanted clean whores and intelligent bartenders who knew more than how to sling flat beer.

He dismounted and, not finding a hitch, tied off his horse to the burned-out structure next door. His companions followed suit. They didn't ask questions, no doubt sensing his tense mood.

The door to the Dragon and Rose was locked. He pounded on it. After no one immediately came, he kicked the door. The hard wood shuddered.

A lock clicked. A bar slid. A round-cheeked, red-haired woman peered out and squinted.

"We're closed."

Angel shoved the door and woman back and he and his companions forced themselves inside.

"Hey! We're not open! Get out of here!"

Marisol closed the door and locked it.

Angel took a moment to survey the place. It smelled as if someone had been cooking. And the woman smelled of boozy sweat.

"We're looking for someone. A couple of someones. They were here last night. Are you the manager?"

The woman scowled. "I'm the owner. It's Lady Sofia to you."

He let out a laugh. "A noblewoman? Running a bar?"

"Not that it's any of your business. No one was here last night. We're months from opening. Now leave!"

Without prompting, his companions spread out and searched the common room. One found a trapdoor behind the bar and went down into a cellar, while Marisol went into the back. She returned a moment later with a pasty greenskin wearing a stained apron. The fel was trembling as she plopped him on the floor in front of Angel.

"Leave him alone!" Sofia said.

Marisol ignored her. "That's it for the kitchen. Looks like they're cleaning up after a party."

Angel was suddenly very interested. "A party? I thought you said this place was closed."

"We're under renovation," Sofia said. "We're trying out some recipes. What's this all about? Who are you people?"

Angel paced before her, his hand casually resting on the pommel of his rapier. On the floor lay what looked like a piece of lettuce and bits of other food. Whatever cleanup they were doing had been hasty. He crouched to inspect the floor behind the bar. The wood was damp as if it had been mopped.

"Must have been a messy party. Does testing the kitchen involve throwing food about? Looks like you've done more than prepare recipes. Tell me, Lady Sofia, who was here last night? We have a friend who vanished. Victor. A little taller than me. Handsome fellow. There was also a girl who calls herself Sprite, but she might have gone by Isabel. He's pureblood and noble. She's a greenskin, like your wash boy here. A pretty thing. There might have been another fel, too. A gravedigger."

"I don't know anything about them."

"No? Well, someone was here. Why don't we start there? Who was in your bar last night?"

When Sofia didn't answer, he made a fist.

She raised a defiant chin. "You wouldn't dare."

He stepped aside as Marisol struck her. Sofia went down. Marisol had wrapped her right hand into a steel knuckleduster. She was crouching to hit her again when the fel shouted, "Stop it!"

Angel motioned for Marisol. His cousin paused, looking disappointed.

"A loyal slave pleads for his master?" Angel asked.

The fel swallowed as if he had too much spit in his mouth. Licked his lips. "They were here, the people you were looking for. Lady Sofia didn't see them, but I did."

When Angel motioned for him to continue, the fel looked like he was about to piss himself.

"The girl came in here first. She had someone after her."

The wash boy stalled out again. Angel felt his patience waning.

"Then the man with the sword came in looking for her," the fel said. "There was a fight. One of the patrons killed him."

It was as if something in the room shifted. Angel's companions looked like they were ready to murder the fel. Angel knew they wouldn't do anything until he told them to, but even their patience would have limits now that they'd heard about Victor's fate.

"Who murdered the noble?" Angel asked.

"He was...a stranger. One of the visitors who came to play cards. I...I didn't know any of them."

"Describe him."

The wash boy's eyes darted from companion to companion. "He was fel."

"You're lying. There was a curfew. No fel would defy the edict for a card game."

"I posted notices," the fel blurted. "I was going to cook. I didn't think anyone would actually come."

Marisol let out a laugh.

Angel glared at her. "So a stranger killed a nobleman last night. A fel stranger. Here. You know what hiding this means?"

The fel wash boy who was also a cook didn't answer.

"The rope. You and every other greenskin at your party will pay with your lives. But perhaps you might find mercy if you tell me what happened to the girl."

Philip, one of his companions, scratched his neck. "Angel..."

"Not now. What's your name, fel?"

"Monty."

"Monty. Right now, Monty, your life is forfeit unless you tell me where she went."

"She went with the one who killed the noble. I don't know where."

"Our friend Victor's body isn't here. So maybe we can start there. What happened to it?"

Lady Sofia was staring at Monty with naked disbelief.

Monty hesitated. When Marisol grabbed Sofia's hair, he cried, "They took him with them to the cart out back."

"A cart? A gravedigger's cart?"

Monty nodded. Marisol released the noblewoman. She looked ready to go out back to resume the hunt. But Angel knew there had to be more.

"Thank you, Monty, that's helpful. But you're still keeping something from me. Last night you cooked for your greenskin friends, spread a feast, played cards, and then joined in killing a pureblood noble. But you never exchanged names? Please. What's this murderer's name?"

"Digger. That's what he called himself."

He stared at Monty, but the fel looked too terrified to be making up such a silly name.

"Digger, you say. A fel who collects the dead is named Digger. I'm sure that will narrow it down. We'll find him even if we have to bring every cemetery worker in for questioning. Anything else I need to know about, Monty?"

Monty shook his head.

Lady Sofia spoke up. "I didn't know about any of this. We'll cooperate with the city guard. This is all a big mess, but I'll get to the bottom of what happened here last night."

"Hmm," Angel purred. "*Lady* Sofia. There must be a reason you're on Loom Island away from your own kind and running a failed bar. What is it the homilies say? We reap what we sow? I'm afraid the time for calling the watch is over. Our companion is murdered and Diregloom has a pair of fugitives on its streets. And while my aunt, the queen, has her own form of justice, I believe we're well in our rights to mete it out right here."

He gave Marisol a nod. She drew her sword and walked behind the fel cook. He closed his eyes and began muttering.

Angel found himself trying to guess what the greenskin was saying.

It sounded like an apology.

Chapter Fourteen

MONTY'S APARTMENT WAS located off a lot connected to the back alley behind the Dragon and Rose. It was a single room up a rear flight of stairs over a shop that manufactured buttons for garments.

Digger had found him the place when they'd both needed to go into hiding. It had been perfect, with few neighbors, a pureblood landlord who was mostly blind and completely deaf, and an entry where no one could see his brother's comings and goings. He had paid Monty's rent months ahead, using up most of his savings earned before returning to Loom Island. His brother had no reason to go out and do anything that might endanger him.

Somehow, it had all gone wrong.

Monty had gotten a job with Lady Sofia, and not just any job. He had to become a cook. And then he had invited every fel in Diregloom to a card game.

Digger paused at the corner to survey the lot to be sure no one was around. The afternoon sun was shining directly on the stairway. He could only hope Monty had gone home and was there now.

"You look angry," Isabel said.

"I'm just thinking. Keep quiet. Your voice carries."

"We lost the people who were after us. Those tourists have no idea who we are."

"Well, there's still the bandits who have it out for you. All they'll have to do is spread some silver around and word will move quickly."

"Not everyone is evil."

He continued to watch. But there were few places worth hiding in daytime. "It's clear."

He led her to the stairs and went up ahead of her. The door was locked. He tapped the wood with a fingernail. Waited. Knocked lightly.

"Monty, it's me," he hissed.

No answer.

The time for subtlety was over. He was readying to kick the door in when Isabel stopped him.

She produced a hairpin from a braid. "May I?"

He stepped aside and watched as she bent the pin and made short work of the simple lock. With a *click*, they were inside.

The curtains were drawn, which was good. The cluttered room had a lumpy bedroll in one corner and a sawed-down table next to a nest of pillows. There were a few lamps and stacks of books and notepaper. Digger felt renewed anxiety as he lit a candle.

Isabel crouched and began to sift through the closest stack. "Cookbooks?"

Digger saw a few of the titles and recognized the colorful covers. Some of these had been from their parents' collection. The only way Monty could even have them was if he had returned to their restaurant and taken them.

He felt his stomach grow tight. "Wait here."

"What am I supposed to do?"

"Nothing. Stay put. Monty's probably still at the bar. I'll be back in five minutes."

All he could think about was how Monty had spoiled a perfect situation. With the current laws, it would be harder to find a new place to conceal him. They were back to square one. His brother was both talented and limited. Their father had said Monty was a natural, their mother had called him gifted. But outside of the kitchen, Monty was lost.

Clutching the shovel, Digger crossed the lot and followed the alley. The back door to the Dragon and Rose was unlocked. Voices came from the common room. Digger's breath caught as he eased across the storeroom floor and strained his ears.

He heard a crisp voice talking, someone used to people listening. Educated. Patronizing. His brother answered, sounding desperate. Lady Sofia also spoke.

Digger peered out and saw a group of tourists. But this wasn't the band who had chased Isabel and him through the streets. The group standing over Monty and Sofia were the same ones who had confronted the sheriff.

He felt a chill in his blood.

These were the friends of the man Digger had killed. Their leader was Lord Angel.

One of them, a woman with braided hair, drew her sword. She moved behind Monty.

There was no time to plan or think. Digger stepped out into the common room. He swung the shovel into the face of the nearest tourist. The metal head smashed into the man's nose with a crunch. Not stopping, Digger charged the next man and brought the shovel up into a high arc.

But the man was quick and rolled out of the way. His sword was out in a flash and he spun, assuming a low fighting stance. The others moved, shoving chairs and tables aside. Shouting. Spreading out.

Monty and Sofia scrambled behind the bar.

Digger ran for the closest man, who was fumbling to clear his sword from the long cape he wore. Digger drove his fist into the man and he went down. He turned in time to see another charging, his sword out and slicing through the air. Digger flipped a chair across the man's path and he stumbled, but Digger almost tripped as he stepped out of the way of the clumsy blow.

"That's him!" Angel said.

The remaining three did as ordered. The woman was closing in. Her sword was poised behind her and her gloved hand was outstretched as if she were feeling the air. The other two followed suit, one to Digger's left and one to his right. All of them were trained. The clumsy tourists he had faced earlier were amateurs in comparison.

Digger had nowhere to go. There was nothing but stacked chairs, tables, and a wall behind him.

Angel pulled his own rapier. His ringed fingers clicked on the weapon's grip. "Drop the shovel. You can salvage this with your life if you surrender."

"It didn't look like you were taking prisoners."

"You're surrounded. You've murdered a pureblood. I commend you for coming forward. Now give yourself up before you and anyone you might know pay the price for your crime."

The woman lunged at him, the sword's tip zigzagging though the air. Digger swung his shovel but she was too quick. She drew back and again thrust her blade, making him lose his balance as he moved to block her. But her sword was everywhere. She was laughing. Toying with him. She was a cat with a mouse.

The other two were holding back. Angel remained behind them.

If all three came for him, Digger might catch any one of them with his shovel as they got in each other's way. But this woman commanded the floor. One mistake and he was dead. A trained fighter like her only needed a single opening.

"Lord Angel, is it?" Digger called while keeping his eyes on his opponent.

Angel smirked. "Have we been introduced?"

The woman smacked the nearest chair with her sword. "You don't address him. Your kind doesn't speak unless spoken to."

"Tut-tut, Marisol. Perhaps our gravedigger friend wishes to know if I'll honor his surrender. Of course I will. You'll see justice. But more importantly, you'll save whatever family you have from a date with the gallows."

"I'm listening," Digger said. The sweat on his brow began to sting his eyes. He fought to blink it away.

"Are you expecting more terms? Drop that ridiculous shovel."

"I don't think so. I'll take one of you with me. But you want something, and I want to know what. If it's revenge, you'd just kill me."

This only appeared to amuse Angel. But his face went stern. "I don't have time to waste, gravedigger. By your admission you killed one of us. That demands justice. But you had a woman with you. My dear Sprite. She had in her possession something I want back."

So they were here for the watch. "What are you looking for, exactly?"

"This is your life on the line, and you ask stupid questions. You were with her. Tell me where she is, and you still have a chance at mercy. Otherwise you die by inches and days. My aunt's tournament will have a new side attraction with you as the star."

"Claudia's your aunt?"

"Queen Claudia to you, fel. Now where's the girl?"

"She's gone. She came in here last night and your friend Victor followed. He was carrying on like you and threatening to hurt people. I stopped him. I put a knife in his guts. It was me, not anyone who worked here. So if you want justice, I'm your man."

Marisol and the other two companions stiffened at his words. He'd just confessed to killing their friend. Digger prepared himself for the assault. The one to Marisol's right appeared the weakest of the bunch. Digger would smash his head in and do his best to buy Monty a moment to escape.

Angel surprised him when he barked, "Marisol! Gavin! Hector! Back away."

The three took a half step back. Neither of the other two lying on the floor was moving.

"It's a gold watch you're looking for, right?" Digger asked.

"Do you have it?"

"I know where it is. Here's my deal. Let those two go and we keep talking."

Angel glanced at Sofia and Monty. They remained behind the bar.

"They're important to you," Angel said.

"They're not involved. You want information? Let's start by cutting them free."

"My dear gravedigger, I'm afraid that's not how this works. You've revealed you know something. All I have to do now is cut it out of you. Or out of them. One way or another, you're going to tell me what I want to know."

Digger adjusted his hold on the shovel. He had blundered by showing he had concern for Monty. He looked for any sign his brother might be ready to act. But Monty continued to grip the bar with his head down. Lady Sofia had a hand on him as if to comfort him.

He hadn't considered the possibility that Monty had more going at the Dragon and Rose than just a place to flex his culinary acumen. Had Monty fallen in love? Now, none of it mattered. Angel was going to kill all of them unless Digger did something.

But here, outnumbered, this was a fight he couldn't win.

A shadow came hurtling from the rear of the common room. The flying table crashed into one of the noblemen behind Marisol and sent him to the floor. A second, ogre-sized shadow stepped into the light.

"I heard I missed a card game last night," Sprat Hellard said. "Why wasn't I invited?"

Chapter Fifteen

IT WAS THE FIRST INSTANT Digger had seen Marisol's attention falter. But with her sword still at the ready, he didn't dare try for her or the others.

Hellard was an imposing figure as he stomped towards them. Quick, too. He scooped up a chair and flung it into the remaining nobleman. He and Angel fell back towards the entrance. Hellard then snatched up a dropped rapier and swished it about in the air.

The silvery weapon looked like a toy in his massive hand.

Marisol stood alone as she pivoted to face him.

Wasting no time, Digger cut loose with a shout as he launched himself at her. She was too fast. She blocked his shovel with her blade and shot her foot out, almost tripping him. But he was bigger than her and got inside the reach of her blade, shoulder-checking her and sending her stumbling towards Angel. Digger almost paid for the move when she spun the rapier in her hand and thrust downward, nearly catching his leg. It was his turn to backpedal as she punched with her pommel and began a flurry of slashes. He dodged one, blocked another, and felt steel cut his right arm as he stumbled out of range.

Hellard had gotten hold of one of Angel's companions and was slamming him repeatedly into the floor. The last companion standing shoved the chair aside and advanced on the ogre.

Digger couldn't do anything while fighting Marisol. He yelled, "Hellard! Look out!"

Lady Sofia charged out from behind the bar and smashed a bottle across the man's head. He went down, groaning.

Hellard raised the man he was holding and threw him into another who was just starting to rise to his knees.

Monty screamed.

Lord Angel had climbed over the bar and was dragging Digger's brother towards the front door. He held the edge of his sword to Monty's neck.

"This could have been easy," Angel said. "But you'd all stand together to protect a murderer. I sense this fel is precious to you, gravedigger."

Digger tried to move towards them but Marisol blocked his path. Two of the other companions limped past her. One couldn't put any weight on his ankle, and the other had an arm dangling uselessly at his side. When Digger tried to sidestep Marisol, Angel pressed the blade tighter across Monty's throat.

"Not a step further. Don't think you've won anything. I'll have the city guard here in moments. Unless you have the watch to offer me."

"I don't," Digger said. "But like I said, I can get it. You harm him, and you'll never see it."

Hellard loomed behind him and began cracking his knuckles. "We could take 'em."

Digger considered it for a moment. But no matter what they tried, Monty wouldn't survive.

Sofia was busy retrieving another bottle.

Marisol finally retreated towards the exit but stood in front of Angel as if protecting him. She whispered something to Angel. He shushed her.

Angel handed his prisoner off to one of his men and Monty was ushered out the door. "Find me the watch. Your fel friend goes free. That's the deal."

"Agreed. Where?"

"Stockade Square. By the gallows. I'll not set foot here again where you can have an army of ogres waiting for me."

"But you'll have the city guard."

"That's a risk you'll have to take. Send it by messenger if you're afraid for your own neck. It doesn't matter to me. But don't be tardy. In two hours your friend hangs. Not quite the spectacle Queen Claudia prefers in her executions, but it will serve its purpose."

"I'll get you your watch."

Angel took a moment to study Digger. "I'll remember you, gravedigger. If you try to run, there's no place you can hide from me when this is done."

"You hold up your end of the bargain. I'll see you at the gallows."

THEY STEPPED OUT IN time to see Angel, his prisoner, and the three companions gather their horses and ride off.

"Who were those people?" Lady Sofia asked.

Digger could only shake his head. "Some damn noblemen chasing a fel woman who ran into your bar last night."

"I figured that out. But why here? What does Monty have to do with this?"

"He made the mistake of being open for business with his card game."

Sofia followed Digger inside and gave him an angry push. Hellard was standing next to them and she switched targets and punched him. The ogre flinched as if wounded.

"I thought I told you to get out of my bar."

"I left," Hellard said. "I was hanging out in a nearby alley when I saw those men coming this way. I thought there'd be trouble."

Digger took the bottle from her hands. "Look...Lady Sofia, I'm Monty's brother. He probably never mentioned me."

Her eyes were glassy with tears. "He talked about you all the time."

"I'll get him back. I promise."

She marched past them. The two remaining injured noblemen were still breathing but unconscious.

Sofia made a helpless gesture. "What am I supposed to do with them?"

"We hold on to those two," Digger said. "Bring them with us as part of the exchange in case Angel tries to screw us."

"What chance is there he'll honor his deal?"

Digger tried to conjure a lie but failed. "Little to none."

"YOU KNOW IT'S A TRAP," Hellard said as he trailed after Digger through the back alley. He carried the two men, one on each shoulder, as easy as if lugging sacks of grain. "We should tuck his friends away someplace safe. Keep them as hostages. That way the swap is on our terms."

"That's what you and your gang are good at, isn't it?"

"What's that supposed to mean?"

"Your ink. Which crew do you run with? Wharf Rats? Huanghun?"

"Currently unaffiliated."

"Isabel said you were recruiting at her mission."

"I was. I'm starting something real that isn't just a group of robbers looking to make coin."

Digger stopped and clanged the shovel on the pavement before Hellard. He was used to using his size to intimidate, but that wouldn't work with an ogre.

"We had people after us today with tattoos like yours. Too much of a coincidence in my eyes."

Hellard displayed his arm. In the shadows it was hard to clearly see, but Digger could make out the mark of the skull with stars on his skin. "Is this what you saw?"

"Yes."

"Karanog? Are you sure?"

"If that's their mark, then yes."

Hellard made a deep noise in his throat. "Then it means trouble. They don't normally come to Diregloom. When I was with them, we stuck to the wilds east of the kingdoms, the swamps, hills, and deserts. But we avoided the water and the islands."

"You're here, aren't you? So why wouldn't your gang come?"

"Too much competition. Too many rules between the rival gangs. Last thing anyone wants is a gang war, so we kept to our territory."

"So what's changed?"

"Management. If you say they're after Isabel, then the price must be good. What is this watch, anyway?"

Digger picked up the shovel and rested it on his shoulder. There was no way he could trust Hellard. But there weren't any other options. For some reason Hellard was insisting on helping. Plus, getting into a fight with an ogre in a dark alley would be the last in a series of bad ideas that had gotten him to his current predicament.

At least Lady Sofia stood a chance. If she was smart, she'd heed his warning and get out of the city. She was pureblood. She could travel freely and get a fresh start anywhere.

He chose his words carefully. "The watch is just a piece of fancy jewelry. I appreciate your help in the bar. But this is my business, not yours."

"You trying to get rid of me? Looks like you might need an extra set of hands."

"What's to stop you from taking me out once I lead you to Isabel? There's a price on her head and you know it."

Hellard grunted. "If the Karanog are here, then I'm in as much danger as she is. They don't exactly let people quit, and our parting was less than amicable. They want Isabel for a reason. Profit-motivated, so they'll take her alive. Me, they'll just kill."

"Maybe you handing her to them will smooth things over for you."

"I'd be lying if I said that hadn't crossed my mind. You don't know me. But I came to the game looking for fel just like you. Ones who are willing to fight. You want me gone, say the word."

Weighing his options wasn't hard. Having an ogre on their side was a seductive thought. And if Hellard was there for Isabel, there wasn't much Digger could do about it.

"Come on."

He led the ogre across the lot behind the button shop and clomped up the steps towards Monty's apartment. The door stood ajar.

"Isabel?" he hissed. "Hey!"

But Isabel wasn't inside. He checked everywhere, but there wasn't any place to hide.

With her gone, he realized all hope of saving his brother went with her. But there was only one place she would go. The sheriff still had her watch. So wherever the sheriff was, she would be there too.

Chapter Sixteen

HOW EASILY FEL GAVE in once confronted by their superiors.

The fel cook they had taken from the Dragon and Rose remained silent and subdued as he rode in front of Angel, sharing the saddle.

Angel had expected him to fight and struggle but the whimpering greenskin only trembled.

They headed towards the stockade. The afternoon crowd from earlier hadn't abated. In fact, it was worse now that the sun was setting behind lavender clouds and the haze of factory smoke. He had been going almost nonstop since the previous evening, trying to untangle his own situation, and forgotten what day it was.

This was to be a special night for the city. With the start of the catacomb games, the curfew was lifted. The fel were free to be out in the streets. It was the type of evening that perturbed Duke Tito and his court to no end and would give the visiting viscount ammunition for his report on Queen Claudia.

But Angel would have no time to enjoy whatever entertainments Claudia had planned. He spurred his horse and his companions kept up. Gavin and Hector had injuries that needed tending. Only Marisol remained unhurt. Cy and Philip had been left behind.

He glanced at her and saw she wore a black expression.

No doubt upset at abandoning their two friends. They'd get them back, of that he was certain. The fel gravedigger wanted the cook alive. Now that Angel had made contact with the gravedigger, he was beginning to feel in control of the situation, which had been nothing but chaos since Isabel had stolen the watch. The watch would be returned. Red Eye would get paid. And after getting out from under his debt, Angel would make things right with his aunt and be the best nephew she could ever share her wealth with.

He could almost taste it, it would be so good.

Marisol and the others would forgive him eventually. For now, all they had to do was obey.

His aunt's decorations adorned every intersection near Stockade Square, with orange banners, teal ribbons, flags, and floral arrangements decorating lampposts and hanging across the streets. Musicians who made up for a lack of skill with volume were screeching away with violin, guitar, flute, and clarinet. The night was bringing everyone out, and he cursed and kicked as people kept brushing up against him and his horse.

He made a beeline for the stockade gate. There they dismounted, and he handed his prisoner over to a guard who led the cook away without question. Gavin and Hector needed help dismounting and were soon being tended to by the stockade medic.

"We should go back," Marisol said. "We might free Cy and Philip."

"No. The gravedigger will bring them here. He wants to make this deal. He knows how bad it will go for him if he doesn't show up with the watch."

"It was a mistake leaving them behind."

"I can see you're angry, Marisol. I know you wanted to have a go at them. But even if we had won, we'd have lost Sprite and any chance at finding the watch."

"I'd protect you from Red Eye."

He leaned in and gave her a kiss on the cheek. "I know you would. But this is the right way to do this. We start killing everyone, we lose what I'm trying to build here. My aunt's island is looking at a boom the likes of which we've never seen. We're situated to be on top of it all if we play our cards right. But for now we have to follow the rules, until we become the ones who *make* the rules. And don't worry, cousin. We'll rescue our friends soon."

She kept her head low.

He flicked her chin. "Don't pout. It doesn't become you."

Riders were approaching the gate.

Claudia's steward Rochus swung off the horse and marched straight for Angel, then gave a curt bow. He was dressed in a checkered orange vest with gold buttons, bright blue pantaloons, and shoes with curled tips. The outfit was made all the more garish because of his green skin.

"Queen Claudia requests your presence."

"Tell her I'm right in the middle of something," Angel said.

Rochus didn't hesitate before saying, "She followed up the request with these specific words. 'Angel is to get his ass back to the castle or he'll be lucky to be licking the dinner plates after tomorrow's banquets.'" He dipped his head as if to punctuate his aunt's order.

Angel sighed.

This wasn't the time. He was so close to finishing this business. But keeping his aunt happy was a tricky thing. She had been reluctant at first to even allow him to move into the castle. Day by day, tedious meetings over décor and city planning and budgets and guest lists where he feigned not only interest but enthusiasm had finally borne fruit. Now she relied on him to assist with the most mundane decisions around her planned spectacle.

She had only excluded him from one thing: the conversations she had with her game designers. The under-the-castle arena had its own staff and budget and was more closely guarded than the castle itself.

The thought of it made him giddy. Not the facility itself but the amount of silver it took to pay for everything. In addition to what he was privy to, his aunt must have been shoveling a mountain of funds into her catacomb project.

Claudia the Second was so far beyond wealthy, it taxed his imagination to think of what he might do when holding the reins to her little island.

But he had pressed his luck by staying away all afternoon in pursuit of the watch.

Rochus stood patiently. His cool, neutral face dared Angel to try his excuse a second time. What other ultimatum from his aunt might he have prepared?

He'd have to go, he decided. He had given the gravedigger two hours to come to the square. Angel could make it to the castle for a brief meeting with his aunt, soothe ruffled feathers, and be back in time to meet the haughty fel and end this distracting predicament.

To Marisol he said, "Keep an eye on the prisoner. No one gets in to see him. No one. Understand?"

She nodded.

He mounted up and guided his horse back out the gate. His aunt's attendant tried to trot ahead of him, but Angel nudged his horse forward as they cut their way through the crowd and rode up Fountain Street towards the castle.

THE STEWARD ROCHUS ran along behind Angel as he pushed through the front doors of the castle and entered the cavernous front hall. It was empty.

"Where is she?" Angel asked.

"She has instructed for you to wait."

"I'll see her now."

Rochus bodily blocked Angel's path to the stairs leading up to the bedchambers. "She asked for you to wait in the clock room."

"The clock room? Why there?"

The steward spread his hands as if showing he wasn't one to know such truths. Then he indicated which direction to go, as if Angel didn't know. A clock gonged and echoed through the hallway. Angel heard his aunt's voice upstairs. Sidestepping Rochus, he bounded up the steps three at a time as the fel hurried to catch up.

Claudia appeared at the top of the stairway. She wore a shining white gown and had six attendants hurrying after her with mirrors, jewelry, face powder, and perfume.

"It's good enough," his aunt was saying. "You heard the clock. We're late. I'm never late. This will have to do."

Queen Claudia and her procession came to a stop as his aunt noticed him. "There you are."

Angel gave a deep bow. "My dear aunt, my most profound apologies. I was waylaid—"

"There's no time for that. You and I will have a discussion. You might have ruined everything."

"I can explain."

She whisked down the steps past him, amazingly spry for a plump older woman with what must have been enough clothes, jewelry, and hair accoutrements to outweigh a suit of steel armor. Her attendants scurried after her, and Rochus fell in next to Angel as he tried to keep up.

"There was an incident," Angel said. "One of my friends was hurt. I had to deal with the city watch, help keep the peace."

She stopped at the bottom of the stairway and faced him. "These are the games. My games. This is the opening festival. You have no idea what you've done."

Before he could interject, she raised a hand.

"You will wait for me here. I have to go and deliver my opening speech. Greet the contestants. Display the prizes. But one of them is missing, Angel. I am very cross with you."

She took a final glance at the three mirrors her attendants were holding before rushing out the door and down to where her carriage was waiting.

He felt his heart hammering. She had found out. He was sunk. He'd have to pull out all the stops or he'd be sent back home, his chances of winning his aunt over ruined, and his debt unpaid.

Why did God hate him so?

None of the attendants made eye contact as they dispersed.

Rochus waited on him.

"What do you want?" Angel asked.

"I give counsel to the queen. I'm available if needed."

"I don't want anything from you, fel."

"As you wish."

Rochus retreated but lingered, standing by a wall as Angel tried to decide what to do.

Getting the watch back was still his immediate concern. But if he left the castle, he'd be violating a direct command. He could only hope Marisol was keeping the cook safe. Once Claudia returned, he could make matters right again. Tell her that he had everything under control. The watch would be back so she could award it to the winner of her games.

He'd stolen the wrong bauble. Surely some other treasure in the palace would balance his debt with Red Eye. He paced the grand hallway and made his way down to the clock room. He was about to enter when he saw a light in the library a few doors down.

Curious, he went in to find Viscount Ilario sitting in a cushioned chair with a giant tome in his lap. Several candelabras spilled their orange light onto the hundreds of books lining the shelves. Sitting on an armrest was a boy with bright lipstick and garish red-painted cheeks, wearing what appeared to be a satin bathrobe. The count was pointing to a page and running his fingers along the words.

"'The pro-phet pur-sue-ed the vis...the vis-e-on...'" the boy read.

"Vision," the viscount corrected. "Good. 'The prophet pursued the vision.' And where did it lead him?"

"'It led him for twen-ty days and nig-nie-nights until he came to the sea.'"

"Excellent, Peter. You have a gift for this." He stroked the boy's head. Then he squinted as he noticed Angel standing in the doorway.

"I'm sorry for disturbing you, Viscount Ilario."

"It's no disturbance, Lord Angel. We're reading Third Scripture. You could join us. It seems the chapel sees little of you, according to Lady Claudia."

Angel gave a humble nod. "I've been remiss. I've allowed myself to become distracted. Perhaps tomorrow morning we can take our prayers together."

"That would please me. Duke Tito was most worried about your spiritual state. I find it troubling that in addition to everything else wrong with this island, faith has fallen by the wayside." He caressed the boy's head again. "But even a dying ember can be rekindled."

Angel bowed and excused himself. He entered the clock room. The chorus of ticking from the many timepieces was a tide of noise. He hadn't realized before how irritating it was. He almost jumped when the silver wall clock gonged eight times.

He was supposed to be at his aunt's side this evening. It was her grand event, what she had been planning for all year long. He had tried to share in her excitement, to be involved in her preparations, to be integral. But instead she had ordered him to wait here while she began her festivities without him.

He could have stolen any number of pieces of jewelry and she wouldn't have missed a single one. Why had he taken the centerpiece of her catacomb prizes?

Fear, he decided.

Red Eye had scared him and made him react instead of thinking his way through the problem.

There'd be no more of that. He had been provided with the finest tutors in Bahia, trained in mathematics and philosophy. He was no fel rube but a pureblood noble. The time for fear was over.

He placed his hand on the front of the wall clock. Felt the shifting works inside moving as if a mechanical heart beat within. The sounds almost drowned out the noise of the growing party that carried up the hill from the square.

Tick, tick, tick.

His aunt hadn't dismissed him. He still had the opportunity to fix the problem. No more fear, no more mistakes. There was time to make this right.

Chapter Seventeen

A CURSORY SEARCH OF the streets near the Dragon and Rose hadn't turned up Isabel.

This didn't surprise Digger. Despite their discussion at the hangman's bar, Isabel remained fixated on the watch. So he and Hellard hurried towards the stockade. There was no way to keep their two prisoners with them, so Hellard found a shed behind a metalworker's shop and locked them inside.

Digger felt a growing anxiety as they crossed the city. If Angel spotted them without Isabel, what would stop the nobleman from killing his brother? And even if they found her and managed to confront him, Lord Angel hadn't hesitated to leave his own men behind. There was little chance he would honor their deal.

His thoughts grew dark as they turned down the final alleyway towards the stockade.

The square had pink and purple lanterns suspended along wires above the streets. A crowd of people jammed the main thoroughfares, some wearing masks and others holding aloft sticks that threw off white sprays of sparks. At least three competing bands played music that blended into a frenzy of sound.

Even the alley had partygoers.

Fel and pureblood locals mingled with tourists. A group of teens raced past laughing, their faces painted in colorful monster makeup. A vendor with a grill was stoking a coal fire next to another who was exchanging sausage skewers for scrip.

Digger felt a growing confusion as he tried to make sense of the scene. He grabbed a fel who was getting his two children bundled against the chill air.

"What's going on?"

The man gave him a look as if Digger had asked why the sun had set. "Claudia's announced a free festival for the opening of catacombs."

"Curfew's in a couple of hours. It looks like this is just getting started."

"You deaf? No curfew bell tonight. They've had criers out all day. Claudia's given out scrip to all who attend. It's free food, and anyone's a fool for missing it."

The father hurried his children out the alley.

Some were using the alley as a changing room as they pulled on costumes. One was a dragon with a tall stuffed head that would tower over everyone. Her partner was preparing to be the rear half of the serpent. More than a few donned elaborate bespoke gowns and suits of rough fabrics festooned with streamers and bows, as if putting on mock noble apparel. Some seemed to be trying to look like Queen Claudia herself.

Hellard was attempting to lurk nearby, but folks nudged past him with little care.

"You see her?" he asked.

Digger peered out the alley. Between the masks and the crowd, spotting Isabel would be difficult. Digger's apprehension twisted his stomach. Angel and any number of soldiers could be concealed among the partygoers. The Karanog were certainly out there if they were still after Isabel. He could only assume that he too was now on their wanted list.

"You might want to wait here," he said.

Hellard didn't comment as Digger left him.

Stockade Square was as crowded as any Saturday. The weekly executions were perversely popular. Diregloom had fallen into the custom once the fel realized it was one of the few times they could congregate in large number, enjoy music and the vendors that favored the pureblood markets, and forget the drudgery of the week, even as the gallows collected a life or three as toll.

Digger hadn't missed one since going into hiding. His new job demanded it. But he also felt a certain obligation to bear witness to each death at the hands of Diregloom's lawgivers. The edict that had taken his parents' restaurant and had allowed for their murder when they protested had become part of the rotten foundation of the city's control over his kind.

Pureblood and fel were now separated not only by districts but by laws differentiating between the two. Purebloods of even the lowest birth could escape an infraction with a literal slap on the wrist or a boxed ear. His kind went into the cart.

But the queen's fascination with her catacomb games was evolving. Rumors were impossible to verify and harder to ignore. What had she been building in her castle for so many months? There were few facts, and only the early rounds of the games from months prior hinted at what she might have in store for the nobility's entertainment.

The only certainty was it would cost fel lives.

He snatched up a dropped scarf and wrapped his face and head. He paused at the stand where children purchased the sparklers and bought one. The vendor appeared pleased to receive a copper coin when so many were pushing scrip at him.

A group of city guards gathered near the gallows. They were making room, moving the partygoers back. Digger elbowed his way forward as the crowd grew dense. From up the hill, beyond the square in the direction of the castle, there came a flourish of bugle calls.

"The queen's coming!" a giddy pureblood girl said.

A cheer went up from the crowd.

Queen Claudia would attend each Saturday. Her mood was somber then. She would often speak, declaring the necessity of such actions to keep the peace, to teach the unruly, to correct the incorrigible. But then she would remind the crowd of her care for them, that they were her children under her protection from the rest of the world. Her voice would take on the tone of a vexed mother speaking with children in need of the rod.

Blah, blah, blah.

Digger remembered the clause of Duke Tito's Thirteenth Edict as it was recited by the knight's commander who had presided over the dissolution of his ranger unit. Digger and his fellow soldiers who had mustered into the fort had then been placed under arrest. Digger had known what it would mean for his parents on Loom Island. They had intermarried in violation of an earlier decree.

Their lives and their property were now forfeit as the new law had teeth.

He had escaped and returned to Diregloom, but not in time to save them. He had hoped—prayed, even—that the lady of the island would stand up to the duke.

The best she had ever done was provide lip service as the duke's magisters seized all fel property and Claudia's soldiers arrested any who resisted. His parents' restaurant had coincidentally been at the waterfront, which was now undergoing its renovation into the centerpiece of Diregloom's booming tourist business. The fawning new owner had paid the city a pittance for the title deed. Digger had made it to the island in time to find Monty and this new owner fighting. His brother had drawn blood. Digger stepped in to finish the job. But before they could escape, the magister and two guards had come to complete some minor paperwork.

How Digger had raged.

He pushed the memory aside. He was fighting a lack of sleep and hunger and had to focus.

There.

At the edge of the crowd past the gallows stood the sheriff. He wore his green hat and appeared worn and disinterested in the spectacle. Digger hunkered down to conceal himself.

If the sheriff was here, Isabel would be too. Her blue cloak would have been easy to spot, but with her new outfit she would be invisible.

From the top of the square a cheer erupted. A sparkling carriage clattered down the street. The musicians stopped playing. Digger struggled to see and got up on his toes. Something about the oncoming vehicle was unusual. As the carriage entered the square, it became apparent what it was.

The carriage wasn't being pulled by horses but by trolls. The two enormous man-shaped green creatures wore harnesses around their bodies. They would be as tall as the gallows platform if they stood erect, but they were stooped and laboring as they hauled their burden forward. The creatures had dark green skin like many fel, their heads covered with mops of black, tangled hair. Someone had painted bright teal and orange flowers on their bodies.

The crowd parted. An older boy stood transfixed in the path of the carriage. In an instant he was trampled and crushed as the trolls stomped forward. His body went under a wheel and remained underneath the carriage as it came to a stop. None of the guards in the square appeared to notice.

The crowd fell into a hush.

A gaily dressed attendant opened the carriage door and pulled out a step for the passenger.

The queen emerged. She was radiant in a white, flowing dress, her bleached hair a bundle of complicated curls tucked around her head. Her body jiggled as she took the attendant's hand and descended to the cobblestones. She waved, her face beaming, her precise crimson lipstick the only color on her stark white face.

The crowd applauded, but enough were intoxicated for the ovation to evolve into a roar. Whatever momentary shock and horror in their hearts at seeing the boy trampled had vanished. More attendants appeared and began to throw out tiny orange cloth bundles of wrapped goodies into the crowd. The men and women closest to Digger jumped up to grab the party favors, and more began bumping him as they scurried about on the ground for any that had been dropped.

One of the trolls reached beneath the carriage and began to tug the dead boy closer. The carriage driver smacked it in the head with a long stick and the troll flinched, grunted, and settled down on its haunches.

Digger had only ever seen one of the monsters before. Supposedly they lived in the water, but the only one that had ever showed up in the city had been part of a traveling zoo attraction when he was very young. He had then thought it cruel how such a large creature had been stuck inside a cage. That one had been lethargic and sick and covered in its own vomit. A child who had gone through the line ahead of him had been disappointed the monster hadn't reacted when poked with a stick.

"My children! My children!" the queen was saying as she walked a circle, waving the whole time. "The catacomb games begin tomorrow! I welcome visitor and friend, one and all. Tickets are available tonight. Let's make this the best season yet. I have such surprises for you!"

She pulled one of her gown sleeves up to the elbow, displaying a series of sparkling jeweled wristwatches.

"These are tomorrow's prizes. And this is just a taste of the treasures which can be won. Be you fel or pureblood, the catacombs await."

More cheers drowned her out. The queen beamed and waved the crowd quiet.

"But first, would you like to see your monsters?"

From the stockade marched guards festooned with garlands around their helmets. They were escorting a group of fel. The prisoners wore manacles and face paints that made them look like fanged demons with menacing eyes. Teal and orange ribbons hung from their tattered clothes. Around each of their necks was a collar with a gold token.

The crowd applauded.

Digger edged sideward away from the crush. He had lost sight of the sheriff. He pushed along until he made the steps of the gallows. They were crowded with spectators, but Digger pushed some aside and climbed a few steps until he was high enough to see over most of the heads. There, moving away through the crowd, he spied the green hat.

He jumped down and hurried to follow.

Had Lord Angel known about the throng that would fill the square? How couldn't he have? Digger guessed they had an hour before the exchange. An hour to catch the sheriff and convince him, one way or another, to surrender the watch.

If his words failed him, he had his shovel.

Chapter Eighteen

AS DIGGER SHADOWED the sheriff, he realized someone was tailing him and creeping closer. He paused at a corner and sprang out, almost colliding with Isabel. She wore a mask and had her hair up beneath a papier-mâché top hat. She had replaced his blanket with a black wrap but hadn't bothered to conceal her face.

"I thought that was you," she hissed. She tried to step past him.

"Hold it. Why didn't you wait at the apartment?"

"You were taking too long. Let's go before we lose him."

She hurried past and he kept up. Telling her about Monty and what had happened at the Dragon and Rose would only confuse matters. For the moment she might prove useful in getting hold of the watch. But now he needed it more than she did.

The sheriff was making his way down to the harbor. Every time Digger paused at a corner to wait for the man to make some distance, Isabel darted ahead. While she moved quietly, the sheriff had but to turn his head to spot the same two figures stalking him.

Diregloom's sheltered bay on the south shore of the island had become a crowded place during the past few years. The harbor was chock-full of boats, a hodgepodge of barges, sailing vessels, prams, and cargo ships. A few were little more than shanties on pontoons. Many of the vessels were home to new arrivals along with those who couldn't afford the rising rents and refused to live near the slums. Planks connected several by common accord, shared easements that were often wide enough to accommodate handcarts.

Digger had collected his share of corpses from the harbor and still found the place confusing.

The district held the poorest of the city alongside the newly wealthy and newcomers in search of profit or catacomb fame. The Wharf Rats and other gangs competed for customers for their drug and prostitution business, and more than a few brawls had broken out across the boat decks. Because of its makeup it remained less patrolled than the rest of the city.

The sheriff was walking onto one of the fixed docks that led to the heart of the harbor. Normally by this time of the evening the boats would be bright with lamplight, but many vessels remained dark. The sounds of renewed music from the festivities carried down to the water.

Isabel led Digger to the corner of a dock house out on the pier. Here on the wooden planks her shoes made too much noise. He walked gingerly across the groaning planks after her. Fortunately the boats made their own regular bumps and creaks and the dock was far from lifeless. Voices and sounds of evening chores came from all around them, along with children laughing, a few dogs barking, and a baby or seven crying.

The sheriff headed up a gangway that ran across the bows of several barges. The raised passageway allowed no place to hide.

Digger nudged Isabel. "Hold back."

She nodded and then broke cover, scurrying towards the gangway. He muttered a curse and followed. They moved up onto the walkway. But up ahead the sheriff had vanished from sight.

Had they lost him?

There were several intercepting planks leading every direction off the gangway. None were lit. The locals must have realized that anyone that belonged there would know where they were going. Or, more likely, no one wanted to pay for a lamp and oil. Plus, the last thing boat dwellers would want was an unattended fire, no matter how small.

The footing was precarious as the gangway extended beyond a second row of lashed-together boats and along a row of pilings before passing between a few larger vessels.

Isabel paused at the rope ladder to a barge. She put a finger to her lips before climbing up and vanishing. Digger hurried after her. At least the barge would afford them a better view.

The dark vessel had activity on its deck. A nearby man with a knit cap and apron was crouched over a brazier loaded with glowing hot coals. Small fish sizzled before him.

There were several other grills on deck, as if more than one cook might work his trade at any given time. Against the far railing were nets, poles, and other equipment lashed to racks. Laundry dried on clotheslines. Inside a hut at the far end of the barge, a curtain snapped closed.

Even as Digger's eyes adjusted, he knew there were too many places to hide. They were vulnerable. This was a perfect ambush point and they were backlit by the lights spilling across the docks from the city.

Just as he was about to get Isabel to retreat down the ladder, he spied another gangway on the opposite side of the barge connecting to a single sloop.

"You saw him come up here?" he whispered.

She nodded and approached the cook. He glanced up at her as he turned his fish. Then he picked up a metal bowl and began to remove them from the grill with a set of tongs.

"Any food for sale?" she asked.

He waved his hand dismissively and shook his head.

"Too bad. I have coins and I'm hungry."

The cook paused. He reached into a pouch and produced a sheet of dried seaweed, then filled the wrapper with one of the fish. "Two pennies."

Isabel fumbled with her clothes.

Digger saw scrip in her hand but no coin. He went to his own coin pouch and paid the man. He then nodded towards the sloop.

"Is that boat for rent?"

"Nuh. She's occupied."

"Are they home?"

The cook shrugged. Using the tongs, he pulled a solid lid across the coals.

Digger handed over two more coins. "I'm going to have a word with your neighbor. If that's okay with you, of course."

The cook appeared to not have heard. But he took the money.

Digger and Isabel moved past him and prepared to descend the gangway to the sloop. It was a precarious balance. But Isabel didn't hesitate, hurrying along its length to the deck of the other boat. The wood bowed as Digger placed his weight on it. He inched forward. The sloop began to bob in the water as he got close.

If the sheriff was on board, he would surely know they were there.

Digger got his shovel ready and used it to keep his balance as he prepared to finish his crossing.

Isabel was waiting for him. "Come on," she whispered.

Behind them, the cook banged his tongs in a rapid staccato beat.

Tap-tappity-tap-tap. Tap. Tap.

Digger swore. He knew a signal when he heard one.

The sheriff appeared on the deck of the barge, his cudgel and knife out. "There are advantages to knowing your neighbors. And I saw you following me. Can I help the two of you with something?"

Digger pivoted carefully while struggling to keep the plank beneath him from wobbling. "The watch you took from the Dragon and Rose. We know its owner. We'd like to get it back."

"And what makes you think I still have it?"

"Do you?" Isabel asked. "It's important."

"I can see that. Fel are practically ordered to attend when the queen speaks, and yet the two of you are here, and on an open night without curfew."

"We have coin," Digger said. "We can pay. A fair reward for finding it, which we're happy to share."

"And is that what you had in mind with your visit? What's the shovel for?"

"My work. I didn't want to leave it anywhere to be stolen."

"Of course you wouldn't. But two fel coming in the night...it's like a story my mother would tell us as children about how it used to be. When your kind ruled. A cautious man would be concerned about your intentions."

"I'm here to make a deal. The watch is nothing but trouble. You give it to us and we pay you and go our separate ways."

The sheriff casually rapped his cudgel against his leg. "How interesting. I imagine that's how things are done with the city watch. A pity, really. Once folks believe that they need coin to get their city servants to do their job, so begins the spiral of corruption. But I'd meet this watch owner. I have questions. How about you two come with me to the stockade where we can have our discussion?"

"We'd rather not. Time is an issue. That watch belongs to a noble who doesn't want to get embarrassed."

"Well, now you've just stirred my imagination. Did this noble lose it, perhaps, in your card game? Then why didn't the winner claim it?"

"I won it," Isabel said. "I was showing it off. But when you came into the bar I thought you'd arrest me if I tried to stop you from taking it."

"I see. I still think it's best if you come along with me. This will get sorted. Your noble will get his watch. Everyone will be happy. Agreed?"

The sheriff stepped aside and gestured for Digger and Isabel to return to the barge. As Digger got close, the man held his hand out.

"Your shovel, please?"

Digger handed it over. As Isabel stepped past, she jumped at the sheriff. She was wielding a leather blackjack, which she swung at his head. He was ready. He blocked the blow with the cudgel and knocked her in the forehead with the knife hilt, sending her to the deck. Digger tried for the shovel but the sheriff sidestepped and slashed with his dagger, forcing Digger back.

Isabel groaned. She was having trouble standing.

Digger picked up a boat pole. It was heavy but too long. For the moment it would have to do.

The cook went charging past them and scurried off the barge. He was screaming for help.

Digger got his footing and watched the sheriff. The man wasn't going to attack. All he had to do was wait until more guards came. Digger could only hope they were all busy with the queen's party.

He swung the pole down but the sheriff edged away out of range. Digger thrust the end of the pole and advanced, trying to get the man off-balance while careful of his own footing. The sheriff moved deftly around the metal brazier and didn't allow himself to get hemmed in.

The sheriff hopped over another grill. "So how is it a menial laborer learns to move so quickly? It's as if you had training. Were you a copper before the edict?"

Digger refused to be distracted. He shoved the pole forward. The sheriff chopped into it with his dagger and grabbed it. They both tugged. Digger proved stronger, but in yanking the pole free he lost his balance. The sheriff took the opening and moved inside the pole's reach. He swiped at Digger's leg with the cudgel and smacked him on the thigh. Pain exploded up his leg. If it had been his knee he would have been crippled.

Digger punched him. The sheriff shifted so the blow landed on his shoulder, but it made the man back off. Digger threw the clumsy pole away with the dagger still stuck in it. But before he could press forward, the sheriff surprised him by launching at him while swinging the club. It was Digger's turn to retreat. He quickly found himself at the edge of the barge, where the railing was missing.

The black water waited.

If he fell in, it would be over. He would either drown, be crushed by the shifting boats, or get captured. Or the sheriff might just kill him. No questions would be asked. Another dead fel for the communal grave. Angel would kill his brother and it would be as if his family had never existed.

Someone began blowing a metal whistle. Whatever guard detail patrolled the harbor was now coming.

The sheriff was poised to strike again, his cudgel firm in hand.

"You keep the gold watch," Digger said. "No other guard needs to know about it."

"What they know and don't know matters little to me. But we both seem to know what this watch really is. It doesn't belong to any nobleman, does it? Rather, it appears to be from the collection of the lady of the island. Queen Claudia is renowned for her love of timepieces. You still expect me to believe it showed up at a fel poker game?"

The sheriff backed away and hauled Isabel to her feet. He gave her a quick pat-down and tossed aside a knife. Guards were climbing onto the barge.

Digger took a last look at the water. There was a chance he might make it by leaving Isabel, but then he'd have the guards hunting him, assuming he survived the swim. The alternative was getting arrested. He and Isabel had assaulted the sheriff, so it was likely they'd face the noose in the morning.

But this sheriff wasn't part of the city guard. He wanted information from them. Digger tried to get a read on the man. If the sheriff wasn't interested in working with him, he'd take his chances in the water.

"I'll tell you about the watch, Sheriff. You're right to be concerned. Because the people who are after it will do anything to get it back. You'll need our help in making this problem go away."

As the group of guards clomped across the barge deck towards him, the sheriff raised a hand for them to wait.

"Explain yourself."

"You're no nobleman, judging by the fact you're living in the harbor. I saw you earlier today dealing with the princeling who lost the timepiece. My kind has gotten good at seeing what purebloods do when they lose face. How much more so when it's a noble."

The sheriff gave the smallest smile.

"I have to be the one who gives him the watch," Digger continued. "He's threatened others. He won't care who you are once he finds out you have it."

The sheriff scoffed. "You'd do that for me?"

One of the guards had a bow and he proceeded to nock an arrow. Approaching below, two guards in a narrow rowboat closed in as they rounded the barge.

"I'm not worried about you, Sheriff. What I want is your word that none of my friends who were at the bar will get hurt. They had nothing to do with this. But this Lord Angel will go through them to get to you."

"That's something I'll deal with. You want a promise from me? Okay, fel. I give you my promise. We'll settle this matter between ourselves. I have so many questions and you, it seems, have answers. But I warn you not to waste my time. Because if it turns out you two are nothing more than a pair of thieves, I'll be sure it doesn't go easy with either of you."

Chapter Nineteen

"WAKE UP," ANGEL'S AUNT said.

She was working a series of hairpins out of her elaborate coiffure and setting them on the display case.

He wiped spittle from the corner of his mouth and almost fell out of the chair. He rose and looked about. They were alone. He resisted the urge to ask what time it was.

The sounds of the queen's big bash had faded. The clocks struck one.

He hadn't meant to sleep. He was well past overdue for his meeting with the gravedigger. If he could only get his aunt to forgive him. Convince her that he was going to make everything better. Make her see that her favorite nephew Angel was there to take care of her.

She lit a lamp at the desk. "Come here, Angel."

He stepped closer and looked down at the desk as if there was something there to capture his attention. They were alone. He didn't see the long ivory hairpin in her hand until it was too late. She grabbed him by the shirt and yanked hard, pulling him down to his knees. Before he could react, she pressed the hairpin against his cheek, the tip poking him below his left eyelid.

He gripped her hand but couldn't dislodge it.

"Be still, my sweet. You wouldn't want me to have to take out both eyes to make my point?"

"Please! No! Aunt Claudia, don't!"

"Shush. Shhh. No more talk out of you. No more excuses. No more acting the boy when you want to be a man. Boys sometimes give in to foolishness. You're no fool, Angel. I have many a bore in my family but we raise no dullards. Unless you believe you're the exception?"

She shook him when he didn't answer.

"I'm no fool," he said.

"Good. Then I won't repeat myself. You stole from me something more precious than you can imagine."

"Yes. The watch. I know who took it from me. I was getting it back when you summoned me."

He screamed as the blade prodded the skin.

"Stop sniveling. My patience is spent. My night is ruined. I planned for this for so long, and with one act you put my games at risk."

"I'm going to make it right!"

She let out a sharp sigh. "You still don't know what you've done."

The hairpin lifted and she released him. He caught the desk to keep from falling to the floor.

"You have a minute to explain."

He looked up at her and the clocks. *Tick, tick, tick.* The sound was once again oppressive.

"I took credit from a gangster and then lost big. I needed the watch to pay my debt. But then a girl stole it from me before I could do it."

She pulled one of her sleeves back and her arm sparkled. She was wearing her collection of wristwatches. These were all smaller than the centerpiece he had taken, but each must have been worth enough to cover what he owed Red Eye.

"So you broke into the case and took the watch," she prompted.

He nodded. "This gangster is going to kill me. But the girl and her friends...I'm supposed to meet them at the square. I'll get the watch back. I'll bring it to you. I'll find another way to pay off the gangster."

She was scowling. Didn't appear to care about a word he was saying. What did she want from him?

"You have seconds left, and still you don't understand what you've done."

He fell to his knees. "I violated your trust. I sinned against God."

"And what did you do after you removed my prize from the case?"

He reviewed the event in the moments he had left. She was almost done with him. What else was there besides the stolen watch that could infuriate her so?

"Your steward Rochus came in. I wrapped the watch with a piece of paper so he wouldn't see."

"Yes!" She punctuated the air with her hairpin, causing him to flinch. "Oh, my sweet nephew, you make me crazy sometimes." She raised the rolltop desk and moved the lamp. When she next spoke, her voice was eerily placid. "You took a piece of paper from here?"

"Yes. I thought the desk might have a key in it to the case."

"Of all my treasures, what I have in my desk is most precious."

He realized she was talking about the paper. "What was on that page?"

She was smiling now as she tidied a stack of notes and paused to admire the one on top. It was a scribbled diagram or chart with labels. She showed it to him. There were so many notes running slapdash up and along the sides of the page that it made no sense. He could barely read her disorderly script. But as he peered closer he made out a few of the labels.

Frog Room. Chamber of Riddles. Skeleton Ambush.

What madness? What fiction was she writing? Not fiction—there were dimensions to the geometric shapes, and he understood then that these were rough blueprints, along with notes upon notes. But this couldn't be the castle. Her white keep had no more room within its walls, unless she was planning to demolish it.

He continued to study the page.

Catacomb West Wing, the top of the page read.

"It's your games," he said. "The rooms of the catacombs which you haven't let me see."

She took his hand in hers. "You know this is my passion. But no one else gets to peek at this, not even you. Especially not even family. If the surprise is ruined, it will spoil the fun. This is for the next season. I have such plans. So much work to do. But if word of the expansion gets out, it could create an obstacle which might cause delay."

"Why? Who would stop you?"

"You think it's easy to rule Loom Island? Balancing the needs of my people and my ambitions is a never-ending juggle. Suffice to say, if word spreads before I'm ready, it will upset me."

"You want the page back."

She was gripping his hand tight. Squeezing. He fought the urge to pull away. Her hairpin began pressing into his wrist.

"Do you feel it?"

"It's very sharp."

"No, silly. Alive. Knowing that another ounce of pressure and I tear your artery open. Doesn't each beat of your heart become precious? The air of each breath sweeter?"

"Yes. I feel alive and am glad to be."

She pushed his hand away and giggled. "Off with you. Get my watch back. The page too, you dizzy goose. You've made me sad, and I'll not allow anything to ruin tomorrow's games."

He nodded and thought it best not to say anything as he stumbled out into the hall. He hurried to find his horse and leave the castle. There would be no returning into his aunt's good graces without both the watch and the page of plans. But even as the bleary-eyed stable attendant brought him his mount, Angel realized that he needed to reassess his future in Diregloom.

Because his rich aunt was hopelessly insane.

Chapter Twenty

DIREGLOOM RARELY INDULGED criminals by placing them in carts or on horseback after their arrest. But the sheriff seemed to be making an exception for Digger and Isabel. They were shackled and led to the dock, where they waited until a jail wagon arrived, drawn by a pair of stunted ponies.

Both horses had orange ribbons tied into their manes and the wagon driver wore a top hat with a patterned band. Was the wagon to keep their capture secret or did the sheriff want the extra security?

The guards shoved them inside the cramped space. There they waited as the sheriff and guards conferred with each other out of earshot.

The lump on Isabel's forehead where the sheriff had struck her had grown large and red. Digger touched her shoulder and she jerked away from him.

"Why didn't you fight?" she asked.

"I would have lost."

"You barely tried. And what did you mean when you said 'friends' to the sheriff?"

"What?"

"You said you wanted his word that your friends won't get hurt. What's going on?"

"Lord Angel was at the Dragon and Rose," he said. "Hellard and I fought his men. He captured my brother and took him."

"Why didn't you tell me?"

"Because I need your damn gold watch to get him back. So what is it about that thing? No thief would go through this much just for an expensive trinket. And don't tell me you're willing to risk your life on the chance a gangster will get your revenge on Lord Angel for you."

She didn't say anything for a while, just stared out the tiny barred window in the back of the wagon. "Remember I told you about Count Barca's son Jamie? I received a letter at the Black Rock Mission that he's coming here to Diregloom."

"Of course I remember. His father's out to kill you. And he's Lord Angel's brother. How'd he find out where you were?"

She sighed. "Jamie's not a bad man. He just won't stand up to his father. I wrote him secretly. Told him where he could reach me."

"So you're both stupid. Love does that, I'm told. There's plenty of fel and pureblood that still live together."

"Yeah, those who are rich or inconsequential can manage. It's not just that Jamie wants to come here. We could have figured something out. But Jamie's got it in his mind he's going to win the catacombs. To show his father. He wrote he wants to become famous enough that he can defy the duke and marry me."

"This boyfriend of yours is one of the contestants?"

"Yes. Supposedly he arrived this evening. So not only will taking that watch turn Angel's gangsters against him, but I was going to give it to Jamie."

"Why would you believe giving him a prize would change his mind about winning and becoming famous?"

"Maybe you haven't been paying attention, but rumor has it this round of catacombs is going to be dangerous even for the contestants. I don't want to see him die, okay? And then when I heard it wasn't just any prize Angel had taken but the grand prize, I thought maybe if the queen never got it back, the games might be canceled."

"Hmm. The games are going ahead as planned. Angel is now coming after you and me. And your Jamie is going to be a contestant. But there's nothing we can do about it now. You should have told me everything a bit earlier."

She thumped a fist against the wall of the wagon. "I'm sorry for you and your brother."

"Yeah. Me too."

THE RIDE UP TO THE stockade was rough and bumpy. With nothing to hang on to, Digger and Isabel were bounced and slammed against the walls and floor of the wagon. A duet of trumpets were playing a jaunty tune. The crowd was as loud as ever as the wagon was drawn through the throng to the stockade gate and into the courtyard.

The driver got down and spoke with someone, but the wagon remained sealed. Digger strained his ears and moved to peer out the window but could only see a wall. Some time passed. The trumpets were replaced with a cacophony of flutes and whistles. A chorus of a song began but this devolved into riotous laughter and shouting.

"The queen knows how to throw a party," Isabel said.

Bootsteps approached. A guard unlocked the wagon and hands grabbed Digger and hauled him out. His legs were numb and he almost fell as he was shoved towards a doorway off the courtyard. He tried to look back at where they were taking Isabel, but one of the guards cuffed him across the head.

"Eyes forward!"

The tiny room was lit by a lantern on a writing desk with a pen and inkwell. His manacles were attached to a ring on the floor, so he could either sit or kneel. He tried to get comfortable as feeling returned to his legs.

Finally the sheriff arrived.

A guard closed the cell door behind him and then they were alone. The sheriff removed his green hat and hung it on a peg. Then he sat on a stool and began to scratch notes on a piece of paper. He filled half the sheet before he began tapping the pen against the desk and wiping its tip with a cloth. After a moment of fiddling with it, he dipped it into the ink and continued writing.

Digger watched in silence.

Finally the sheriff sat back and considered his prisoner. "This city has a flavor to it I can't place. Your people are subjects under Lady Claudia. She demands obedience from fel and pureblood alike. Yet as is apparent from tonight, she is celebrated."

"The people like their parties."

"So it appears. I apologize for the cramped cell. It places the accused in a stress position. Anyone left chained like that for a few days will admit to most any crime. Unfortunately, it's the only room I was provided for our conversation. May I fetch you water?"

"Maybe later."

"Good. To the matter at hand, then." He removed the watch and unwrapped it. "From Claudia's collection. Stolen by the young lord, who had it taken from him. And it winds up in the Dragon and Rose at a poker game."

"Yes."

The sheriff tapped the pen on the paper. "Who brought it there in the first place?"

"One of Lord Angel's men came to play and wasn't put off by playing with fel. He lost his purse, then the watch. Got angry. Nearly wrecked the place before we threw him out. He was cursing us when he left. Said he'd return and we'd all be sorry. Then you arrived."

"That explains the mess. So which one of you actually won the watch?"

"Isabel did."

"What game?"

"Five card."

The sheriff still wasn't writing. "And what did you have to bet that would cause him to put up something so valuable?"

"Twenty silver tencoins. He was already broke and drunk. Had just enough for the ante and didn't want to lose to, what were his words? A filthy greenskin. The watch went on the table. He had no hand and lost. Tried to take the watch back. I didn't let him."

"More the fool you for getting yourself into your predicament."

"A few hours ago, Lord Angel came and grabbed my brother from the Dragon and Rose. He's holding him prisoner and told me to meet him here, watch in hand. The girl you arrested went along with me because Lord Angel threatened to burn down the bar if we didn't bring him the watch."

"Did he now?"

"You don't have to believe me. That's why we came for it. It's not like the city guards were going to help a couple of fel recover a stolen piece of jewelry."

"I suspect not. And how is it a menial worker who uses a shovel finds himself so flush with silver coins?"

"I know how to play cards."

"But still, the law is the law. You shouldn't have fought with the nobleman. And then you should never have come after me."

"I understand. I can write a confession if that makes your job easier. But you need to let my friend go."

The sheriff continued to tap the paper. "So it started with a showdown between you and this nobleman. Victor, I believe his name is. You don't know what happened to him after he rampaged and left your bar?"

"Drank more and drowned his sorrows, I suspect."

"Your winning hand—what was it?"

"Two pair, queens high."

Rising, the sheriff pushed the desk to where Digger could reach the paper and pen. "I remind you that I'm not the law here. But perhaps I can give the city guard a push when it comes to your friend in custody. So write your confession and I'll present it. Is there anything you'd like to add which might give me extra leverage in assisting you?"

"I don't know what you mean. I admit to attacking a pureblood in the bar. And coming after you. Isn't that enough?"

"It's a trite expression, but it's so often true: baring one's sins lifts a weight off a man's soul. This of course might be blasphemy to the ears of others, insinuating a fel possesses anything as sacred as a soul which comes from the Divine. But if you have more to tell, please do so."

"Why are you here in Diregloom, Sheriff?"

"To solve a murder. It's a matter which has fallen to the wayside of the city guard's attention. They're overtaxed when it comes to complex matters not involving suppressing fel dissent and breaking up fights among drunken tourists. But nothing which concerns you."

"I'm curious."

The sheriff took the hat from the peg and brushed it clean. "A magister and his two guards vanished. It was a month after the Thirteenth Edict some two years ago."

Digger kept his expression neutral. The three men were in the ground not far away from where the missing nobleman from the Dragon and Rose was buried. The magister had been the one who had presided over the forfeiture of his parents' restaurant. Near them in a neighboring plot rested the pureblood who had purchased the restaurant.

"Loom Island has always been a dangerous place," Digger said.

"To body and soul both. I'm going to speak with your companion. Compare notes. You can write? Then put your words to the page and be specific. I'll be back soon."

Digger was left alone with the desk and paper. He realized his mistake in oversharing. Isabel wouldn't know the cards of his winning hand or would come up with a different lie. They weren't going to get out of this.

Then he noticed the crumpled page that had wrapped the watch. He stretched to grab it. It was covered with what at first appeared to be confused scribbles. But the longer he squinted to make out the chaotic notes and lines and labeled circles, the more he realized what he was staring at. It was plans for an expansion of the game vaults beneath the castle. He studied it for a moment longer before tucking the page away.

Someone was coming. From the opposite side of the door, the sheriff was speaking to another.

The second voice was Lord Angel, and he sounded angry.

Chapter Twenty-One

HIS MAD AUNT WAS GOING to kill him.

Her turn had been so sudden, her mood so fierce, that Angel found his hands were shaking as he rode towards the stockade.

Fleeing the island was still an option.

Get away from his aunt, let her rage about the missing watch. The accusation might make its way to the duke's court, but he'd endured gossip before and the duke wouldn't bother with such trivial squabbles. He left his extended family to solve their own personal crises.

But even back home he wouldn't be out of reach of Red Eye. He didn't believe there was a servant he could ever trust again to not have a vial of poison or a knife meant for him.

This was all that gravedigger's fault. He and that fel girl of Jamie's. Curse them both.

At first he hadn't even recognized Isabel, the night she had stolen the watch. He had been too drunk, too happy, having taken the watch from its display, the end of his debt in reach. Why shouldn't he have partied? No whore would steal from a customer who was going to spread silver coins her way and risk losing a good client. But then, even after realizing who she was, he had indulged in her presence and the possibilities of torments he might relate to his brother.

But she had been the one who had played him. Targeted him.

It was as if she had known he had his aunt's prize. But how could she? He had just stolen it hours before. Rochus, the steward, might have discovered the theft. Angel's companions knew, but they had been partying it up alongside him in their townhouse by the waterfront.

He was missing pieces of the puzzle. He hated puzzles.

The streets were still lively and well illuminated. Too many of the revelers were fel.

Time to focus his anger. Time for the cook he had taken from the dive bar to spill his guts about the gravedigger, Isabel, and anything else he might know that would lead Angel to the watch.

As he rode up to the stockade gate, the two guards out front stiffened. With ribbons on their helmets they looked stupid. He dismounted and wound his reins to a hitching post. Gavin and Hector were waiting for him but had nothing to report. Angel marched past the two guards and went into the stockade. The courtyard was filled with the sounds from the streets beyond but there was no one in the shadowy corridors. He headed for the far building where he had left Marisol and their prisoner.

"Lord Angel."

It was the sheriff, still wearing his ridiculous hat. He hadn't seen him there in the shadows. It was as if the man had materialized out of thin air.

Angel tried his best to conceal his ire. "I'm here for the report on my missing friend."

"Ask the guard captain. I've heard no news. I've been making inquiries of a different nature. This bar—the Dragon and Rose—keeps coming up. I understand you brought in someone and have him held here."

"The fel cook who works at the bar. I'm going to have him questioned."

The sheriff appeared to perk up. "And what line of questions might you have for him? I ask because there may be some overlap with my own work. Missing property."

"I don't have time for this."

"Of course not. It's probably a minor matter. A bauble taken from someone's jewelry collection. A watch, if the reports are correct. As you know, the lady of the island has a famous collection of watches. Didn't we see some on her very arm as she showed them off to the crowd?"

Angel felt ice in his veins. What did the sheriff know? If he had a lead on the watch, then there was hope in Angel recovering it. But if the sheriff found it, it would spell disaster. Angel would lose all hope of returning to his aunt's favor. And Red Eye would be out for blood.

"My aunt, the queen, entrusted me to handle this matter. A misplaced timepiece from her catacomb prizes."

"Yes," the sheriff said smoothly, "I heard something similar. Would you happen to know anything about it? Was this a theft? The guard captain assures me they've received no complaint from the castle. But my source says this particular prize appeared at the Dragon and Rose the same night your friend Victor disappeared."

Who else could know about Isabel and what she had taken? None of the fel they had fought would dare talk to the lawman unless they wanted their friend killed. Perhaps the pureblood bar owner had come forward. He'd have to deal with all of them once he got the watch back.

The only other possibility was the gang member his companions had left bleeding out. But surely that wretch had perished. Was the sheriff looking to connect him to a murder?

"What's the source of your information, Sheriff?"

"A separate crime completely, actually. An earlier assault. So this watch...?"

"I heard the same rumors but my aunt has me helping her. While her watch might turn up as merely being misplaced, if you have information, you'd do well to share. While you're at it, ask your suspect about my companion. But right now, I can't help you. I have my own business to attend to with the guard captain."

"A pity you can't help. Good luck in your investigations, Lord Angel. My best to Lady Claudia."

Angel was glad to be free of the man as he entered the guard offices. Marisol was kicked back on a stool near the cell where they had the chef prisoner.

"Did the sheriff talk to the fel?" he asked.

Marisol got up to face him. "No."

"What about you? Did he ask you anything? He wanted to know about the watch."

"He didn't. Angel, where were you? I've been here all night."

"Mind your tone, cousin. This sheriff—he knows something. He's going to be trouble."

"We've been a little short on that tonight. Why not pick a fight with him and the guards? Maybe we should just hit the streets and start beating up every fel we run into?"

"Don't get sassy. I'm working on it. We'll get Cy and Philip back. I wanted to make sure you were still here watching the chef. I'm going outside to see if the gravedigger is out there waiting. If not, I'll be back and we'll make the chef tell us everything he knows."

"Let me go with you."

"No. I don't trust the guards or the sheriff. Sit tight."

He went back outside and cut through the courtyard and exited into Stockade Square. The music had stopped. People were going home. The celebration was just a taste of how crazy Diregloom would become over the weekend as the catacomb games commenced.

How had his own good time on the island become such a disaster?

He and his companions Gavin and Hector scoured the square. They checked a few of the drunks who had their faces hidden and even went down the numerous alleys in search of the gravedigger. Had the fel decided to give up on the exchange?

Angel felt his annoyance building. If the gravedigger had fled, that would mean any chance of finding the watch would vanish. He wrote Cy and Philip off. For all he knew, the ogre had eaten them. Angel would accumulate more friends. That part was easy. But navigating his aunt's wrath and Red Eye's assassins was going to make life precarious.

By his estimation it was well past the start of the third watch. Dawn was a few hours away. He began thinking of boat schedules and which would be first off the island. He still had time to deliver some pain to the cook, though. The fel probably knew nothing, but the distraction would be welcome.

The sheriff emerged from the stockade on horseback. He led a second horse with a bound figure seated on it.

Angel hurried over to see.

There in the dying glow of the strung lanterns rode the gravedigger. The sheriff was taking him away. But where?

He grabbed one of the guards. "Where's he going?"

"No idea, sir!" the man squeaked.

Angel's two companions brought him his horse.

"They're heading up Fountain Street," Gavin said.

Angel swung up into the saddle. He kicked his horse into motion. The animal's hooves skittered on the damp cobblestones as they raced into the chill night in pursuit.

The sheriff had lied.

He had the gravedigger in custody, the one soul who knew everything about the watch, and he was taking him to the castle. The why of it didn't make sense. But Angel had to catch him before his own situation spun even further out of control.

Chapter Twenty-Two

"SO I'M NOT TO HANG in the morning," Digger said as he fought to keep his balance on the horse. With his hands manacled behind his back it was either that or fall, and he'd collected enough bodies from stupid horse accidents to want to avoid suffering such a fate.

The sheriff never took his eyes off the road. "I took the liberty of speaking with the guard captain. Seems there's no report of a theft of a watch."

"Sounds like you get a raise. I'm sure there's a fence or two who will deal with a lawman looking to move a fancy piece of jewelry."

"How little you know me."

They were passing the many spewing fountains on the boulevard leading up to the castle. Digger processed what he had heard of the exchange between Lord Angel and the sheriff. Monty was a prisoner in the stockade.

"I've cooperated," Digger said. "What about Isabel? And Lord Angel has my brother."

"It gets a little more complicated, I'm afraid."

"What's that supposed to mean? We had a deal."

"Which has saved your neck so far. Isabel will remain a prisoner of mine while I find out what she knows. She was unwilling to be as forthcoming as you." He paused to ride around a group of lingering revelers. "But this cook is Lord Angel's prisoner. I have no say as to what he does with him until the prisoner is accused."

"That doesn't explain why you're taking me to the castle."

"It's undisputed that you attacked me. I thought I'd return the favor and deliver you up where you'll be able to have a fighting chance at freedom.

Unless you'd prefer a turn at the gallows. But with the games on tomorrow, the audience won't be very enthusiastic at seeing a simple hanging."

So that was it. The sheriff was bringing him to the castle. As a fel condemned to the games, his chances at survival were slim. There he would fight or die.

Each season of catacomb games were different, according to the stories. Only the richest of Diregloom's inhabitants could afford to watch as spectators. Queen Claudia was good to her word and released all fel who survived, but the numbers were few. His fellow gravediggers who had helped with the cleanup had shared what they had learned. This round of catacomb games was supposed to be more extravagant and deadly than any of the previous years.

"I thought you'd be groveling by now," the sheriff said.

Digger didn't respond. What was there to say? He had failed to save himself and his brother. And now he faced a likely death sentence.

The manacles binding his wrist remained as tight as ever.

They rode through the castle gate. The inner courtyard was alive and busy as servants rushed about with purpose. Long drooping streamers ran down from the corners of the rooftops to the tops of the walls. Every window and doorway was covered in elaborate floral arrangements. And there, between the keep and the western guard tower, was the entrance to the catacombs.

The gray stone archway looked like the gaping mouth of a demon clawing its way up from the ground. Through its teeth were a set of stairs descending into shadow. The demon's eyes held lanterns that shone like twin beacons.

A man with a clipboard was staring up at the stone face. He waved to a worker who turned the lantern in the right eye slightly. Others were putting the finishing touches on a display of flowering thorn vines that may or may not have been real. Stuck in the vines were swords, shields, and skulls, all presumably from adventurers who had failed to even make it through the demon's mouth.

If Digger's stomach could have sunk any further, it would.

A fel in a fancy outfit approached them. He had dark lines under his eyes.

The sheriff dismounted. "I have an additional entrant for tomorrow, steward."

The fel only glanced at Digger for a moment before signaling someone. A guard hauled him off the saddle.

"What's the charge?" the guard asked.

"Assaulting a pureblood."

No further questions were needed. As the guard pushed Digger towards the keep, another rider entered the gate and cantered over. Lord Angel barely stopped his horse before swinging off the animal and storming towards the sheriff.

"Sheriff! You insult me!"

"Not on purpose, Lord Angel. If I give offense, I beg forgiveness."

Angel's face had turned a shade of deep red. "You didn't say you had a prisoner. You can't release him here!"

"Release him? As you can see, he's been remanded to the queen's authority to face justice. The condemned chose the catacombs."

Digger saw pure hatred in the nobleman's eyes as Angel marched towards him.

"The watch. Where is it, you filthy fel?"

"I'll tell you," Digger whispered. "It's close. But you have to promise me..."

Angel leaned in ever so slightly. It was enough. Digger slammed his forehead into the noble's nose. Felt the cartilage crunch like an egg.

Blood bursting down his face, Angel howled. He could barely keep his eyes open, but he pulled his dagger from his belt and came at Digger. The guard holding Digger stepped back. Digger prepared himself for the assault but knew he stood no chance. He kept his knees bent and hunched forward. But with his hands restrained behind him the outcome was inevitable.

"Lord Angel, stop!" the steward bellowed.

Angel didn't waver in his course. With one hand on his bleeding nose, he advanced with his blade out at his side. Digger backed up towards the mouth. The workers moved out of their way.

The steward charged up to Angel. "I order you in the name of Queen Claudia to stop! To disobey me is to defy her. He's for the games."

"He's a fel. I can do with him as I please."

"Not when he's the queen's property. Put your blade away."

The nobleman flicked blood away from his upper lip and spat. "Where is it?"

Digger just watched Angel for the slightest move.

"Lord Angel," the sheriff said. "Perhaps this will quell your rage." He produced the watch. "I believe this is a missing timepiece lost from Queen Claudia's collection. I'd like to return it."

"No," Angel said. "Give that to me."

The steward took the jeweled timepiece and examined it. By now more guards had arrived. Two grabbed Digger by the elbows. More surrounded the steward as if to protect him.

"Seems the queen's grand prize has found its way home again," the steward announced. He held up the watch.

Digger tried to make sense of the scene. The watch had been instantly recognized. Had Isabel been correct in her assessment?

Lord Angel was trembling. He turned on the sheriff. "You had it?"

The sheriff straightened his hat. "The queen's misplaced watch has been returned, Lord Angel. Choose your next words wisely."

"You'll regret this."

"On the contrary, this should make for an engaging game this weekend. I understand the winning contestant with the most tokens may choose this very timepiece as their prize, not that I can afford a ticket to the show. Perhaps, if you want, your aunt will permit you a late entrance so you can try your hand?"

The steward handed the watch to a waiting attendant, who held it delicately and rushed it inside the castle with a pair of guards following.

Digger was jerked along and marched away, but not towards the demon's mouth. The steps on the side of the keep were unadorned, but Digger knew the entrance to a dungeon when he saw one.

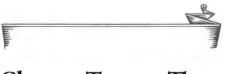

Chapter Twenty-Three

ROCHUS THE STEWARD was smirking.

Angel forced himself to regain his composure even as the steward handed him a second handkerchief to stanch his bleeding nostrils. He could do little as the sheriff climbed back on his horse and rode off.

He had to think quickly. He brushed past the steward and hurried up the stairs, clamping down on his aching nose and fighting to see past the streaming tears.

"Lord Angel, where are you going?" Rochus called.

Angel ignored him. The attendant with the watch wasn't heading for the clock room but instead was moving down towards the ballroom. The large chamber overlooked the rear terraced garden, and it was filled with long tables and extravagant floral centerpieces. Fanciful weaponry and pieces of mock battle-worn armor hung from the walls. Above the wooden throne hung a dragon skull. To one side of the throne stood a glass case which contained the other timepieces that would serve as prizes.

The paying guests would congregate here before the games commenced.

Angel watched helplessly as the watch was placed with the others.

He turned and almost collided with Rochus. "Where's my aunt?"

"She rests and ordered no one disturb her."

Angel pushed past him and made his way up the stairway towards the bedrooms.

The attendant outside his aunt's room sprang up from a chair. "She's asleep!"

"Then I'll wake her."

He tried to step past, but the attendant was physically blocking him. Rochus had topped the steps and was closing in fast. Shoving the attendant aside, Angel pushed the double doors open. The lavish bed was still made. His aunt was sitting at a dressing table with a rosewood jewelry box laid open. She was putting on a dangling earring with orange gemstones.

He paused to gawk. "You're awake."

"Obviously," his aunt said, barely taking her eyes off her reflection. "And your nose is bleeding."

The attendant and Rochus barged in behind Angel.

"My lady, my apologies," Rochus said. "The young lord was most insistent."

"It's fine. Leave us, Rochus."

The steward bowed and took the attendant with him as he closed the doors.

"I know it's late—" Angel began.

"It's 3:48. The problem with you is a lack of precision."

Her response flustered him. "Yes," he managed. "I don't carry a watch."

"You should. What do you think I attribute my success to? None of this breaking the day into 'after breakfast' or 'before supper.' Can you imagine living so aimlessly? Such nonsense. You should carry a timepiece and be more exact." She turned to face him. "Well, then. I'm a bundle of nerves and now you're here. I'm guessing by the manner of your entrance you have nothing to tell me which will make me happy."

"Actually, Aunt Claudia, I've brought your watch back. It's in the ballroom display."

"Did you? I'm surprised. I was afraid you were becoming boring. And how, exactly, did you manage to recover it?"

"I tracked it down to a bar. There was a fight."

She leaned forward and folded her hands, suddenly interested. "A fight? *You* got into a fight?"

"The bar was full of fel hooligans. My five companions and I were outnumbered. We had swords. They had savage strength. And an ogre."

"I don't believe a word of it. The ogre is a nice touch. Do go on."

"Two of my men were injured. The fight was a close thing. We held them off until I captured one of them. Their leader, as it turns out. His life for the watch."

She clapped and giggled. "And they made the trade?"

"No honor among the lot of them. We still have their leader. In fact, the sheriff brought him up to be entered in the catacombs. He's opted to be in your contestant pool. He's a big one."

"Oooh, I like the sound of him already. He's not hurt, I hope."

"Not at all. But I wanted you to hear the news first. You're pleased, aren't you?"

She rose and went to him. Planted a wet kiss on his cheek. "Very, my sweet. I'll be a wreck come dawn without rest, but I'm far too excited. Let's go down to the kitchen, shall we? We'll get that nose fixed. And then I'll have Chef Miriam whip us up some sopapillas and you can tell me every detail of your brave battle."

Chapter Twenty-Four

"WAKE UP."

From the light shining through the high bars, Digger guessed it was morning. He hadn't quite meant to fall asleep when he'd lain down on the hard bench. His manacles had been removed. His head was stuffed with wool, his mouth and throat dry, and now there was a strange fel in his face. He had bright eyes and a thin white beard.

He pushed the man back and blinked his eyes clear.

The cell was much larger than the one in the stockade. Roomy, even. Ten other fel men were standing, sitting, or reclining on furniture nicer than anything most slum dwellers had in their apartments. A round table was covered with food, pitchers, and a flower arrangement.

Digger shook his head to clear it. Then he realized there was a metal collar around his neck. They all wore collars.

"I thought you were going to sleep forever," the bearded fel said. "Food's here. Don't want you facing the day on an empty stomach."

Digger tugged and pried at the collar. "And why is that?"

"Because we're going to be fighting soon and we might need to rely on each other. Can you hear it?"

From outside came the sounds of a crowd—talking, laughing, shouting. Someone was playing guitar and flute. The festival atmosphere from the previous night was going strong.

"We're in the castle still?"

The bearded fel nodded as he handed him a delicate cup with fine lines painted in swirls. There was beer in the cup.

"There's also juice and the nasty herb tea my grandmother used to drink. Thought this might give you some energy."

"Thanks." Digger sipped. It was small beer, not strong, but it tasted as good as the stuff at the hangman's bar. Some of the other fel were picking at the offerings, eating fruit, fish, bread, pastries, and an assortment of sliced meats and finger foods.

"What's your name?" Digger asked.

"Paulus. And now that you're awake, maybe you can help convince these other fine fellows we all need to work together if we're going to survive the day."

"Why haven't you done that?"

"Because they won't listen to me."

THE OTHER FEL WEREN'T interested in Digger's words either, not that he tried hard. He was too hungry to give a speech, so he ate. The guitarist and flutist finished up. A string quartet began playing a happy minuet. Hardly what he would have imagined he'd have to fight to. Or die to.

He was continually distracted anytime bootsteps passed outside the cell door.

Meanwhile the other ten collared fel ate, drank, and spoke loudly. Some even laughed. They all wore collars. On the back of each dangled a gold token the size of a silver tencoin. Only Paulus didn't appear nervous. He was leaning against a wall, eating from a bunch of grapes.

The cell door creaked open. A guard pointed to two of the fel. Other armed guards waited outside. Neither fel moved.

"Go on, boys," Paulus said. "You've hours before the match. It's time they spruced you up."

The two marched out without any goading from the guard. The cell door slammed shut and was locked.

Digger leaned next to Paulus. "You know what's going to happen?"

Paulus showed a forearm tattoo. The word "Pardoned" was wrapped in scrollwork and wings. Digger had met a few fel who had such tattoos, having gotten them after receiving a rare lenient judgment not ending in a hanging.

As if the tattoos would sway the city guards if they caught any of them committing another actionable infraction.

Digger grunted. "Yet here you are."

"Yeah, and I was here two seasons ago and survived. They're going to clean us up so we look good for the crowd. If we're lucky the game manager will give us some pointers on what we're supposed to do. Last time I even got a clue, but don't believe everything he tells you. They want sport out of us and a good match. They don't care how unfair the game is going to be, and it'll favor the contestants."

One of the younger fel stopped chewing. "I thought we're the contestants."

Paulus shook his head. "We're the monsters. That token on your collar is the treasure. We're going to have to fight to keep them from taking our heads off to get them."

"How did you survive?" Digger asked.

"By doing anything I could not to die. But listen, there's parts of the game that will favor us. It all depends on where we're placed in the catacombs. There's traps. There'll be others, too. More prisoners. Some might not be on our side. It all depends on what the queen wanted when she set the season up. The first day I fought no one died. Some of us got wounded, some knocked out, and the contestants made it past our room without having to finish the fight. But we were thrown back in the next day, and that was when things got bloody."

Paulus had all their attention.

"I was the only one who made it."

Digger studied Paulus. "So why're you back?"

"Because I got piss drunk a week ago and punched a pureblood barmaid in the face."

The young fel next to Paulus turned to face the others. "We're fel, aren't we? We're stronger than them. Tougher. Our forefathers used to hunt theirs. Don't be afraid. We got this. It's like the old man says, we stick together!"

Digger heard a slight slur in the young man's words. How much had he had to drink? Was the food drugged?

"That's the spirit," Paulus said. "But keep your head and your wits about you. The queen isn't interested in any ordinary pit fight. She's designed these games to test the contestants, but also to give the paying tourists a show. It means we stand a chance, but it's stacked against us."

Digger sniffed at the plate of sliced goat meat. "What can we do to prepare?"

"Fill your belly. Rest up. It's going to be a long day and a longer night."

Chapter Twenty-Five

AUNT CLAUDIA APPEARED to have exhausted herself. She had talked for almost an hour, sharing her catacomb ideas with Angel as he listened intently. The fried dough treats were all gone, their tea drunk, and it was still before dawn when his aunt nodded off with one of her notebooks in hand.

Whether his renewed favor would keep remained to be seen, but the day was off to a promising start.

But he wasn't out of trouble yet. There was still Red Eye and his debt.

He rubbed his eyes. The attendants had slacked off. Even the help needed sleep, he supposed, but the kitchen was going full bore and had been all week. The number of delicacies being prepared was massive. Pheasants were being stuffed, whole pigs roasted, candies and pastries meticulously assembled. The cost of the event continued to amaze him.

It could all be his, if he could only avoid getting his throat cut by gangsters.

In the ballroom, a complement of alert guards were watching him closely. All pretense of deference to rank of birth were gone. Rochus must have spread the word, but he hadn't gotten to his aunt. If the steward tried to contradict him, it would be a matter of his word against Angel's.

He went up to his room. His trunk he had brought with him from home held the bare essentials: his collection of ties, seven outfits, and twelve pairs of shoes. But he felt grimy. Time to wash up and change. His pillowy bed beckoned. A short nap would clear his head. He took off his tunic coat and unbuttoned his shirt. Dried sweat coated his body.

He moved to pull on the cord that would ring an attendant. But before he could do anything he heard someone moving in the bathroom.

"Hello?" he called.

One of the house girls emerged with an armload of towels. She squeaked in surprise. She was a young thing he hadn't noticed before. Alluring, big eyes. A figure barely contained by her uniform.

"I'm sorry, lord, I didn't hear you enter." She curtseyed and kept her gaze low. "We're behind on our rounds with the number of guests and preparations."

He'd remember to ask for her later, but for now he was beat. "Hardly an excuse, girl. Draw me a bath. Easy on the perfume. Make it hot."

She dipped again, set down her towels, and went back into the bathroom. Soon water began running. He stripped down to his undergarments and left them on the bed so she'd take care of it. He tugged the ribbon free from his ponytail and shook his hair loose as he entered the bathroom.

The servant faced him, a single towel folded over one hand. He didn't catch the bunched shoulders and hard stare until it was too late. She threw the towel down and slashed at him with a knife. The blade caught him across his stomach as he slapped her away. Trying desperately to retreat, he tripped on a rug. He went down.

She turned the blade in her hand and launched herself at him. He caught her by both arms, the weapon inches from his face.

"What are you doing?" he cried. "Stop!"

She kneed him in the thigh, just missing his tender parts. Pain blossomed up his leg, almost making him lose the pushing war against the knife. How could this woman be so strong? The answer was simple. She was fel. The cursed people infested Loom Island. What they had lost in wits and soul they made up for with raw strength and viciousness.

He couldn't force her away. The knife blade pressed down another inch. Struggling to turn the blade, he leaned up and bit down on her wrist. She screamed and the knife dropped. He let one of her arms go and slammed her jaw with the heel of his hand. Her teeth clacked and she reeled. Her grip on him slackened and he twisted out from under her, then rolled on top of her with his hands around her throat. He squeezed.

"Red Eye? Was it Red Eye?"

She gagged and scratched but weakened with every passing moment.

"Who sent you?"

But he didn't dare let up. Who knew what other tricks she might have? He clung to her until her face purpled, her eyes bulged, and she went limp. Finally he let go and got up on shaking legs. The gash on his stomach covered his belly in red. His nose was once again bleeding, and now he had scratches along his arms.

He gave the body a final kick. He almost rang the bell that would send up a servant. But then he paused. How many more assassins had Red Eye hired?

Sitting on the corner of the tub, he picked up a washcloth and cleaned his wounds. Soon the tub water was pink. But the slash along his front wasn't deep. He cut strips of towel and formed a makeshift dressing for the wound. It hurt to move. He finished washing, turned off the water, then stepped over the dead servant to go put on a fresh outfit. Once his rapier was strapped on his belt, he went to find Marisol and his companions.

They'd have to help watch his back. Even in the castle, Diregloom was a treacherous place. They'd all have to be ready for anything.

Chapter Twenty-Six

SPRAT HELLARD DECIDED he liked catacomb season.

With so many fel and purebloods intermingling in Stockade Square, he was free to move about with little notice. Sure, things might be trickier when the sun came up, but for the moment he lost himself with the revelers and the food and the music. Pretended he belonged. But as the last musical troupe put their instruments away, he knew it was time to go back to work.

Digger had vanished. The sheriff was gone too. He had missed them and didn't spot Isabel anywhere in the crowd. More than a few faces glanced up at him now that the singing and music were over. Their giddiness of being out after curfew was yielding to cold sobriety and the realization that an ogre walked among them which wasn't on anyone's leash.

It was only a fantasy to assume these people would ever grow accustomed to an ogre in their midst. Even in a city with a large fel population, he would never fit in. Diregloom was a lie, and he couldn't fathom how these people endured and celebrated games that required their blood to be spilled.

Try as he might, he hadn't made any headway in finding others who would do anything to change matters.

He imagined for a moment how it would be if fel ruled the island. Purebloods would be sent to live in squalor while his kind could be out on a night like tonight. He chuckled at the thought. Maybe they'd have their own games, pureblood versus pureblood, and the winner would get to spittle-shine the boots of every fel who toiled in the factories and workshops.

He dismissed the fantasy. The reality was that there would have to be a fight or the fel would be gone in another twenty years, outlawed, worked to death, or hunted. Much as ogres had been. The fel on the mainland were already devastated and freely killed by Duke Tito and the other pureblood rulers.

He had tried to convince his former bandit gang of the need to unite the fel, but they were too shortsighted to see beyond their next opportunity for pillage. And then the Karanog had started allowing purebloods to run with them.

But Diregloom at least held the promise of a few who might be swayed. Just finding any brave enough to stand up to a pureblood had been hard enough, until he'd come across the card game at the Dragon and Rose. Digger and his friends had done just that. Now he had to find out where his new friends had gone off to.

Someone bumped into him. As he looked up at Hellard, the light of the overhead lanterns revealed a youthful face. The young man's smile faded and his expression quickly filled with terror.

"You can scream now," Hellard said.

The man fled. As Hellard watch him go, he spied another among the diminished crowd who glanced purposefully away. The figure wore a broad hat and high-collared coat and a sword dangled from his belt. But Hellard also spotted a dark mark on the side of the man's face. In the poor light, he could have been mistaken, but he guessed it was a tattoo. It was time for Hellard to get out of the open.

Hellard began to move back towards the alley where Digger's cart waited.

He paused to sniff at a freestanding floral arrangement the flower seller hadn't brought inside. The man with the hat was coming his way.

The cart stood where he had last seen it. Hellard rounded the corner at the back of the alley and pressed himself against the wall. It didn't take long. The man walked quietly, but the alley amplified each step as he came to the corner.

Hellard lunged for him, fists clenched and swinging.

The man was fast, but not fast enough. As he blocked Hellard's haymaker, he stumbled. Hellard pressed his advantage and shoved the man hard against the opposite wall. Before the man could react, Hellard clamped a massive hand on his throat.

"Who are you with?"

"Guk! Guk! Guk!"

The man went limp. Hellard slapped him a few times. Realized he wasn't faking.

"Crap."

Hellard put the unconscious stranger down. First he checked every direction to see if anyone had noticed the fight. They were alone. Hellard patted the man down, pocketed a coin purse, and took the sword. He was about to snap the man's neck when he paused to look at the tattoos. The man wasn't Karanog. Some other gang, no doubt. So why was he interested in him?

After a moment of deliberation, Hellard began to strip the man down. He paused for a moment to admire the fine stitching and exquisite fabric of the stranger's gold shirt and cape. He placed the naked body in the cart. Using the sword, he sliced up the cape and bound the man. Then he leaned on the corner of the flower shop and watched as the night stretched on and the crowd thinned further, his eye out for Digger, Isabel, or anyone else who might be looking for them.

THE STOCKADE REMAINED busy. Several drunks were hauled in by the city guards.

Hellard was too far away to see their faces.

Others were watching the stockade as well, purebloods by the look of it, and dressed the same as the crew he had helped fight in the bar. They'd recognize him if he got too close. He'd watch them, he decided.

Then the prison wagon appeared and vanished within the stockade. The sheriff followed. Not long after, Lord Angel rode past, also going inside. He emerged minutes later. Then he and his companions went out around the square, busily checking faces.

Hellard thought this might be a good opportunity if the nobleman had been alone, but with three of them he would be overmatched.

He wheeled the cart into the back of the alley and took a circuitous route up the castle hill. The man in the cart groaned.

"Shut up or I clobber you."

He lingered near one of the fountains. Splashed water on his face. He was no sneak thief but he had to know whether Digger and Isabel were among those captured. Just then, the sheriff rode by heading towards the castle and leading a manacled prisoner. It was Digger. Hellard started to pursue them, but then Lord Angel also trotted past.

Hellard could follow, true, but there wasn't much chance he could bluff his way into the castle. So he wheeled the cart down towards the stockade.

The nobleman's companions were nowhere in sight as he approached the two guards at the gate. They perked up when they saw him.

Hellard stopped the cart and gestured towards the tied man. "Contribution for the drunk tank. Was carousing in the graveyard and scrawling on the tombstones."

One of the guards peered in the cart and looked up at Hellard.

Hellard tried not to smirk. "Leaving your mouth open like that will let the flies in."

"What?" the guard asked.

"I said do you want him or do I drop him on the cobblestones? He's pissed himself and covered in vomit."

"Take him inside," the second guard said irritably. "Talk to the sergeant."

Hellard wheeled the cart into the stockade courtyard. He didn't see any sergeant. The covered walkway had numerous doors, some of which had padlocks and long bars.

"This is where you get out."

He dumped his prisoner onto the ground. Then he wheeled the cart around the courtyard. Surely there were dozens of men stationed there, but they must have been outside on duty or inside one of the numerous offices.

A woman with a ponytail was seated on a stool by a cell door in the corner. She was one of the nobles from the bar, the one who had almost killed Digger. Her sheathed rapier was resting on her lap.

"Any bodies?" Hellard asked.

She barely stirred. She waved him off. He stepped under the overhang and seized her, slapping the sword away and shoving her up against the cell door. She began to scream but he slammed her hard, knocking the breath from her.

"Not another peep. Who do you have in there?"

Her eyes flared as her fingers dug into his hands. "The cook."

He banged her body again and she stopped clawing at him. Reaching over with one hand, he tried the solid door. It was locked. It lacked any window so he could see inside.

"Monty?" he hissed. "It's Hellard. Are you in there?"

"Yeah," Monty said from inside. "Can you get me out?"

He shook the woman. "Where's the key?"

She was fighting to breathe. Her hand reached for a hilt sticking out of her boot. He gave her another hard shove and smashed her onto the stone floor. She groaned as he patted her down, throwing the knife away. No keys. The door was solid with metal hammered over wood, and there was no handle to grip. He'd need a crowbar or tools.

Voices echoed from across the courtyard. A pack of ten guards had entered the gate. They stopped when they spotted the tied naked man.

Hellard pressed his face to the door. "I'm sorry, Monty. It's no good. I'll figure something out."

"Don't leave me!"

But there was no time. He scooped up the woman and plopped her into his cart and headed for the guards. To a man they acted like a bunch of cats and almost scattered as he approached. Hands went to weapons.

Hellard went for the friendly ogre routine: a wide, toothy smile, palms out, slow movements so as not to scare the children. "Sorry about leaving him there. He got wiggly."

"Who are you?" a crooked-nosed older guard asked after composing himself.

"Grave duty, but I got a few scrip notes to drop off some drunks. Him, and this one here," he said, pointing to the woman with the ponytail.

"Well, you can't just dump him! Pick him up. Drunk tank's this way. Need to lock her up in one of the other cells."

"Give me the keys and I'll take care of it."

"Are you daft? Follow us and we'll show you."

The group of guards lingered. Who knew fear of an ogre would get them to bunch up like that? He saw no opportunity to relieve the guard of his keys as he was taken to two cells on the far side of the courtyard. The guard watched closely as Hellard dumped off the gangster in the already occupied drunk tank and Lord Angel's lethal lady friend in the neighboring cell.

"Now get that stinking cart out of here, fel. There's no bodies to collect."

He held his hand out. "Come on. How about a tip? It's been a long night."

"Scram!"

He pushed the cart out the stockade gate. Monty was safe for the moment. Isabel was no doubt in the stockade somewhere. That left Digger. A rescue from the stockade might be feasible with enough men. But springing Digger from the castle was going to be impossible.

At least the guards hadn't batted an eye at an ogre working as a gravedigger. He now had a cover. And with anonymity came the potential for so much mischief.

Chapter Twenty-Seven

THE GUARDS FINALLY came for Digger and Paulus.

In an adjacent room, a group of women waited. Digger was sat on a reclining chair. Immediately the women went to work, brushing out the tangles of his black hair, scrubbing his fingernails, plucking eyebrows and nostril hairs, and then washing him down.

Four armed guards were assigned to watch just him.

Digger tried to relax as he was dried off and his hair was rinsed.

A coiffeur began cutting, shaving the sides of his head and teasing and trimming the rest of his hair so it formed a ridge from front to back. Then the man tried to apply makeup. Digger waved him away.

"It's for the dramatic lighting," the coiffeur said.

Digger began to remove the cloth thrown around his neck. "I'm allergic."

The coiffeur gave one of the guards a pleading look.

"Let him work or get thumped," the guard growled.

Digger sagged in his chair. The makeup work took longer than the rest of it.

In the second seat, Paulus was getting his fingernails buffed. Then one of the women began to paint the nails black. Moment by moment, his fellow contestant was turning into a fierce monster before his eyes.

By the time Digger was allowed to get up, he could only guess he appeared similar to Paulus.

They weren't returned to the holding room. Instead they were brought into a dark corridor and led down a ramp into a barred jail cell with benches.

Six of the others were there already, similarly painted and preened into sinister greenskin monsters.

A stack of weapons lay on the ground. Digger picked up an axe. It was made of wood but painted silver.

"Fake."

"Yeah," Paulus said. "Those are props for our showing. We don't get the real thing until later, assuming we get any arms at all."

The comment caught the attention of the others. Digger selected the heaviest of the bunch, a faux longsword with a solid handle. After an hour they were all together again.

A brightly dressed castle attendant appeared on the opposite side of the bars. "Okay, monsters! It's almost time for your showing. Look fierce." He took a moment to consult a notebook. "The game theme is the Nymph's Grotto. You are her defenders. Imagine yourselves the last line of defense between your mistress and those who would steal from her and threaten her virtue."

"What?" the younger fel asked.

"Act mean," Paulus murmured. He picked up a fake axe.

Moments later a line of tourists came down the hallway. They were dressed in fine suits and skimpy dresses. They giggled as they openly stared. Paulus surprised Digger when he roared and smashed his costume weapon against the bars. The men and women jumped and then laughed as he reached for them through the bars.

"A spirited one!"

One of the women scribbled a note on a page. Others did the same as they walked past and examined all of them.

"Put on a good show," Paulus whispered. "Don't just stand there."

"What's the difference? Either way we're going to be thrown into the catacombs."

"They're making odds right now. The better you look, the better chance we have of being placed somewhere where we get an advantage."

"Like what?"

Paulus gestured with his axe. "Something with an edge. It's the sad sacks who get put out front for the early stages."

Digger let out a bellow as the tourists flowed past but couldn't muster the same enthusiasm as the older fel. All he could hope was that the sheriff had honored his promise and his brother would go free. He was doomed to play out this farce and didn't want to waste energy he would soon need just so some purebloods could get a thrill from his demise.

More groups of tourists came and went. Some made comments about their size and what would happen to them in just a few hours. Others chimed in on their favorites and who they were betting on. A few threw coins, or candy. One young woman flung a garter belt at Paulus, to the delight of her pack of friends.

Paulus kept up his performance and didn't comment as Digger fell silent. From down the corridor came the sounds of other prisoners, but these were pleading and crying. He realized they weren't the only group of monsters. Judging by the scoffs and laughter of the tourists, these were scoring poorly.

"Hey, greenskin, catch."

A woman leaned past Paulus and threw a wadded lacy handkerchief at Digger. It bounced off his face and landed on the floor. Digger lunged at her and caught her wrist. The woman was petite and wore an abundance of jewelry. And now she screamed. Digger yanked her against the bars and grabbed her throat. The other tourists were shouting. A guard got his hands through the bars and tried to pry Digger's hands free. More guards entered the cell and Digger felt a hard rap on his head, followed by more blows as he was beaten down into a spinning haze.

The woman, now free, was sobbing.

"Grab that one," a guard said.

He was hauled to his feet and dragged out of the cell.

"Where to?" a second guard asked.

"Preliminary round. And hurry up. We start soon."

The world spun. But he managed to smirk. At least now they'd get it over with quicker.

Chapter Twenty-Eight

THE COOKS AND SERVANTS hustling about the castle's kitchen bumped Angel aside anytime he got in the way. Perhaps they didn't notice who he was. In their breakneck rush and with so many of them dressed in fancy attire above their station, it didn't surprise him. Still, it didn't mean he wouldn't give some of them a thrashing later, but for now he was hungry.

As he squeezed past a chef shucking oysters and others stirring steaming pots and working at the ovens, he wondered who else in the castle might be an assassin.

If Red Eye couldn't be appeased, it meant Angel would have to fight back. The thought unnerved him. Red Eye was one man, but he'd been proven to have a long reach.

Angel snagged a meatball from a chafing dish. It scalded his tongue as he tried to chew. The cook who was working at the dish gave him a look but said nothing. Even bowed her head deferentially. At least someone in Diregloom knew their place.

The preparations were for the banquet, which would be an ongoing parade of dishes for the mainland royalty here for the games. Even now there was a mass of visitors in the courtyard outside. These were here for the early viewing of the monsters. They would be milling past the kitchen windows in costumes or their Sunday best, wearing high hats, plumes, corsages, ruffles, and shining pieces of decorative armor. More than a few carried swords, mostly rapiers or foils. Some were contestants wanting a look at the opposition. Among them would also be the bookmakers who would be setting the odds, so even those not rich enough to buy a ticket could place a bet and listen to the news of how each round's contestants performed.

Angel could have been out there with them enjoying the party. He felt the tug in his heart at the thought of action. He had a good eye for a racehorse, so picking which fel was going to score the most hits on overconfident pureblood contestants would be a piece of cake.

He shoved the urge aside.

He was back at square one. Somehow he needed to earn enough coin to pay off his debt. He needed to find his companions, retrieve Marisol, and question the fel cook one last time before disposing of him. The gravedigger would see his end soon enough. That only left finding dear Sprite. Perhaps the sheriff knew something of her whereabouts. Then he could exact his own justice on her.

A trumpet played a short trill outside. Round one of catacombs was about to begin. He wanted to be with his aunt during the games. Snatching a glass of sparkling wine from a tray, he headed into the banquet room.

Claudia was there, along with Rochus and a few of the senior matrons who oversaw the staff. She was busy doling out orders as she inspected the lavish tables being set with dishes of food. She didn't even glance at him as her procession passed him by.

The trumpet signaled again.

He fell in behind them and followed as they went out to the front courtyard and faced the crowd.

A cheer went up. Aunt Claudia plucked a handkerchief from her sleeve and waved.

A bald servant with an earsplitting voice said, "Let the catacomb games begin!"

The attendants waited until the ovation died down before conducting the crowd towards the open maw and into the catacombs. Claudia continued waving until they were all filtering away. A roar from the entrance echoed through the courtyard and caused the crowds to hush. It was one of the carriage trolls from somewhere below. The spectators then broke out in laughter and howls.

"My money's on the troll!" a loud voice shouted.

Angel would have bet against him. His aunt had always made sure the contestants had the upper hand. But would she risk one of her prize pets?

The staff got their final orders and hurried off. His aunt brushed past him but he caught up to her.

"Aunt Claudia, did you get any rest?"

She looked at him for a moment, her expression impossible to read. "Just a little, dear. But there's so much to do. The preliminary round is to start in twenty-two minutes. And then we have our first banquet."

"A moment of your time."

"I'm really quite busy."

Whatever affection he had rekindled the night before was gone. But with assassins out for his blood, he couldn't put off talking to her.

"I'll be brief."

Rochus glared but didn't say a word.

Claudia motioned Angel to get on with his request. He cleared his throat. He wished he had her alone, but it wasn't possible.

"I need to borrow money."

She giggled. "You want a loan? After what you did?"

"It was a mistake. I made up for it, didn't I? The watch is back. Your game day is turning out to be a smash. I've never heard such a buzz. And all of these are ticket buyers."

"Hmm. The margin on this will be thinner than I'd like. The stone workers have never been cheap."

"I've got a few ideas that could help. We could do all the books ourselves, control the bets. It's something I understand well. But right now I need a few coin to help clear up some final details of my trouble with getting the watch back."

Her face clouded over without ever losing the smile. Her eyes grew cold. She waved Rochus back and wandered to a banquet table. There she took a moment to adjust a silver serving spoon so it lined up with a set of forks.

"I'm surprised to see you this morning," she said.

Angel was confused. "What do you mean?"

"I mean I enjoyed hearing the tale of your adventure. It would have been a fine way to remember you."

"I don't follow, Aunt Claudia."

"You got the watch back. But my plans are still lost to me. I've never been good at remembering details. That's why I put them to writing. That page was worth more to me than any trinket. If only you had died with some dignity. It would have added spice to the day's festivities."

He felt a chill in his gut. "There was an assassin in my room."

"So you got my little gift."

"You sent her?"

"Imagine how it would have played out! A noble-born killed by a fel rogue in the heart of the castle. An escapee from the catacombs snuffs out a life in its prime. Imagine the horror, shock, and rage! I've met some of the contestants. Oh, but for the warriors of old who hunted wild fel in the deserts and mountains. But we have to settle for our sport. This would have stoked a furnace in the bellies of my contestants, something no prize can ever do."

"You...tried to kill me."

"You believed bringing the watch back would earn my good graces. Now we understand each other."

He remained stunned. Rochus stood nearby, perhaps close enough to hear. Also close enough to stop him if he tried to strangle the deranged woman in front of him.

Angel dropped to his knees and grabbed a hand. Kissed it. "Please. What can I do to make it up to you?"

She ripped her hand away. "I don't know. What *can* you do?"

"What if I can retrieve that paper? The gravedigger might know where it is. He's here, in the catacombs."

"You don't have much time. I guess you can enter as a contestant and find out. Finding my lost page would please me."

"It's still the first round. I'll talk to him. Maybe one of his friends has it."

But he saw he no longer had her attention. Rochus was signaling her. More servants had queued up for their instructions, along with a few guests. Her smile brightened as she went to welcome one of them with a hug. Angel almost didn't recognize Viscount Ilario. Still wearing his austere suit, he had a ribbon on one wrist and the young boy on his arm.

At least someone was having a good time.

But then he saw waiting with them his older brother Jamie. Seeing him there didn't make sense. Jamie—the soft-headed puppy who had fallen for his fel nursemaid. So why was his delicate sibling here?

The answer was all too obvious when he saw the fancy rapier with the silver handle on his brother's belt. He also wore a wide-guard dagger.

Claudia gave Jamie a hug. "What a surprise! My steward mentioned your letter. Said you'd visit and that you wanted to be a contestant. How wonderful!"

Jamie bowed and gave a dimpled grin, which waned ever so slightly when he made eye contact with Angel.

"You see, Angel? Now you can enjoy the spectacle even more now that you have someone to root for. Oh, my sweet nephews, this will be so much fun. But Jamie, the games are starting and I'm sure you don't want to be late. While we might not catch the first round of the preliminaries, I'm sure there's time to see you inserted so you have a chance at winning. That is what you want, isn't it?"

"More than anything, Aunt Claudia," Jamie said.

"Then off you go. I'll be cheering for you."

As his brother was ushered along by an attendant, Angel asked, "Have you spoken to her?"

Jamie stopped in front of him, his mouth tight.

"Your Sprite is here somewhere, brother. What do you hope to accomplish by entering the games? Hmm?"

"Don't call her that. You almost cost Isabel her life."

Angel shook his head. "Not me. You're the one who expressed his love for a fel. And then Father did what Father does. By the way, does he even know you're here? And how will Mother react when she learns her dearest has run off to fight in Aunt Claudia's contest?"

"I didn't tell them."

"Of course you didn't. Because Father would have stopped you. Can't have both his boys running away to the decadence of Loom Island. But whereas he won't even write me, he'll send for you. And what will you do then?"

"What I do doesn't concern you."

"No? I'm your brother. Of course it concerns me. What prize here calls you? Gold? Is it fame? Is it making a name so you can try to openly declare your love to a greenskin?"

When Jamie flinched, he knew he had hit paydirt.

Angel gave a satisfied nod. "I guess all things are possible here. But the edict stands, even in Diregloom. But more importantly, how are you going to even find sweet Sprite when she's gone missing?"

"What did you do? Where is she?"

"I've been asking that same question. Seems she's gotten mixed up in some trouble. At least that's what I've heard. But I'll keep my ears open. Maybe I'll find out before you have to go fight. But don't let me stop you from stepping into the games."

Jamie looked as if he was ready to burst. But he never would. A weak retort would follow, or even better, tears. "You're trying to trick me. I'm going to play in the games. I'm going to win. And then I'll find Isabel and keep you and Father from her forever."

Angel applauded. "Then bravo. I too will cheer for you. Remember, the pointy end goes towards the monsters."

Jamie marched off with the attendant.

Claudia stood at Angel's side. "That sounded a bit cruel."

"I was hoping to talk him out of playing. He's only an average swordsman. He lacks the stomach."

"A pity. He'll have to take his chances, I suppose. So if we were to run his odds side by side with yours, who would the bookies favor?"

Before he could ask her for clarification, she hastened away with Rochus. The games wouldn't start without her.

Angel dismissed the thoughts of his brother. Goading him had been a momentary distraction. He couldn't help himself. But now he had to consider his next step.

If Claudia had sent the assassin, it meant Red Eye wasn't the threat Angel had believed. He had to find this page of hers. That piece of paper could be anywhere. It felt like he was back at the beginning. Isabel could have it, or the sheriff.

But it all came back to the gravedigger.

Angel had to speak with him before the games started. He still had the cook as prisoner to use as leverage. What was this piece of paper to the fel? There'd be no reason not to hand it over if it meant saving someone the gravedigger cared about.

He made his way outside and headed for the demon's mouth.

Perhaps one of the monsters unwittingly held the key to Angel's good fortune.

Chapter Twenty-Nine

DIGGER COULD HEAR THE crowds.

He had been thrust into yet another cage, this one wrapped in a dark curtain. Three other prisoners huddled nearby. These hadn't been preened and pampered as he and the others had been but instead reeked of sweat and their own filth.

He tried to get their attention but none would even make eye contact. They were sullen and terrified, and why not? They were about to die for the pleasure of a bunch of noble purebloods.

Sunlight shone in through a gap in the fabric, revealing a ramp leading up. Twisting decorative vines ran along the walls. He heard the echoes of people talking above, as if there was a second room looking out over the hallway beyond the curtain. The sounds only grew louder as the unseen gallery filled with spectators.

Something roared. The crowd cheered. The monstrous growls diminished, but Digger concluded it had to be one of the queen's trolls.

He felt a moment of pity for the brainless creature.

After a while a large group descended the ramp. Scores of spectators, some wearing masks and others elaborate makeup, came down into the hallway.

One of the fel next to Digger began sobbing.

A few in the crowd peered behind the curtain, but a guard shooed them away.

"No previews. Go further down the main corridor. Then take the stairs to the left. And keep your tickets out."

Most wore pink tags pinned to their collars or sleeves. As the last of the crowd left, someone ran down the ramp, pushing past a pair of guards.

"Preview is over!" one of the guards said. "Hey!"

Other soldiers intercepted the lone figure and a terse discussion followed. Then one of the men pointed towards Digger's cage.

"He's in there," a guard said. "He's up for the first round."

Lord Angel threw the curtain open. "Remember me?"

Digger backed up. Lord Angel's nose had been straightened but both his eyes were dark and his face was swollen. He could only hope the nobleman would once again get close.

"You look like you lost a fight," Digger said.

Angel ignored the comment. "I've come to make you a deal."

"You see where I am. What do you have that I could want?"

"You're part of my aunt's game. I can't stop that now. But think of your friends."

"How do I know they're not dead?"

"Because I have the cook locked away in the stockade. That can change. That is, unless you don't care about him. But I have a suspicion you do. And it's only a matter of time before I find this ogre of yours and Isabel. I can call off the hunt."

"You got your watch back. Or at least the queen got it back."

Angel looked at the nearest guard, who took a few steps away.

"There was something else," Angel whispered. "Something which can save your friends if you just tell me where it is. It's a piece of paper with some notes. Tell me what rubbish heap you threw it in. That's it. You save three lives."

"What's so important about that piece of paper?"

Angel licked his lips. "Nothing. Not to you or anyone else. Just me."

"So plans for the expansion of the catacombs wouldn't interest the queen's subjects?"

A flicker of recognition crossed the nobleman's face. "You have it?"

"If I do, then it seems you'll be able to get it from my corpse soon enough. If it's of no consequence, then I'm sure you can wait until then to go through my pockets. But you coming down here now means there's something on that page you want to keep for yourself. Get me out of here. Release the cook from the stockade. Put us both on a boat, and I'll make sure you get your page back."

Angel smiled but his eyes remained hard. "That's not going to happen. Tell me where it is. Save your friends grief and pain. Or, as you say, I'll find out soon enough whether any of you have it."

"Not if we put it somewhere where it can be discovered."

"True. But while your death is imminent, I'll drag it out for the chef. Once I catch Isabel, I'll be sure she lingers for weeks. I'm sure one of them will tell me to relieve their suffering."

Digger leaped forward, his arms reaching for Angel's face. But Angel deftly stepped back and chuckled.

"So you do care, fel. Under your brave face, you're as scared as these other wretches. Maybe not for yourself, but for your friends. It will please me to no end to inform them that you died telling me one of them has what I'm looking for."

Up the ramp, a series of bells rang.

"I'm sorry, Lord Angel," the guard said. "It's time to clear out. It's about to begin."

The guard left the curtain open and escorted Angel down the hall where the other spectators had vanished.

Digger clenched his jaw until his teeth hurt. The piece of paper with the catacomb plans was still in his pocket. If Digger died, Angel would reclaim it. It was only a matter of time before the nobleman discovered Isabel was also a prisoner in the stockade. If Monty was still alive, Digger had no doubts that Angel would carry through with his threat even if he got the page back.

It was at that moment Digger decided he needed to survive.

Chapter Thirty

"WELCOME, ONE AND ALL," a voice from the gallery boomed. The clear, crisp words cut through the din and the crowd went silent. "I say again, welcome to the newest, greatest season of catacombs."

Applause and cheers broke out.

"Queen Claudia the Second has once again prepared a feast for our eyes, thrills for our appetites, and an experience for your memories. A few words for your safety. Keep away from the bars. The catacomb games are a dangerous place, and projectiles and monsters have occasionally hurt those who have leaned in too close. What you are about to experience is not for the fainthearted. There will be violence, but then again, all of you probably know this."

The crowd chuckled.

"This afternoon is our preliminary first round. It will give the contestants full flavor of what awaits them tonight, if they don't bow out. It will also give us, the audience, the opportunity to see the true mettle of those who would dare enter the nymph's lair.

"For below is no castle basement or dungeon, but the home of a most dangerous sea spirit. With her song and her touch, she lures young purebloods away to their doom. Her pit is home to monsters and torments. Only a brave few dare enter. And why?

"Adventure? A chance to see this beautiful creature of legend with their own eyes? Or is it her treasure? What tempts these warriors to their greatest challenge is their heart, is it not? But only the truest of spirits will persevere."

"Get on with it," someone yelled.

The game caller wasn't fazed. "What weapons will work here? What perils lie ahead? For our first round, a group of fearless souls pass along a beach where the echoes of the nymph's song linger in the rocks and cliffs of her haunted isle. They discover an entryway concealed in washed-up seaweed. A mouth of a giant frozen in stone submerged in the sand."

The sunlight was obscured, throwing the hallway beyond Digger's cage into shadow. Digger pressed against the bars to make out anything in the dark. A few minutes passed. Then he heard shuffling and several footsteps coming his way. A nervous laugh. A light began to shine until the bottom of the ramp was once again illuminated.

A group of ten figures appeared carrying lanterns.

They wore all manner of gear, from simple tunics to full metal chest pieces. At least one was a woman. They all held weapons, and Digger guessed they were all real.

From above, the game caller said, "But little did our adventurers suspect that even the tiniest of sand crabs would signal their arrival to their nymph mistress. These would also be her first line of defense."

A creak of ropes sounded from above. A cascade of hundreds of tiny objects fell on the contestants. They began screaming and swatting at their clothes. Some tore off helmets to swat away whatever was covering them. One of the ten let out a shriek and ran back up the ramp.

The spectators in the gallery roared in delight.

"Psst."

The whisper came from the back of the cage. Something was shoved at Digger and he grabbed it. At first he thought it was a piece of wood, but it had the distinct shape of an enormous bone. The other fel were likewise presented similar weapons.

"I'm opening your cage," the voice hissed. "Anyone who doesn't step out gets skewered. Bit of advice? Wait for the signal. Go for one of their tokens. Might save your skin."

The fel who had been sobbing finally stopped. No one said a word or made a sound.

Meanwhile, one of the contestants was pulling his shirt back on after having shaken it out. It was then that Digger realized the man was wearing a token clipped to his belt. Each of the other contestants had one too, on either their helmet or armor.

"Crabs." The man pulling his shirt on laughed. "It's just a bunch of tiny crabs. Pick up your weapons, guys. This place will have to do better than that."

As if he had been waiting for the contestants to compose themselves, the game caller announced, "With bravado, the remaining nine steel themselves up. Fear only claimed one, who is now disqualified. But what other threats await?"

From down in the darkness a chorus of bellows erupted. Men's voices, fel perhaps. Someone was putting on a display that gave the nine contestants renewed pause.

A soft metal squeak sounded and the curtain was pulled away. The cage door was loose. The clamor held the contestants' attention. They weren't looking at the cage.

"That's your signal," the voice whispered.

Digger adjusted his grip on the bone club. It had heft and felt solid but unwieldy.

"But the nymph had other defenders," the game caller shouted. "Suitors. Sailors who she had seduced to dive from their ships, who had survived the swim through treacherous seas to woo her. These smitten lost souls would do anything for their mistress even as she corrupted their flesh. Mad with lust, she sends them out armed with whale bones to kill those who would pillage her sanctuary."

The shouting down the hallway sounded like it was getting louder. Digger saw this as an opportunity. The ramp was right behind the nine contestants. He could make a break for it. But surely there were guards ready for just such a violation of the game rules. They wanted them to fight.

Digger stepped from the cage. The others followed.

It was the weeping fel who attacked first. He let out a mad cry and launched himself at the group.

"Raaah!" Digger screamed as he ran at one of the contestants. His overhead swing caught a man on the shoulder. The man cried out in agony and dropped his lantern, which popped on the ground. The flame went out.

Digger didn't hesitate but swung again, smashing another across the side of the head.

The other two fel were slow to press the attack. The contestants easily parried with their swords.

Meanwhile the weeping fel had taken down two people. He was laughing wildly when he was caught under the ribs with the thrust of a rapier. He crumpled to the floor.

Digger blocked an incoming blade and ducked. When he swiped his club, his opponent retreated. It gave him a moment to catch his breath. From further down the entryway the shouts of his fellow monsters had faded. Had it merely been a distraction? He realized the game wouldn't stack the odds too highly against its contestants.

One man stopped to yank the token from the dying fel's collar.

The two other fel were surrounded and starting to tire.

The spectators above were cheering, but the sound was muted. Digger could only see the humans in front of him brandishing their weapons. One had a short stabbing spear. He jabbed at Digger. Digger's own massive bone club threw him off-balance every time he moved to block a blow. The man was toying with him as another with a longsword moved around Digger's flank.

"Piss off, his token's mine," the spear wielder said.

The swordsman scoffed. "First come, first serve."

Not waiting for either of them, Digger brought his club down on the spearman's foot. The crunch of bone was satisfying, but his club cracked and was starting to split. The spearman hobbled back as he cried out.

The swordsman sliced the air as Digger stumbled away. He fell over one of the downed contestants.

A gold token sparkled on a necklace.

But there was no time to retrieve it. The swordsman pressed his attack and Digger barely avoided the blade as he picked up a dropped rapier. He wasn't trained with the fiddly light weapon, and his opponent appeared to know it, based on the man's growing smile. The enemy's sword jabbed repeatedly at him. As quick as Digger could try to block or parry, the man would smack Digger's sword aside and slash at him.

The blade caught Digger's cheek.

The crowd in the gallery began clapping and hooting.

Digger chopped at air. Missed. The man was too quick.

He heard another of the fel cry out but didn't dare take his attention off his opponent. Digger tore his shirt off and bundled it in one hand. The swordsman licked his lips as he followed Digger into shadow. Digger fought to calm himself. Tried to probe his opponent's defenses. The man appeared to know what Digger was thinking and his sword slapped Digger's weapon almost hard enough to knock it from his grip. A few more steps and he would be boxed into the cage.

"Stay in the entry chamber," a voice from the wings hissed.

The crowd no doubt wanted to see what was happening. Someone from above lit a nearby sconce torch with a long pole lighter. The spectators gasped and murmured.

The new light illuminated one of the dropped clubs. Digger kicked it up towards the swordsman. As the man easily knocked it away, Digger charged. He caught the edge of the longsword with his shirt-wrapped hand and knocked the man in the head with the pommel of the rapier. The man grunted and faltered.

Digger didn't hesitate. He lunged and tackled the man and began to pound his head against the stone floor.

A tepid cheer went up from a few in the gallery but there were more cries of shock. The swordsman had gone limp. Digger tore the token and necklace free.

He grabbed the heavier longsword. Tested its heft. He had trained with longswords as one of the duke's rangers. It suited him fine, and he turned to face the others.

Only two of the pureblood contestants remained standing. A pair of others leaned on the wall nursing wounds. The last of Digger's fellow monsters had somehow gotten lucky, but he was now crawling towards the ramp. The two were following him and jabbing their rapiers at the ground, making him flinch.

Digger marched towards them. "Hey!"

He could only imagine how he looked between his makeup, his bleeding cheek, and however much spattered blood now marked his body.

"This token is for him."

He flipped the token towards the fel.

"He's free. I'm fair game."

The two men turned, ready to fight.

"Kill him!" a voice from above shouted.

Digger stood perched on the balls of his feet and ready to strike the first man who came in range. From what he had seen, this group had been taught a showy version of swordsmanship. He was banking on them making the first mistake. But even still, his odds against two opponents were slim at best. At least he'd take one of them out before dying.

He was surprised when both ran up the ramp.

"Two more disqualifications!" the game caller announced.

The spearman with the crushed foot limped past, as did two more. The remaining contestants weren't moving. Neither were the other fel. He went from man to man and collected tokens.

A single bell chimed.

"We have a monster victory! The entry to the nymph's grotto has been defended! What an upset! But lo, Her Majesty's champions and new treasure seekers approach! What fresh challenges await? Buy your tickets for this evening's next round of catacombs, my dear friends. You won't want to miss it."

The crowd murmured and there was a smattering of applause. This was clearly not the result most had expected. No doubt few had bet on a monster victory so early in the games.

Digger crouched to assist the surviving fel.

A doorway next to the cage opened. Attendants moved into the chamber.

Digger stood to face them but then turned his attention to the gallery. "Wait!"

His shout caught everyone's attention. He showed his handful of tokens and nodded towards the fel at his feet. "I've won his freedom. I also want to buy free some of my friends. Two of them are being held in the stockade."

"That's not in the rules," the invisible game caller said.

"Then change them."

"These are the queen's games. She sets the terms of play. You can buy your freedom and his. You can also give your tokens away or save them. Then you can purchase a prize."

"I don't want your damn prizes." He doled out two tokens and placed one on each of the other wounded fel. He could only hope they'd survive. "They're free. Get them a doctor."

"That's three monsters who have purchased immunity and release. And what of your own freedom?"

"Freedom is overrated." He then hefted his sword and went to the closest wounded human. He smashed the sword down, splitting the man's skull.

The crowd cried out in horror. Before they could finish reacting he moved to the next man and did the same. A third died before the game attendants rushed to save the last one and pulled him away. Digger unceremoniously cleaned off his weapon on one of the corpses. He pocketed the remaining tokens.

"I think I'll stick around. I'm sure this earns me another death sentence. If Lord Angel is up there, tell him I'll be down here waiting." He fished the page of notes from his pocket. "Oh, and tell him I have what he's looking for."

The vocal spectator cackled. "A challenge! Brilliant!"

Digger almost skewered the game attendant who tried to take his sword.

An older fel in bright clothes interceded. "Put the weapon down, friend. It's over. You won. But for now you have to come with me. I'll get you cleaned and stitched up. Because in a few hours you're coming back for the next round, like you asked."

Chapter Thirty-One

"WHERE ARE YOU GOING?" Queen Claudia asked.

Angel had tried to slink away from the remaining cluster of nobles mingling with his aunt in the gallery above the catacombs. The opening round had concluded and it had been a disaster. The gravedigger had survived. He also had the page and had announced it to the world.

Angel licked his upper lip. "I'm not feeling well, Aunt Claudia. A headache. Please excuse me."

She strode towards him, a flute of sparkling wine in hand. "Poor boy. Perhaps you'll find some rest in your room. A nap is always curative, in my experience." She leaned in close. "Does our brave victor have what I think he has?"

"Yes. I'm going down to his cell and taking it from him."

"Hmm. You'll do no such thing."

"What? Why ever not?"

"Because this has been the most thrilling round in any of my games. You heard the crowd. They're excited!"

"He just murdered four purebloods! A fel!"

"And bravo for him. He also beat the odds and declared his intention to not buy his freedom. Isn't it magnificent? It's the best season yet. He's staying in the game."

"Aunt Claudia, all I have to do is go down there and get it back."

"No. He's resting up. He'll need time to prepare for this evening and I won't have you hurt him."

"I'll ask nicely."

"No one's allowed into the lower levels that doesn't belong there."

Angel glared at the various nobles keen on the conversation until they looked away. "You've sent an assassin for me," he whispered. "Now I have what you want in reach and you'd have me wait?"

"Oh, there's no wait unless you choose to. By all means, take your nap. Maybe your widdle headache will feel better. But there's a way you can claim the page without breaking any of my rules."

He closed his eyes and sighed. "You'd make me fight?"

"Your brother has spunk. Maybe he's the one who deserves a place on my island. The catacombs await, dear. Besides, we might have a few contestants give up their places after hearing about that slaughter." She gripped his arm and gave the muscle a squeeze. "But you're strong and a trained swordsman. I'll even place a wager on you if it makes you feel better. It's your choice, of course, my Angel. No matter your decision, I'm having the best day ever. You playing catacombs alongside your brother will only be the icing on top of it."

He couldn't believe he was actually considering it. No bucket of crabs was going to scare him off. He knew he could beat the gravedigger in a straight fight. But what other surprises awaited those who played the evening round of his mad aunt's game?

"The tokens he captured are for the taking?" he asked.

His aunt hitched up her dress and began mounting the steps out of the gallery. "Of course."

"And the prize watch. How many tokens?"

"Ten. And only for a contestant who survives the final chamber."

"Okay. I'll do it. I'll play the game. Win that watch. But there better be room for my companions."

Her smile couldn't get any wider. "Oh, super. I'm sure we can squeeze them in. Now I have to hurry. I have my game keepers to talk to. We'll need to work on bringing up the lighting in all the rooms for when the action starts. Plus it was a bit chilly down here. I wonder what the oddsmakers say now that we've had this upset."

She kept talking. Rochus had appeared from some recess of the gallery and was taking notes.

Game time for the evening was two short hours away, after the banquet. He had time to get Marisol and Gavin and Hector. They needed to be ready to fight.

If there were no more snags, Angel was starting to see a way out of his predicament. He'd enter the game, kill the fel, take the cursed page and give it back to his aunt. And then he'd buy the watch and pay off Red Eye.

Everyone would be happy.

Simple.

"Aunt Claudia, I'll do it. But I have one small favor to ask first. And I think you'll like it."

Chapter Thirty-Two

PAULUS WAS STROKING his beard as the guards brought Digger to the waiting room. The lounge had been straightened out since Digger had left. The table had fresh platters of fruits and meats. Full pitchers of beer and decanters of wine were set next to stemmed crystal glasses.

"You've earned us the royal treatment," Paulus said.

The others appeared nervous. All of them were looking at Digger.

"You heard us shouting?" Paulus asked. "We had you in mind. We were told we'd stand a better chance if we made a good show. That's what they want from us, you know. Didn't expect you to survive. No one did."

The cell door slammed and locked behind Digger. "I wasn't expecting to either."

"Is it true?" a green-eyed fel asked. He hadn't been among the earlier inductees. "Heard you killed half a dozen purebloods."

Paulus chuckled. "And was too efficient about it. They want a show, lad. Taking them out after they've fallen is bad business."

Digger eased down onto one of the couches. "Bad business? This is murder. Why shouldn't they get a taste of what they're dishing out?"

"Because believe it or not, we might survive the day if we do our part. You fall, you scream, you bleed a little, and then you play dead."

"What are you talking about?"

"Come on. You were the first to see those contestants. The 'adventurers.' Young kids with weapons, most drunk or stoned. They want to hear us squeal and cry for our mamas. Take our token. Buy their prize. No one cares that we're not really dead. And we go free after it's all done."

"You saying it's all an act? That's not what I've heard."

Paulus shook his head and scowled. "How long have you been in Diregloom? They have real weapons. Sometimes we do get killed. But it sure beats a noose."

The green-eyed fel looked confused. "How do you know so much? Did you work at the castle?"

"He was a monster in a previous season," Digger said. "So what can we expect later?"

"It's always a closely guarded secret. We have the defensive advantage, but the game's rigged in favor of the contestants. I guess that was put to the test with your performance."

"Then why don't you look pleased?"

"Because at the end of the day, the queen hates to have her team lose."

THE TWO STITCHES IN Digger's cheek were oozing. As he sat he tried to stay alert, ready for the moment when the guards or game attendants came for him. He had been told it would be two hours, but he knew he couldn't believe anything from those involved with the catacombs, the castle, or the queen.

Plus, Lord Angel might show up at any moment to claim the page.

But that was a long shot.

Why would the nobleman risk himself when he could pay off anyone to murder him? Even one of Digger's fellow monsters might try something if it meant their own life would be spared.

He thought of Hellard's appeal to him and the others at the Dragon and Rose. As if fel would ever be united in a cause against purebloods. If generations of being hunted down hadn't done it, if losing their hold on Loom Island hadn't changed their collective minds, then it was every fel for themselves.

Take the lesson humans had known since spawning from the dust of the ground in the times before the fel walked the earth.

Trust no one.

Rely on yourself and never be disappointed.

A wave of tiredness almost sent him to sleep.

It wasn't just his body. It was the same feeling that had coursed through his veins after putting the magister and his guards into the ground. Something had left him since he learned his parents had been murdered. His spirit felt weary. And now he taken more lives, and the day wasn't over. He feared he had lost a part of him he would never regain and now he was giving up the final pieces of his soul.

Paulus poured him a beer. "Don't worry, it's small."

Digger sniffed it. Tasted it. It was excellent, hoppy and malty and smooth without being too strong.

But after a couple of sips, he paused. "We can't lose our edge."

"Maybe so, but it'll calm the nerves."

He waited for Paulus to eat something first. Then he followed suit, slaking his thirst and eating. Like everything else he had been served since being brought up to the castle, it tasted fabulous.

Chapter Thirty-Three

HELLARD PUSHED HIS cart next to a few other people waiting by the side gate to the castle. They had similar carts, and they had a look about them as they stood there. They wore hoods over their heads even though it wasn't cold. Their clothes and boots were brushed clean, but a sheen of dirt remained on all of them. At least one of them had a pick and shovel inside his cart.

Just the people he was hoping to find. Graveyard workers like his new friend Digger.

A fel smoking skunkweed from a curved pipe looked up at him. "Who're you?"

Hellard settled in and tried to look bored. "Queuing up for the inevitable bodies."

This caught all the gravediggers' attention.

"Don't remember any new drudges hired by Xavier. You for East Hill?"

Hellard didn't know any Xavier. He had heard of East Hill but wasn't aware of any other cemeteries on Loom Island. "Yup. East Hill cemetery. Xavier told me he was short a man."

The fel blew smoke. "Mind your place in line. I'm sure there'll be plenty to go around."

A guard opened the gate and waved them and their carts through. On the side of the keep opposite of the party was a set of steps descending to a lower gate. Two of the gravediggers were escorted down. The fel with the pipe took a last puff before knocking the ashes out against his cart and putting the pipe away.

"How bad does this get?" Hellard asked. "I have a delicate stomach."

"Guards do the cleanup. We just pick up the bodies."

As if to underscore his comment, the two fel emerged again with a shrouded dead body, which they flopped into their cart. They went down and brought out two more and then began to tarp the three corpses. The fel who had been smoking went down next.

One of the other gravediggers was grinning. "This should be a good weekend."

Hellard peeked under one of the shrouds. The body appeared to be pureblood.

"Hey! Hands off!"

"Relax," Hellard said. "Just looking, not taking. I'm wondering who will mourn these poor souls? Also I thought the games were rigged in their favor."

"They are. One of the game attendants just told us a fel cleaned house in the preliminary round this afternoon."

His companion, a woman with a toothy underbite, looked glum. "Figures. I bet the sure odds the monsters would get wiped out."

Hellard chuckled. "That'll teach you. Did anyone say which monster made it?"

"Why?" the woman asked suspiciously. "You know some of the felons in there?"

"Maybe if word gets out that one of ours has taken out a pureblood or two, we might gather our own cheering section."

"False hope, ogre. Why don't you just focus on the job?"

The other gravedigger came back up the steps with a body over his shoulders. A green hand dangled from the cloth. "That's it for this round. The other dead purebloods are being taken back to the mainland. Sorry, new guy, you'll have to wait for the next round in a couple of hours. But it looks like you're closer to front of the line."

Hellard checked the dead fel's face. It wasn't Digger.

A guard began to escort them back out the gate. The buzz of the crowd carried on the evening air. A few of the attendees were visible past the guards, mingling near the front of the keep.

Lord Angel appeared with two of his rapier-carrying associates on his heels. He marched through the crowd in an obvious hurry. He looked angry.

Hellard hunkered down and watched him exit through the main gate.

There would be no way he could beat the man to the stockade, assuming that was where he was going. Monty, unfortunately, would have to fend for himself. He still had Lord Angel's two friends tucked away inside a shed. But Hellard wasn't going to try to make any kind of deal on his own. If Digger was out of the picture, Hellard knew what to do with the hostages. He wished he knew where Isabel was.

The bandit in him told him to cut and run. Diregloom was a big city and he'd find others who might be roused to his cause. The odds of freeing Digger from the catacombs weren't good.

But just maybe, just maybe, an opportunity might present itself if he was patient and kept his eyes peeled.

In the meantime, he had an excuse to make new friends.

Chapter Thirty-Four

THE GAME ATTENDANT was a diminutive man with a knobby nose and wearing a jester's cap. He led Digger and the group of monsters from their waiting room through a narrow corridor and out into a wide faux cave with stalactites and sparkling ropes of ornamental seaweed.

Guards followed. And judging by the sounds, more were watching from the walls.

The center of the room featured black and pearlescent squares in a grid pattern. A closed portcullis lay beyond. Anyone trying to make the gate would have to cross the grid.

"Watch your step here," the attendant said, pointing to the grid. "Safety's on; should be safe, but it pays to be careful." He only stepped on the black squares.

Digger's makeup had been reapplied and a gold medallion hung around his neck. No one had explained anything about it. The other fel were chatty and jumpy, nudging one another as if they were about to go out on a date rather than face sword-wielding tourists out for their blood. Paulus once again appeared calm.

They stuck to the black steps and crossed the grid. The attendant showed them a rack of weapons.

"Your choice here, except for you." The attendant handed Digger his broken whale bone.

Digger grabbed it. "It's busted."

The attendant shrugged. "All eyes will be on you. It's now your brand. You can upgrade like you did before, if you wish, once the round is underway."

The others picked up large tridents and unwieldy chopping swords that looked like kitchen utensils or something a child might draw. The weapons seemed heavy enough that they could do damage, but against rapiers and swords they'd be too slow.

Digger looked at the empty weapon rack. "Give me my sword back. I won't pick it up until the round begins."

"That's all you get. Now listen for your cues. Fight on this side of the game board only. Stay hidden until the contestants begin to cross the board."

Gripping the bone, he considered the possibility of smashing the attendant and making a run for it. But up in the high gallery, guards shifted and whispered. No doubt there were arrows or crossbow bolts pointing at them in case anyone got a crazy idea.

The attendant went from prisoner to prisoner, straightening collars, wiping hair from faces, and brushing crumbs from their clothes. "Make it a good show. We're all counting on you."

Digger thought about killing the man on principle.

Two clusters of stalagmites on their side of the grid were actually hollow and made of wood, with blankets laid out on the floor. Their hiding places, from where they were supposed to spring up and scare the contestants. Digger walked back to the portcullis. It wouldn't budge. The fake stonework was stucco over wood. There were more than a few real rocks strewn about for decoration. Most were unwieldy but a few were throwing-size. He began to collect them and brought them to one of the hiding places.

"What are you doing?" one of the fel asked.

"Taking every advantage we've got."

Paulus picked up his own collection of stones.

The lanterns shining above the chamber dimmed. In the poor light the seaweed glowed. It truly was a marvelous effect. Sparkling glass set into the wall twinkled like stars or gemstones. Candles flickered to life above them as the gallery was illuminated. The spectators began coming down the steps, a warm buzz to their conversation. Judging by the noise, it was by no means a packed house.

Curious.

Digger crouched to examine the nearest white square. It didn't appear any different than the black ones, but he didn't want to press on it to find out. He then hurried over to where Paulus was taking cover.

"Stay hidden," Digger said. "Wait for me to throw my rocks. Then you go. We take out the first ones across. Bottle them up."

Paulus pulled one of the nervous fel along with him and got him situated behind the stalagmites. "Sounds like a plan."

They hid and waited.

From somewhere distant rose echoed cheers. The muffled voice of the game caller could be heard, but the words were indistinct. More cheers followed. The ones in the gallery above must have skipped whatever new first round was taking place in order to get to this chamber and front-row seats.

He guessed there may have been other rooms beyond the first which didn't involve the monsters. The voice of the announcer continued to echo along with still more cheers.

Almost an hour passed before the gallery began to fill up.

One of the new spectators spoke with a loud slurred voice. "I don't care what you say. The first round one was better. This was all swinging dummies. My niece could have pushed her way through that!"

"Yeah," someone answered. "But that slime was funny."

"Sit down, both of you. It's about to start."

The buzz above grew to a crescendo before falling to a hush. Digger focused on slowing his breathing. Ignored the growing cramp in his legs. The fel next to him kept making wet mouth sounds.

"Stay close," Digger whispered. "Watch my back and I'll watch yours."

The fel nodded.

"Ladies and lords," the game caller said, "the adventurers have moved beyond the entryway and into the heart of the evil nymph's lair. Her first line of defense has fallen. What new surprises lie in wait for our contestants? As a reminder, keep your hands within the bars at all times. This round will see our catacomb goers make their way into the chamber of secrets."

As if on cue, a soft whispering came from all sides of the chambers. A faint screeching began, as if a violin was being played purposefully out of tune. The gallery applauded. Blue light rose up from behind some of the larger stones.

Digger could only guess at how many secret chambers and compartments were hidden away around him.

More lights illuminated vermillion figures carved in the walls. Men, some appearing beastlike, were all making their way towards a beckoning woman who dominated the scene.

The game caller said, "Here is where the nymph selects the best from among her suitors. She tests their skills, their strength, their cunning. Only the most virile will gain her favor. No intruder has ever entered this part of her grotto and lived to speak of it. Yet even now, our brave catacomb runners approach!"

The applause quickly died down when a distant door creaked open. The gallery lights dimmed to near black as lanterns approached the opposite side of the board. The prisoner next to Digger peered out to see.

Digger nudged him. "Stay put."

He collected his rocks and strained his ears.

Three contestants were speaking in hushed tones. They sounded young.

"The sign says 'Black bishop's crossing.'"

"I don't see anyone here."

"That's because they're hiding. It's an ambush, stupid."

Their conversation fell to a low murmur.

"Get on with it!" a spectator jeered, but he was hissed at and shushed.

"It's a draughts board."

"Bishop's crossing? I thought we were facing a nymph, not clergy." The contestant chuckled at his own joke. "Let's go."

Digger couldn't follow what happened next, but there was a click, a snap, a hiss, and a wet smack in quick succession. Then came a howl of pain.

"Ah! Ah! Ah! I'm hit! I'm bleeding!"

A general commotion from the adventurers made it hard to follow what they were saying. But one of them was hurt. Digger clutched his rocks and strained his ears. Timing would be everything if he wanted to beat them.

"It's just a dart," one of the adventurers said. "Let me help."

"No! Don't pull it out! Stop!"

"Calm down." Digger recognized Lord Angel's voice. "It's not checkers, it's chess. He triggered the trap by stepping on white. Try staying on the black. Jamie, you stay behind me."

The wounded adventurer let out a pained laugh. "Why don't you go first?"

"Hector, Gavin. Step only on the black squares along the diagonal."

Footsteps were coming closer across the game board. Digger rose and spotted two of Angel's companions stepping from black square to black square as the rest of the party of contestants watched from the opposite side.

One of the adventurers pointed at Digger. "There! One of the monsters!"

Digger chucked the first rock. It barely missed the closest man. The second hit him in the chest and caused him to stumble. The floor clicked. A dart flew out of the nearest wall and struck his arm. He screamed, sidestepped, and triggered another dart. It struck his ear. He stumbled and fell back, and two more darts hit him as he dove off the far side of the board.

Blade out, the second companion had come leaping towards Digger and was almost across. Digger threw his third rock. The swordsman deflected it with the guard of his rapier. The man would be on Digger in an instant. It was either grab another rock or pick up his weapon.

As he reached for the whale bone, Paulus sprang up and threw his own rock, nailing the companion on the head. Blood poured from the man's forehead as he hesitated. Digger approached the contestant only to stop in his tracks as the man slashed wildly.

Lord Angel sounded furious. "You young lords want your tokens? He has them. Attack!"

Marisol drew her foil and a thin dirk in her left hand before leading the charge. Two of the others began jumping squares and passing her by. They held short swords and wore bright green masks that covered their eyes.

The game caller resumed his narrative. "The defenders have revealed themselves! These are no love-mad slaves of the nymph but her personal body servants. Trained. Lethal. Beast men whose minds have been twisted after years of service. These know the catacombs and will die defending its innermost mysteries!"

"Go monsters!" the heckler from above shouted.

Digger ignored the renewed clamor from above. The swordsman in front of him wiped blood from his eyes and began to advance on Digger. Another step and he'd be off the grid. Digger charged. His opponent blocked the swinging whale bone but wasn't prepared for Digger throwing his full weight into him. They collided with a thud and went tumbling onto the board. Squares sank and clicked beneath them.

Darts hissed and flew overhead. The whale bone slipped from Digger's grip, but his opponent's sword was also knocked away as they grappled.

The contestant closest to them screamed as darts hit him. He dropped his rapier and tore the darts away. He stumbled back and retreated, almost colliding with Marisol, who shoved him aside.

The man next to Digger tried to stand, hands and feet on the black tiles. Digger sprang up, feet planted on two black squares. Marisol and the others were closing in.

Where were the other monsters? He didn't dare look behind him. He had no choice but to retreat. But any advantage the board provided would be lost once the contestants came across.

He leaped at the closest adventurer. They collided and Digger smashed his skull into the man's face. Something crunched. Blood sprayed and teeth *click-click-clicked* across the game board as they tumbled to the floor.

Darts went zipping everywhere. Some *tinked* on stone and others struck the wood facades of the cave. More of the oncoming contestants were hit. Marisol had ducked to the floor nearby.

The man beneath Digger squirmed until Digger landed a series of quick, savage punches. The contestant went limp. Digger thrust him aside and reached for the only weapon close to him. The broken whale bone.

Marisol was the only contestant on the board not struggling to pull darts from her body. She crawled a few squares closer and paused as she pressed down on a white square. It clicked but no darts flew.

"Angel!" she cried. "Everyone! Come on! The darts are empty!"

Digger rose and hefted the club and began to retreat.

Angel, Marisol, and over a half-dozen armed purebloods were coming for him, and now there was nothing standing in their way.

Chapter Thirty-Five

DIGGER HAD BACKED AWAY almost to his stalagmite hiding place as the humans grouped together and cautiously crossed the checkered floor. Most of those who had been struck by the darts were coming too, as the missiles had not done more than superficial damage.

The shock of the trap was gone. Digger had earned their wrath.

Angel was content to allow the others to precede him, but he continued to hold one of his fellow players back. Marisol had risen and again advanced ahead of the others, her two blades out to either side, her face all business.

"Paulus," Digger hissed. "They're coming."

The opportunity to hem the contestants in on the boards was lost. Now they'd be facing superior numbers among the decorative stones and frescos of the chamber of secrets.

The game caller spoke. "The nymph's twisted game table barely challenged our group of fortune hunters. Only a lone defender stands in their way..."

Marisol hesitated once she was off the board. She scanned the ground and the rocks and set her foot tentatively forward.

Digger reached his hiding place. Two of the fel were still taking cover. Digger didn't look at them. Instead he beckoned Marisol forward.

As she advanced, one of Angel's companions passed her by. He still had a dart dangling from his arm. He charged at Digger, chopping the air with his rapier. But his movements were sluggish. Digger easily avoided the attack. The man was panting heavily, his teeth clenched. His footwork was sloppy.

Digger blocked a thrust and stomped on the man's foot. The companion howled.

But before Digger could press his advantage, the other fel burst from their hiding places. One smashed the companion with his oversized blade and proceeded to beat him senseless.

Two more of his fellow monsters went for Marisol but were stopped short as she expertly parried both in a flurry of motion. Paulus stormed towards her and threw his last rock. It smacked her in the head and she fell. But before any of them could finish her off, the rest of the contestants came charging at them.

A few of the waiting fel shouted and bellowed. One of them who appeared to have drank more than his share beat his oversized blade against a nearby fake rock. The display of bluster caused the oncoming purebloods to pause. Angel pulled Marisol to her feet and hauled her back.

The gallery above filled with whispers.

"That's it for tricks," Angel said. "There's as many of us as them. And none of them knows how to fight."

The group of adventurers hesitated. The pureblood Angel had been protecting tried to move forward but Angel caught his arm and hissed for him to wait.

"Come on, you pansies!" the heckler called.

"Why didn't you attack?" Digger whispered to Paulus. "We had them bottled up."

"No one wants to be first to die. Plus, with all the tokens in your pocket, I thought you'd make a good distraction."

The two lines of combatants waited for someone to make a move. Then one of the contestants who had been struck by a dart wavered. Another stepped back and vomited.

"The stings of the trap begin to leave their mark!" the game caller announced. "What poisons course through the veins of our adventurers?"

The contestant who had puked looked up at the gallery. "What did you do to us?" He wobbled and had to be steadied by another.

"Now!" Digger shouted.

He swung his whale bone and connected with a poorly timed parry, knocking a swordsman's rapier away. He then smashed the club across the man's hand and wrist. Bones popped. The man cried out and stumbled aside. Digger didn't follow but switched targets, shoulder-checking a wobbling contestant who wasn't able to bring his sword up in time. The man went down with a blow from Digger's club.

The rest of the fel charged.

Paulus smashed a rapier aside with his oversized weapon. But his opponent was fast and soon they were sparring. Fel and men shouted and cursed as they collided.

Digger caught a pommel across the brow. It was the young man Angel had been holding back. But the new opponent wasn't fast enough to get away as Digger caught a sleeve and brought his club down across the young man's back.

They separated.

"Jamie, get behind me, you fool," Angel ordered.

He and Marisol were fighting side by side. Two fel lay at their feet, both writhing and bleeding. Another tried to parry Angel's sword and strike at him, but as the nobleman stepped away, Marisol lunged and stabbed the fel's arm with her foil. Lightning fast, her dirk followed, piercing the fel's chest. He screamed and reeled but she delivered a series of quick stabs before he could escape. The fel tumbled to the floor.

Panting hard, Digger faced Jamie.

"You're Isabel's lover."

Confusion crossed the young man's face. "You...know her?"

"We're friends. You shouldn't be in here. You're going to get yourself killed."

Jamie was panting hard. He glanced towards his brother.

Digger saw the hesitation. Knew there wasn't any more time to waste. He smashed the butt of his club into Jamie's chest and followed it up with a wide swing that caught the man across the brow. Jamie went down and Digger backed away.

Meanwhile Angel, Marisol, and two of the remaining contestants were facing Paulus and the four last fel. One of the fel attacked.

Angel got under his guard and stabbed him. The fel cried out and backed away, dropping his weapon and clutching his bleeding abdomen. The other two contestants with Angel were light on their feet and wary. Marisol lunged forward, slapping at weapons with her dirk and thrusting her foil. She was a flurry of motion. Angel and the others followed. The fel retreated.

"Could use your help!" Paulus said.

One of the wobbly adventurers had gotten back up to face Digger. He was blinking rapidly as if trying to clear his eyes. But his rapier was steady and every time Digger moved, the man thrusted his weapon at him.

"Busy," Digger grumbled.

From above, the game caller purred. "The adventurers rally. The nymph's minions begin to fall back. Will they let their mistress down? Will these invaders find their way to her treasure chamber?"

Lowering the tip of his club, Digger baited his opponent, trying to get him to commit to an attack that might throw his balance off. The man kept his eyes locked on Digger's and didn't fall for it.

Digger took a step back, reached into his pocket, and threw the five tokens out on the floor. "That's enough for one of your prizes. Take them with your life. It's that or I beat your brains in."

The heckler guffawed and clapped, the lone spectator to do so.

Digger took a step back over one of the fallen contestants. The swordsman facing him bent to pick up the tokens. Boos erupted above them. Digger snatched the token from the collar of the fallen man at his feet.

"Hah!" Marisol shouted as she launched a fresh assault and caught one of the retreating fel. Angel dodged a clumsy blow and struck another one down. The other two contestants were closing in on Paulus and the last pair of prisoners. They were backed up against the portcullis with nowhere to go.

With his opponent distracted, Digger advanced towards Angel.

The nobleman turned to face him. "You wanted me down here. I'm here."

Marisol almost got past Paulus's defenses as the older fel swung clumsily at her. The heavy weapons were taking their toll. Exhaustion was setting in.

Digger paused. He motioned for Angel to come at him. When he didn't, Digger bent down next to one of the dart-struck contestants. The man lay prone and was gasping as if having a hard time breathing. Digger jerked him to his feet.

Angel swirled his blade in the air. "Stop wasting my time."

"Free my friend. You get the page. You walk out of here with your life."

"I let him go already. I have you now."

"I don't believe you. We still have your companions."

Angel spread his arms. "Where does that leave us then?"

"Me taking that sword from you and breaking your neck. But him first." Digger shook the man, who moaned and gagged.

"Do what you want with him. I don't know him. But this can go easy for you. Hard for your friend, though. I'll still get what I want."

Digger pressed the edge of the club against his captive's throat. Squeezed. Heard the man start to choke and felt him shudder.

From the gallery a woman shouted, "Let him go!"

Digger glanced up at the shrouded audience but couldn't see who was speaking. He shook the man in his grip. "He came for our blood. Why should I?"

The crowd was silent but for the lone woman. "He's down. Let him live and I'll pay out your freedom."

"That's not the rules," the game caller said.

"I don't care! He surrenders. Lord Gomez's son surrenders. Have mercy, I beg you!"

Digger hesitated. "How does that work?"

"It doesn't," Angel said. He ran Digger's prisoner through. The man screamed and crumpled to the gasps of the audience.

Digger released the man and barely blocked a sword thrust. He fumbled with his own off-balance club as Angel chopped it hard. Another blow struck the club and it broke. Digger pulled the fallen man away and snatched one of the darts from his shoulder. Angel pressed his attack, his rapier probing as Digger continued to back up. But then Digger stopped and heaved the dying man at Angel, catching him off guard. As Angel tried to dodge, Digger leaped at him. They collided. Digger jabbed Angel in the arm with the dart and tried to get an arm around the nobleman's neck.

Angel slammed the pommel against Digger's head repeatedly. They clung to each other, Digger squeezing and clawing but unable to protect his head from the hammer blows. He could only hope whatever drug coated the dart's tip was still present.

The crying woman in the gallery was drowned out by the crowd's renewed cheers. The other sounds in the chamber became a blur. Crashes.

Shouts. The caller was saying something. But Digger could only hear his own bellows of rage as he twisted and broke the dart in Angel's arm.

Angel was howling and finally his blows weakened. Digger felt dizzy. Blood and sweat stung his eyes. But as he tried to rise, Angel caught him in the side with a small knife. The blow was weak but the sharp blade pierced his shirt and flesh. Digger smashed the knife hand against the floor. The knife tumbled. Angel scrambled away. Digger's own strength began to ebb as he fought to rise. He found Angel's dropped sword.

But Angel was standing now too. He began limping away.

Digger knew he was about to drop. It took all of his concentration to keep the blade from slipping from his grip as he headed for the portcullis.

Paulus was the only fel still standing. Marisol was leaning on a nearby wall with a hand pressed against her ribs. She had blood on her lips and was breathing hard but still held her sword. Digger warily stepped past her.

"Finish it!" the heckler called.

More jeers and shouts punctuated the taunt. But Marisol limped away and helped Angel to sit on one of the fake rocks.

Paulus was working tokens free from the two fallen men at his feet. Somehow he had exchanged his own game weapon for a real short sword. Next he relieved the tokens from the dead fel.

He raised his head towards the gallery. "I want...I want to buy freedom."

"The round isn't finished," the game caller announced.

"What have you got left?" Digger whispered to Paulus.

Paulus shook his head. "Not much."

Digger examined the portcullis. The lights had once again adjusted and the alcove was well illuminated. The grating appeared heavy, but he tried to lift it. It didn't budge. But then he noticed a polished brass plate with a slot. He put his hand to the medallion around his neck.

"Are they supposed to be doing that?" someone in the gallery asked.

Digger tugged the chain around his neck free and untied the medallion. It fit perfectly in the slot. He dropped it in.

The game caller announced, "The nymph's slaves and the adventurers fought each other to a standstill."

"A tie?" the heckler said. "Come on! Fight!"

He was shouted down.

Once the crowd quieted, the game caller continued. "The portcullis, with the master slave's token, opens easily."

The gate began to wind upward by unseen mechanisms. The dark hallway beyond had torches that ignited with amber flames, illuminating a long corridor of white stone. Paulus helped Digger as they exited the chamber of secrets.

A chime rang.

"Is it a victory?" the caller asked. "A reprieve? The slaves retreat into the deeper chambers. With the round over, the adventurers have time to regroup. Perhaps a call for new comrades will bolster their numbers. Because their greatest challenge lies ahead of them. And what of our monsters? Will their mistress be pleased they escaped with their lives? Tomorrow's catacomb games will reveal all."

Chapter Thirty-Six

APPLAUSE FOLLOWED DIGGER and Paulus as they hobbled down the corridor. The portcullis slammed shut behind them. Whispers could be heard around them and then a metallic scraping sound. Bright lanterns shone in Digger's eyes. They were confronted by crossbow-wielding guards and seized by attendants who pulled the weapons from their hands.

Paulus held up his hand and showed the tokens. "Freedom. I buy my freedom!"

An attendant examined the tokens. "Save them for the game master. She'll decide."

A guard pushed them towards a section of wall that stood open. "If you would have tried that gate before fighting, we would have had to shoot you. Sounds like you made your fellow monsters improvise, though. Impressive. The crowd likes you."

Digger limped along, his hand clutching his bleeding side. He wasn't having any problems breathing and guessed Angel's knife hadn't punctured too deeply, but the pain was almost overwhelming. His jaw and cheek ached where Angel had struck him.

The back corridors of the catacombs were narrow and at times they walked single file. But Digger saw no chance of escape. Finally they were placed back in the waiting room. The queen stood inside with a single attendant, a man in orange and blue dressed like a clown. His face was stern and he kept his eyes low and his head bowed. The queen, however, wore a broad smile as she gave both of them a hug.

Digger had crossbows pointing at him the whole time.

The queen snapped her fingers. "You men, leave us."

The clown cleared his throat. "My queen, is that wise? These fel are dangerous."

"You can stay, Rochus. I'm sure you'll protect me if I need it."

Digger could hardly believe it when the guards obeyed, leaving them alone with her. The queen of Diregloom. The noblewoman who could have stopped the murder of his parents with a word.

"What a show! An upset! Two monster victories! I can scarcely contain myself, I'm so pleased. And this time you didn't start executing the contestants. That was distasteful, I must say. But this round more than made up for that unpleasantness."

"We've earned our tokens," Digger said. "Those other condemned fel who fought with us—we have enough to free them too."

"Not quite. You lost more than a few tokens when you distracted poor Lord Baldros. However, I'll allow you to buy off as many as you'd like. Yourselves as well. But I want you to consider staying."

"Why?"

"Money. Gold. Rank, if you survive. There are those of your kind in my service who bow to no one but me. Ask your queen and she might grant it."

"There's nothing you have that I want. I don't speak for Paulus here, but I'll take freedom."

"How much gold?" Paulus asked.

The queen's eyes shone as she nodded at him. Digger didn't believe for a moment they weren't being watched. Could he break her neck before a crossbow bolt struck him? But there remained a chance his brother could be freed. With the tokens in his pocket and the queen's blessing, he could get out and spring him from the stockade.

Using a frilly handkerchief, she dabbed sweat from Digger's face. "Take your rest, brave monsters. Have your hurts cared for. Eat. You can decide in the morning."

Rochus fell in behind her as the cell door was opened. They watched her leave through the bars. The door opened again and attendants with pitchers, fresh food trays, and other items entered. Digger was encouraged to sit. His wounds and bruises were washed. A salve was placed on his side, which stung momentarily before a welcome numbness made the pain vanish. He received more stitches.

The medic checked the rest of his body. "It's a deep cut but the bleeding will stop. No broken bones. Nothing to stop you if you decide to play on."

Digger was offered wine and this time he accepted it. He was famished. Thirsty. His aching body yearned for sleep. The medic was helping set one of Paulus's fingers that appeared to have been broken.

"You seriously considering it?" Digger asked.

Paulus waited for the medic to step away to his doctor's bag. "One more fight? I think I can survive it. It won't take much gold to keep me and mine from working another day in the factory. Stay with me. Think of what we can do with our wealth."

"You'd still be a fel in Diregloom. And less than nothing if you leave the island no matter how much gold lines your pocket."

Paulus grunted as a splint was fixed to his left hand.

"Is that your fighting hand?" A spectator had appeared on the opposite side of the bars. "Any other injuries?"

Paulus showed his right hand and flexed it. "That's my fighting hand."

The spectator made notes in a book. Others arrived to peer at the pampered monsters. Some held flutes of wine while a few smoked. A trio of women were laughing and making hushed comments. One of them whispered to a guard.

"Ask him yourself," the guard said. "But he's not leaving the cell."

Whatever request the women had in mind never came. They tittered some more before leaving, only to be replaced by a new group of gawkers.

The medic packed his bag and the attendants finished up. The scent of flowery perfumed water lingered on Digger's skin. He looked at his fingernails and saw them perfectly clean and buffed to a shine. He was tired. It was late. Nothing else was happening, so he got comfortable on one of the couches and tuned out the tourists.

Some time passed and he drifted, and then his eyes popped open at the sound of jingling chains. The spectators were gone. Guards were marching a new group of prisoners past. The fel were dressed in elaborate costume armor. They kept their heads down and looked miserable.

Digger rose and pressed his face against the bars to watch. How had the queen managed to get so many new fighters for her game?

Lord Angel trailed along behind the procession, his face puffy and his eyes black. "Hold up, sergeant."

The guard stopped the prisoners. Angel went to the front of the line and plucked off a helmet. It was Monty. Digger's brother looked shaken and worn and kept his head bowed. Angel smacked him.

"Hey!" Digger called. "I'm right here if you want a fight."

"And so you are. But it's hands off the monsters, by rules of the game and order of the queen. How simple it would be to come in there and kill you. But you've made a name for yourself, not that it'll last past tomorrow. So much grief could have been avoided."

He again slapped Monty, this time across the back of the head.

Digger clenched his jaw but said nothing.

"This chef tells me he's your brother. Imagine that. It explains so much. And when I made it clear to Monty here what was about to happen to him, he looked like he was going to start crying. Isn't it pitiful having a weak brother like that? I feel your pain, gravedigger. Monty also had a hard time believing all his misfortunes could just go away, except for the fact you won't give me a piece of paper. I would have gotten it from you today but you ran. Tomorrow there will be no escape. I'll take what's mine and make you watch as I spill your brother's guts out on the floor to the applause of the queen's guests. My aunt agreed to my little idea of plopping a few extra monsters into the final encounter. How do you think that'll play out?"

"Cut him loose. You get your page, right here, right now."

"It's too late for that. My aunt won't allow it. Besides, I want to win my treasures, fair and square. Unless, of course, you buy out in the morning. Nothing I can do to stop that. But I don't see any among this lot of sorry fel who won't piss themselves scared once the curtain rises."

Angel walked along the line of prisoners and stopped at the rearmost monster, a woman dressed in a seashell gown, her hands manacled. Wearing a mask that looked like an octopus's tentacles and with her hair braided and wound through with green ribbons, Digger almost didn't recognize Isabel.

She spat at Angel.

He punched her stomach, doubling her over. He then grabbed her by the hair.

"And look who else I found? Seems the sheriff had her tucked away and didn't tell me. But my Marisol found her for me, and not a moment too soon. Seems my little Sprite almost slipped out of the stockade. But she has nothing else I need. So I imagine this will make tomorrow's final round so much sweeter. The queen has even given her a special place in the fight. It'll be such a shame if you miss it."

A guard stepped in. "I have to ask you to step back, Lord Angel. In fact you can't come past this point. It's—"

"I know, I know. Game rules." He shoved Isabel away. "This will only end one way tomorrow. There'll be no more retreating, no more hiding. I'll see all of you in the morning."

The guards got the prisoners moving. Angel offered a final wave before heading back up the corridor.

"Monty!" Digger called. "It's going to be okay. We beat them today. And tomorrow we're going to do the same."

His brother made no indication he'd heard as they vanished down the corridor. Digger stood by the bars until the sounds of footsteps faded. At least Monty was alive. Isabel, too. But for how long? The game would only get more lethal. The odds would stack ever higher.

Paulus grunted. "You actually believe what you say?"

"I'm not sure what to believe, except I hate that man."

"Good. Does this mean you're staying? Because I could use the help and that lot of fresh meat didn't have a straight spine among them. I suppose it's not too late to buy ourselves out."

Digger didn't answer. He returned to his couch and propped his feet up and waited for morning.

Chapter Thirty-Seven

THE NEXT DAY'S CATACOMB run was a breeze compared to yesterday's fiasco.

Angel and a new group of contestants had little trouble with the weak resistance offered by the six fel in the chamber of secrets. The grid and its darts had been reset, but the contestants had hurried across it and surprised the defenders and it had been a slaughter. Only two of his fellow contestants had been hurt. They'd bow out once the round ended.

Digger and the old fel weren't among them. His queen was saving them for later. Angel hadn't heard that they'd bought out their freedom, so he knew they were up ahead at what had to be the final encounter.

Only Marisol had continued on from yesterday. Her cracked ribs hadn't stopped her. Meanwhile his brother Jamie was laid up somewhere in the castle, but Angel had been too busy to ask about him. At the moment, Angel waited as his fellow contestants squabbled over a token and who got to insert the medallion to open the portcullis to the last room.

Marisol grabbed Angel's arm. They hadn't spoken except during the fight. She had remained sullen all morning as they got ready for the game. He thought she might quit on him but she hadn't. But he could guess what was on her mind and he didn't want to hear it.

"Talk to me, Angel. What's our plan here?"

He threw her hand off. Tried not to let his anger show. "What do you mean?"

"I hope it's not lost on you that this place is dangerous. Gavin died of his wounds. Hector's not looking good, and you couldn't be bothered to see him last night. What's our play here?"

"Simple, dear cousin. We win. We beat my aunt's game and we'll be set up. We'll never have to worry about borrowing from scum like Red Eye ever again."

"This last room was child's play compared to yesterday and we still lost two. None of these people listen, and some have never held a sword before."

Loath as he was to admit it, she was right. After a smooth initial encounter with no armed opponents and swinging spiked weights fortified with easily avoided spring-loaded blades, the chamber of secrets had been a cakewalk. Angel's arm still ached where the previous day's dart had struck him. Even a weak dose of the drug had taken hours to wear off. But today he had barely broken a sweat.

The half-dozen defenders had fallen in rapid succession. Angel and Marisol had killed one apiece and he had dispatched two more as they'd dropped their weapons and begged for their lives. Sure, the gallery had booed, but Angel didn't care. The catacombs would pay out whether the crowd loved him or not. He had four tokens and was certain he could collect enough to purchase his prize.

Whatever ignominy came his way from stabbing the nobleman contestant would be eclipsed by the glory of Angel's victory. And Marisol would eventually forgive him. Girls like her needed a brighter star to hang on to.

He forced himself to smile. "We can't lose. Gavin will be mourned. We'll see Hector gets the best care, and we'll find Cy and Philip. But right now you need to focus. That gravedigger is the last thing standing between us and our reward."

"He's not what concerns me. Your aunt wasn't pulling any punches yesterday. We both could have died, and we have no way of knowing what's next."

"We'll beat it."

"You're willing to risk yourself and me."

"Yeah, I am. Nothing's stopping you from quitting. I've never been able to make you do anything you don't want to do."

It wasn't like her to hold her tongue, but she paused as if choosing her words. "You never asked the cook about Cy and Philip. You could have pressured him to tell us where that ogre might have taken them. And then when I told you about Isabel, you threw both of them into the game."

One of their fellow contestants, some third-born baron's son with a ruddy face and shining locks of black hair, emerged from the alcove where the portcullis stood raised. "Hey! You guys coming?"

Angel ignored him. "I did what I had to, Marisol. That fel might have bought himself out. Now he'll be there in the final round. We go kill him now. Then we worry about the others."

"They're your friends."

"They'd understand."

"If I was one of the ones left behind at that bar, would you risk my life like you have theirs?"

"Don't waste our time with dreaming up a situation different than the one we're facing. You didn't get left behind. You're too good of a warrior. You're here with me, and I'm glad for it. You're the best of us with your sword. Soon we'll be done with this game. Hector will get better. We'll hunt the ogre down and save the others. But in the meantime, if you're staying in, then I need your full attention."

He could only hope the flattery would work. He moved past her and shepherded the baron's son with the fancy hair towards the others, who were waiting in the hallway just beyond the portcullis.

The gallery above began to empty. The crowd was moving to where it could watch the next stage of the action. Game attendants emerged to help the two contestants who were quitting. Marisol caught up with Angel, her foil and dirk held ready.

Good.

But Angel was worried too. No season of the games had ever claimed so many pureblood lives. Even with so many casualties, his aunt hadn't called it off. Rather, her enthusiasm had doubled. The crowd's zeal hadn't diminished much either, and he'd had a stack of messages waiting for him that morning from spectators and bookmakers eager to know if he was going to keep playing.

Of course he was.

The catacombs would continue into the final round. With his aunt's wild imagination, anything was possible. What he hadn't told Marisol was that he'd gladly sacrifice all his companions if it meant he could win.

Chapter Thirty-Eight

THE BREAKFAST OF SAUSAGE-and-peppers the catacomb attendants had served them was giving Digger heartburn. He tried his best to ignore the acidy belches, along with all his other misgivings.

He could buy himself free.

What chance was there he could save Monty or Isabel from the game? Somehow he needed to take out Lord Angel, and that would have to happen during the upcoming final round. But the game was rigged. That he and Paulus had survived and had been victorious was a fluke. In an even fight, one on one, he knew he could stand his own against most men. He was trained and experienced in armed combat. The contestants he had faced weren't prepared for his raw strength. But the last encounter would favor the purebloods. Digger and the other prisoners were part of a narrative and no one liked an unhappy ending.

He and Paulus had been dressed in new costumes more elaborate than the prior day's outfits. Paulus was given a polished white breastplate and a helm that looked like a giant conch shell. His weapon was a battle axe, also oversized and poorly balanced with a dull edge. Paulus tested its heft and appeared pleased enough.

Digger had received a fresh whale bone. It was studded with flecks of shining crystal. The dangling plume from his own ridiculous helmet kept getting in his eyes, until he took it off.

"Hey! Put that back on!" an attendant hissed from the other side of one of the walls.

"I can't see with this stupid thing. Plus this way the audience can see me. Isn't that what you want?"

The attendant dropped the matter.

The two of them waited in a wide, plain corridor with barn-sized doors leading out in opposite directions. Was it to be just him and Paulus in the final round? The sounds of busy preparation came from every corner. Workers grunted, tools banged, and machinery clicked.

What felt like hours passed. There was no way to track time.

A muffled cheer echoed around them. Someone, somewhere, was doing something to rile the audience up.

Paulus was trying to sharpen his axe on the stone floor. "What do you think's going on?"

"No clue." Digger spoke up to address the walls. "Hey, whoever's listening. What's the harm in letting us know what's happening out there?"

The game attendant who had chided him earlier spoke. "New preliminary and first round. Simplified, so we can get to round two this afternoon. The contestants are sure to make it here, so be ready."

"New contestants? How many?"

"Probably all of them, including that lord who has it out for you. The queen wants the best finale possible. You certainly gave her something worth remembering. Let's make today special."

"So we're the finale. There's only two of us. Do we get reinforcements?"

The attendant didn't answer.

There was no place to hide. As the first of the spectators began to fill the gallery, there was no way to tell from which door the oncoming contestants would enter. He inspected the lower set of doors and began to probe the walls. Some were stone. Some wood. Only a thin panel stood between him and whatever room the game attendant was hiding in.

"Don't touch," the attendant said. "This is off-limits. You're to wait for the caller, who'll give you your cues."

Scrape marks on the floor showed where a larger section of wall in the center might swing out like a door. He pried with his fingers but couldn't gain purchase.

"Last warning."

He showed his hands and returned to wait next to Paulus in the middle of the room.

"You should have taken your out," Digger said.

Paulus leaned on his axe.

The distant game caller began to give a long explanation to the audience. Something behind the walls shifted. A metallic scraping sound began, along with a series of squeaks that sounded like a rusty winch. Digger guessed it was the portcullis in the chamber of secrets rising. This was followed by the distant chimes of a bell. Round over. They were coming.

More voices filled the gallery. The lights in the corridor dimmed, casting Digger and Paulus in shadow.

Digger caught snippets of their conversations. The spectators were casually talking about the food, money, the spectacle they had witnessed, and what they were planning that evening after the game was done. Corks popped. They sipped their wine, waiting for what was to come next.

A distant wail echoed.

Digger returned to the wooden section of wall and strained his ears. The cry repeated, growing louder. Someone cackled until they ran out of breath, laughing at some unheard joke. Moans and anguished sobs erupted from the opposite side of the wall, causing the crowd above to fall into a hush. Then they applauded.

Dread ran through Digger. Monty and Isabel were beyond that wall, he felt certain.

Paulus hissed to get his attention. "Hey, focus. This could start any minute."

Digger moved away from the wall. The haunted cries continued. He could only hope this was part of the illusion of the catacombs and not real. The lights dimmed further until he could only see the outline of the fel next to him. A rank fish smell permeated the room that he hadn't noticed before.

Gong! Gong! Gong!

As the echoes of the deep chimes faded, a blue glow shone down along the walls. Previously unseen etchings came to life around them. Scenes of a woman adorned in frothy ocean waves filled each panel. In one she was leading an array of sea creatures against a crumbling castle. In another she watched as mermen drowned a group of soldiers. In each depiction the woman presided over various foes and their defeat. The movable wall was the only one showing her facing the room. In each hand she held necklaces and sparkling gemstones. At her feet was a giant clam with a black pearl in its open mouth. Circles of multicolored lights began to swirl about the chamber, giving the figures the illusion of motion.

The crowd responded to the light show with enthusiastic applause.

The game caller's crisp voice rose above it. "Two of the nymph's champions, against all odds, survived the assault of the brave fortune seekers on the chamber of secrets. Hurrying to warn their mistress, they pause to await her instructions."

An echoing woman's voice boomed. "Fight them, my warriors. Stop them. I demand it!"

"The two champions have no choice. Their mistress has commanded it. They are all that stands between the invading fortune hunters and their goddess and her treasure room. The brave adventurers approach..."

Chapter Thirty-Nine

THE PAIR OF GRAVEDIGGERS who had been in the front of the line brought up a third and a fourth body, and there were more to come. Hellard didn't see any dead purebloods among them. Nobody he knew among the victims, at least.

He was patiently waiting his turn, having once again yielded to the other body wranglers and content to not have to answer more questions. The guard at the side gate hadn't even batted an eye upon seeing him again.

Judging by the crowds, the games hadn't lost any of their luster after the violent beginning and the upset staged by the monsters. Hellard guessed there were even more gathered in front of the castle than yesterday. Even those who didn't have tickets and couldn't get through the front gate were keen on the spectacle. The musicians and food vendors from Stockade Square were all present. Street performers joined the mix. Jugglers were throwing bottles into the air, puppeteers reenacted interpretations of what the game reporters relayed, and the people, Diregloom citizens pure and fel alike, cheered.

He masked his disgust with a droopy gaze and a lopsided smile. He also kept his sleeves down lest another sharp-eyed gravedigger notice his tattoos.

Digger's luck was holding. Monty and Isabel were still alive too, after having been hauled into the castle the previous evening. But any bandit worth his steel wouldn't wait on luck to see their way through a tricky day. Hellard knew he had to take his chances and go inside.

The gravediggers finished tucking the fallen monsters under their tarp. They looked disappointed. There was little loot to be had from dead fel prisoners.

He worked to untie two shrouds from the bodies inside an unattended grave cart. Once the knots were undone he pulled the shrouds free and tucked the tarp back over the dead before anyone noticed.

The pipe-chewing gravedigger appeared, hiking up the steps with a fresh corpse on his shoulders. It might have been Digger. But then Hellard saw a dark-green hand dangling, and Digger was light-skinned enough that he might pass for pureblood.

Hellard was next in line. With the stained shrouds under one arm, he moved past the gravedigger.

"Hey, new guy, they don't need you yet. Hey!"

"One of the guards asked for these," Hellard said and hurried down.

He descended into a wide corridor with high barred windows that provided light. Two more gravediggers passed him by, carrying a small body, what could have been a child. He winced at the thought of one so young dying in this place.

One of the gravediggers said, "This is the last of them for now."

Hellard showed the shrouds and kept walking. "Orders are orders."

At the end of the corridor a single guard stood at a small metal door. He wore no signs of rank. His eyes went wide as Hellard got close.

Hellard maintained his smile and spoke slowly. "Sergeant wanted one of us to carry these down for later."

"Leave 'em. There's no more work for you here."

"If you say so. But he said to hurry because they had two more bodies and they ran out of these things. I didn't want to get the sergeant mad at me."

Hellard studied the man's reaction. The unranked guard clearly didn't want the sergeant, whichever one he had in mind, mad at him either. Yet he hesitated.

Unlike the guard at the gate, Hellard guessed this guard hadn't been on duty last night. "I remember where to go. I'll be quiet and drop these off and not say anything to anybody."

"Yeah. They're going to be starting again and they can't have you getting in the way. Hurry up, then."

The guard produced a key ring. But just as he was about to unlock the door he paused. He was looking at Hellard's shoes.

"Why don't you have any mud on you if you were burying bodies last night?"

Hellard shrugged. Then he punched the guard in the head and the man went down in a heap. They were still alone in the corridor. Hellard wasted no time in taking the keys and wrapping the guard up in one of the shrouds. He paused to listen at the door but didn't hear anything. He unlocked it and opened the door.

Hopefully no one would notice he was bringing a body into the catacombs rather than taking one out. But no one would miss the fact that there now was an ogre in the belly of the castle.

Hellard's smile was now genuine. He walked through the door ever so softly and closed it behind him.

Chapter Forty

DIGGER SQUINTED, BUT nothing in the darkness was moving. The whale bone in his hands wasn't heavy but he didn't want to wear out before the contestants arrived. What was the delay?

The wait was over. The spectators and game caller had gone silent. He tried to work up spit in his mouth but couldn't. A sound began behind one of the pairs of double doors. A mechanical whirring and *clank-clank-clank* preceded the doors swinging slowly open. Then the same sound began on the opposite side of the room. Now both ends of the corridor lay open.

From one direction came lantern light. A group of ten contestants stepped tentatively through the doorway. Angel and Marisol were with them. The second doorway on the opposite side of the corridor remained dark.

Paulus edged away from the adventurers. "Come on. Let's fall back. There's nowhere to fight here."

Digger held his ground. "Wait. It can't be that simple."

The contestants received a long round of applause from above.

"They come!" the game caller said as the clapping died away. He cleared his throat. "They come," he repeated. "Having sought reinforcements from the nearest camps of their fellow adventurers, our returning contestants have made it through new challenges. You've seen them defeat more of the nymph's slaves, and pass through several traps. But now they arrive at what will be their toughest fight."

The heckler was back. "There's only two monsters?"

A few people laughed. A woman added, "Yeah, but my money's on them this time!"

The crowd ate it up. Digger saw none of the contestants move. From the other doorway came the sound of clinking chains and a soft, throaty grumble. A game attendant behind a wall was whispering and a sharp *smack* followed. After a moment, he heard heavy feet approaching across the stone floor.

Digger motioned for Paulus to move against one of the walls.

The contestants began spreading out. Only Angel and Marisol held back. But none seemed to want to get closer as the lights bounced and played across their faces.

One masked woman among the oncoming combatants pointed at Digger with her rapier. "It's just the two of them. Get them before they run!"

She and a few of the others advanced. The floor made a familiar click as someone triggered a concealed pressure plate. Digger ducked in anticipation of more darts, but instead the roof appeared to fall in and a wave dropped on the frontmost contestants. The water struck them with a heavy splat, along with dollops of what looked like fish parts.

Digger sniffed. They *were* fish parts. That explained the smell. Half the contestants were not only drenched but covered with reeking guts.

The crowd responded with a visceral "Ewww!"

Fish heads and chunks were scattered everywhere. A growl from the opposite set of doors grew louder as a shadow loomed. One of the queen's carriage trolls emerged into the room. His long arms dragged as he shambled through the doors. He sniffed the air and then stared straight down the corridor at the adventurers.

The game caller chuckled. "It seems one of the nymph's troll thralls has broken free. Drawn by the smell of adventurer blood, the sea troll charges forward!"

It wasn't much of a charge. The dull creature plodded with his nose in the air. But then the doors behind it slammed shut with a crash. Fire ignited on the wood as an unseen archer shot a burning missile into the doors.

The troll flinched, then began to hurry in earnest across the room. He passed Digger and Paulus as if they weren't there. The contestants had time to scream as they raised their weapons and backed away. But the doors behind them banged closed. One man slipped on a fish tail. The troll caught him and hauled him into the air. The creature's nostrils flared and then the troll bit down on the man's head.

Digger and Paulus ducked against the wall.

Another contestant made it past Angel and Marisol and pounded his fist on the doors. "We're trapped!"

The troll spat out something and threw down the lifeless body. He slapped at the nearest adventurer and clambered after him. The man had time to stab the troll with his rapier before the monster's mouth engulfed him. It began to make a loud slurping sound.

The other contestants spread out around the creature. Angel locked eyes with Digger, but there was no easy way past for the moment.

Digger hit the swinging wall with the image of the nymph and her treasure. It proved to be made of wood and hollow. "This is our way out."

He pushed at it. If the door remained off-limits, he would no doubt be killed. But the wall was part of the game. The etchings were a clue. Here the nymph held her treasures close.

"Look for something. Anything which might get this open."

They pried, pulled, and probed, but the wall yielded nothing and wouldn't budge. Marisol was shouting something. The remaining adventurers were succeeding in avoiding the troll, but mostly because he was still busy chomping on his second victim. The troll reached for her. She pierced the monster's palm and he reeled back. Another stab and the troll dropped the man he had been chewing on.

She advanced, both weapons threatening the giant creature. "Press it. Make it retreat."

Angel was right behind her. "Grab something that's burning. Anything."

The troll slapped down a massive hand. The other contestants remained bunched up by the sealed doors. Angel and Marisol were alone in facing the creature.

Paulus murmured in Digger's ear. "This is our only chance. We have to attack them while the troll's still standing."

"Give me another second."

Digger's fingers traced down along the grooves of the nymph's legs, the treasure piles, and each indented shine mark. Then, in the center of the black pearl inside the giant clam's mouth, he discovered a slot in the wood. It would fit a key or another medallion like the one he had used to open the gate from the chamber of secrets.

Neither of them had a medallion this time. He looked up at the troll.

The troll had managed to pull the first contestant he had bitten along with him to the opposite wall. The monster was licking him clean, clearly more interested in the fish guts than in man meat. Around the troll's neck was a collar with three tokens in front and a dangling medallion in back. The creature remained preoccupied with its snack until Marisol tried to slip past. The troll roared and swiped, causing her to dive out of the way.

"Watch my back," Digger said.

He collected the largest pieces of fish he could find. He tossed one towards the troll and it landed next to him. The troll paused and considered Digger before leaning over and sucking up the offering.

He spoke in a soothing voice. "There, there. We're on the same side. Monsters, right? Here, have another."

He threw a second piece of fish. The creature ate it and smacked his mouth, eager for more.

Paulus and the contestants were all watching. No one knew what to do with the monster and were no doubt waiting for Digger to get murdered.

Digger grabbed a handful of guts and held it out. With his other hand he prepared to snatch the collar.

The troll lunged, snapped his teeth, and would have bitten Digger's arm off if he hadn't recoiled. The thing rose and backhanded him, knocking him to the slick floor. Paulus grabbed Digger by an arm and pulled him away as the troll began to suck fish parts off the ground.

Paulus hauled him to his feet. "What are you thinking? You can't tame an animal like that."

"Seemed like a good idea to try something."

The contestants retrieved both their fallen comrades, but neither was moving. The crowd hooted and jeered. The scintillating colors made focusing on anything difficult. Someone ran past along the opposite wall. It was Marisol, and she had just evaded the troll.

Angel clapped, shouted, and stomped his foot, obviously trying to get the troll's attention. But the monster barely noticed as it continued to feed on the scattered fish parts.

Marisol sprinted to the opposite set of doors. The flames had dwindled but still burned. She grabbed a pair of torches from wall sconces. Digger hadn't noticed them there. She lit both and began to return.

Digger stepped out to block her. Paulus had his back, his attention on the troll and the other contestants.

She kept both blazing torches out before her. Digger swiped with his whale bone, but she ducked his tentative blow. A cruel smile spread across her face. Digger ignored it, thinking her mad, and knowing they had to press their advantage to take out one of their most dangerous foes. She had recovered from whatever injuries she had suffered and appeared to be having no problems moving. Drugs could do that, Digger knew. That might be one of the advantages afforded the contestants so they might persevere against their fel opponents.

A man screamed.

Digger caught sight of Angel shoving one of his fellow fish-gut-covered contestants towards the troll.

The man stumbled and slipped, falling within the monster's reach. He was clutching his side and his hand was red with blood. He shrieked as the troll grabbed him. The creature began to tear the man apart in front of his companions, none of whom did anything to help.

The crowd went crazy.

So did the heckler. "Player killer! Player killer! Whooo!"

While the troll was preoccupied, Angel rushed along the wall, heading their way. Two of the others hurried to follow.

Digger's inattention almost cost him a torch to the face. He smacked it aside, but Marisol closed in and nearly knocked the whale bone from his hand with a hard parry. The torch made a surprisingly solid club, but the blow extinguished it. Paulus interceded. He caught her across the back with the flat of his axe. It sent her reeling and she sprawled onto the floor. But she was up in an instant, abandoning the torches and drawing her foil and dirk.

The game caller was talking, narrating the action through the din of the gallery crowd, but Digger tuned it out. He focused on Marisol. She set her feet and blew a loose strand of hair from her mouth.

One of the contestants, a man with black locks and holding a sword, caught up with Angel. He slammed him into a wall. They were shouting at each other. That wouldn't last, but for the moment they were distracted.

"Keep her off me," Digger said to Paulus.

He flung his bone at Marisol and grabbed up the burning torch. It still guttered, and the flame brightened once he held it upright. He couldn't believe what he was doing even as he raced past the squabbling contestants and launched himself at the troll.

Chapter Forty-One

THE PREOCCUPIED CREATURE didn't see Digger coming. He landed on the troll's back and flung the torch forward. The tumbling torch landed in front of the monster. The troll reared up, repelled by the fire. He abandoned his meal and loped backward. A dull moan erupted from his throat. Even as he retreated he swatted at Digger.

Clinging to the creature was like grappling a slimy rock. Digger seized a handful of the monster's hair and hung on. The troll turned and turned, threatening anyone in his path with trampling. Digger managed to take hold of the collar. Trying to get it open would take too long. The tokens were on a solid metal loop, but the medallion was tied on with its own leather cord. He bit down and tore at the cord with his teeth even as a massive hand clamped down on his back.

The troll tore him away. The giant hand squeezed and the creature yowled.

But the cord ripped free, leaving the medallion dangling from Digger's teeth. He had no time to react as the troll flung him against a wall. The monster was on top of him in no time, mouth wide, black teeth and thick tongue looming.

Then the troll shrieked.

Paulus stood behind it, having just smacked the troll in the rear with the burning torch. The troll spun and snapped his teeth and swatted the air as Paulus backed away. Digger wasted no time in moving out of range of the creature.

The other contestants had grouped around Angel. They had their weapons ready and looked like they were about to kill him. They pushed at Angel and he pushed them back.

Marisol was the only one standing in Digger's way. She limped a few steps back as Digger reclaimed his bone. Paulus's earlier blow must have done some damage. But Digger knew how quick she could be and watched her every move. He had to get past her to the wall and the slot. If she didn't know what he was after, she would have no reason to stand her ground.

Meanwhile, Angel was shouting. "Do any of you want to win this thing? Then listen to me!"

"What were you thinking?" one of the contestants asked.

"We're on the same team!" said another.

But the contestant with the black hair pointed the tip of his sword at Angel's throat. "He's a coward. He killed a nobleman yesterday."

Angel slapped the sword aside with a gloved hand. "I only wounded him. That's what needed to be done. Don't you see? None of us get anything if we don't get through these monsters."

"That man you just backstabbed was my cousin!"

"None of you came here because you thought this was going to be easy. If you want to win, you'll need my help."

They all began shouting at once. But the troll appeared content to once again scrape splattered fish parts from the floor. Digger hurried to the wall while trying to untie the cord from the medallion. A series of tiny knots wound around the metal disk. It wouldn't fit into the slot with the cord attached, but he only had his teeth to sever the leather.

Marisol loomed nearby but Paulus kept her at bay. She kept calling Angel's name.

The crowd above them sounded more agitated.

"The monsters are getting away!" a woman shouted.

"Hurry," Paulus said.

Digger spat part of the leather cord out. "Working on it."

A clock bell tolled.

"Time!" the game caller cried. "The nymph has decided her champion defenders are taking too long in dealing with the intruders. Casting a spell, she calls down aid from one of her sisters, who commands the stinging insects of the forest!"

A dart zipped through the air. What triggered it and where it came from was impossible to tell. It struck one of the squabbling adventurers. He screamed and pulled it free. More darts flew, coming from every direction. The swarm of missiles threatened monster and pureblood alike. Paulus yelped. He plucked a dart from his leg before taking cover on the ground.

Marisol, Angel, and the arguing adventurers followed suit.

Digger crouched by the wall and worked the last segment of cord free.

"Got it."

He shoved it into the slot in the wall. His action was immediately rewarded as something beneath the floor clinked and rattled. The wall began to swing outward. He had to scramble back to avoid getting knocked over. The darts stopped flying. He and Paulus got out of the way as the door revealed a new corridor lit with pink lanterns.

"Let's go!"

Paulus screamed. Marisol had appeared from nowhere and had driven her offhand blade into his forearm, causing him to drop his axe. She shoved Paulus so he stood between her and Digger. Digger grabbed the whale bone but there was no opening. The other contestants were recovering from the dart attack and seemed to have forgotten their argument.

Marisol slipped the blade free and brought it up to Paulus's neck.

Digger raised a hand. "End of the round! I buy his freedom!" He fished a token from his pocket and held it up. "This fel is free of the game."

The other contestants paused and looked up at the gallery.

"Congratulations!" the queen called. "He's free. But the next round continues immediately. Off you go. Best hurry."

A clock chimed and a *tick-tick-tick* echoed around them.

Digger nodded and began to head for the doorway.

"Fel!" Angel called.

Digger turned in time to see Angel run his rapier through Paulus. He pulled the weapon free. Paulus fell, his hand clutching a gushing wound.

Angel flicked blood off his blade. "Seems like this is the language you understand. Face me now. Let's get this over with."

Digger watched helplessly as the life left Paulus's face. He sagged and lay still.

He tried to control his breathing. No one running the game did anything. The token in his hand had just proven worthless. Whatever rules they were playing by were gone.

The crowd gasped. Even the heckler was stunned to silence.

Digger backed away into the hallway. Angel moved to follow, as did Marisol and the other remaining contestants.

He heard their footsteps coming after him as he ran, heading towards what had to be the final encounter in the catacombs, one he hadn't expected to ever see. The entire place was a death trap. At that moment he realized there was only one way he or his friends would ever make it out. He would have to kill every pureblood down there.

Chapter Forty-Two

TO GET DOWN ONE OF the passageways, Hellard had to inhale and suck in his gut.

The interior of the castle beyond the door became more confusing as he proceeded. There were dead ends and obvious last-minute wall demolitions revealing new construction and fresh masonry, plaster, and even a few wooden walls. But this was where those who ran the catacombs would operate. If he was going to have any chance at a rescue, this was it.

The space was so narrow, he had to pull the guard off his shoulder and drag him behind.

This particular tiny passage was also crammed with mechanical devices fixed to the walls. There were knobs and switches and even a few fixed crossbows on swivels with tiny viewing slits, presumably to shoot at whatever was going on in the game room.

The lighting was poor. Some sort of fight was going on. Things in the walls beyond his own crawlspace snapped and clicked. He could hear a clock or similar mechanism ticking.

One of the wooden walls shuddered as he brushed against it trying to squeeze past. He discovered hinges and locking pins with his fingers. The entire section of wall appeared capable of opening. He trod carefully around a fire-lighting stick and a long-spouted oil can. Above him were extinguished lanterns on hooks.

His soft, creeping footsteps were easily masked by the sounds of the crowd outside. Every time he peeked, though, he couldn't see them or much of anything else. He just knew the audience was above him somewhere.

Finally he found a peek hole with a metal cover, which he slid aside.

He realized the other vantage points had been blocked by scenery fixed to the wall. Now he could see everything in the game room. A clock gonged. An announcer was speaking.

He watched as a fel contestant with a beard was murdered, to the shock of the audience. And there was Digger, fleeing from a group of noblemen through a large door on the opposite side of the room.

Hellard couldn't tell if his friend was injured. But he recognized Lord Angel and Marisol from the Dragon and Rose.

He hunched down at one of the crossbows. It had a box built around it with a complex spring-loaded actuator. Pulling a pin disconnected the firing mechanism, leaving the trigger free to be operated manually. He managed to swivel the crossbow somewhat, despite its mounting frame. He sighted on Lord Angel. Didn't hesitate to pull the trigger.

Nothing.

He checked and saw there was no bolt or dart loaded. This was also the case with the next two. He was dragging the guard along further when he heard someone ahead of him whispering.

"It's okay, Tonto. You're going to be okay. Shhh. Shhh."

Hellard stopped and listened as the man continued to soothe whoever he was talking to. The action outside was moving away. The crowd above was also on the move, judging by the hollow footsteps. He'd have to hurry if he wanted to help Digger and the others.

"Who's there?" the voice asked.

Hellard cleared his throat. "Uh, body cleanup."

"Get back, you fool. Not until I clear Tonto out of the room."

"Tonto?"

A skinny man stood from where he was kneeling on the floor and stood to face Hellard. "What are you doing in here? You don't belong. The final round is about to start. The bodies are to be—"

Hellard dropped a fist on top of his head and the skinny man went down. A long club clattered to the floor. Hellard stooped to pick it up. It stank of fish. He then went through the man's pockets for anything useful. He found a set of keys and a wad of scrip. He took it all and kept dragging the guard along the corridor until he reached a dead end. He sighed with frustration.

He began to probe the walls and discovered a door that would slide once a pair of latches were thrown open. Before he could, a clatter and echoing whispers made him freeze. Then came bootsteps.

He located another peek hole. A group of ten armed guards trotted past, emerging from a hidden door on the opposite wall of the game room. Attendants followed. They blocked the door through which Digger and the others had gone. Then, after clearing away the fallen fel and a few other contestants, the door was sealed.

This was no good. There would be no easy opportunity to free his new friends, at least not by following so many guards.

And the guards remained vigilant.

If the action had moved past this room, why were they holding weapons? Moments later they marched out, appearing to be in a hurry.

He returned to the unconscious skinny man. Who had he been talking to? He couldn't find a peek hole near him but did find a small hatch in the wall that could be crawled through, if the one doing the crawling was a goblin or a starved, greased-up toddler. He opened it and stuck his head out into the game room.

A large figure hunkered nearby. It grunted and uttered a few nonsensical sounds before lazily reaching for Hellard.

Hellard jerked back but had nowhere to move as a giant troll hand pushed through the hatchway opening. Hellard bounced from foot to foot as long fingers ending in black fingernails swiped at him. But the troll couldn't reach far. Then the creature hooked a finger in the shroud around the knocked-out guard.

The guard was murmuring. "W-w-what?"

The hapless man was pulled through the tiny hatch. He didn't go easily through, but after a few hard yanks the guard vanished. A series of wet smacks followed and a thud. The guard made no more sounds. The troll's shadow eclipsed the hatchway. He began sniffing. A nose appeared at the hatch and the creature's nostrils flared. Reaching through, the troll caught the skinny man by the legs and pulled him out of sight. Then the troll reappeared.

"Just ogre meat here, my friend, and you won't be getting me through that opening."

Hellard wedged himself near the hatch. At any second the guards outside would reappear. Now at least he knew what they were watching out for. The creature kept reaching and scratching. If the monster caught him, it would be like getting hauled through a tiny funnel by a team of horses.

The troll inverted his hand and hooked upward with his fingers. Hellard had to raise a leg and then another. The monster next pulled at the wall. It buckled, threatening Hellard's already precarious purchase.

"Tonto?" Hellard asked. "Is your name Tonto?"

The wall cracked. A moment more and the monster would tear the hatch frame apart and have room to reach inside. Hellard would have to jump for it, but the tight space made it impossible. He wouldn't be fast enough.

Desperate, he fumbled for the skinny man's smelly club. He used it to smack the troll's fingers. The troll jerked but kept probing. The hand vanished and now the troll had his mouth to the hatchway. A tongue the size of a tree branch began rolling back and forth. The thing was snorting and sniffling. When Hellard moved the club, the tongue followed.

"Is that what you want?"

Hellard dropped down and was about to shove the club through the hatch when he paused. The troll was sucking at the opening. Hellard shoved the club into the troll's mouth. The troll clacked his teeth down on the wood and moved away from the wall. Chewing sounds followed.

The club wasn't a club at all, he realized. It was a fish-scented troll treat.

He scoured the narrow hallway. Among the things he had stepped over was a bag containing more of the sticks. It reeked of fermented fish.

A cheer went up from the distant audience. Finding his way out of the present set of corridors and past so many guards in time to help his friends wasn't going to work. If this was the final round, it was already starting. Getting out was the only option. He felt confident he could make it back outside and with a little luck clear the castle.

But something about the troll made him linger.

The brute wasn't much more than a dumb animal. But perhaps he deserved a chance at life as much as anyone else. And what if the creature could cause a little chaos that might distract the purebloods from their celebration of murder?

He felt along the wall until his fingers found the latches. A large panel slid, opening a way into the game room. The troll was sitting on his haunches and appeared content with the stick in his mouth. The guard looked like he'd had all his limbs broken from being pulled through the hatchway. The skinny troll handler lay next to him and likewise wasn't moving. But they hadn't been eaten. Perhaps the rumors of troll appetites were exaggerations.

Hellard waved another stick to and fro. He steeled his nerves as he stepped out into the game room.

The troll perked up. He had the first stick in his mouth like a piece of candy but was mesmerized by the new offering.

Surely the creature hadn't entered the chamber via the tiny corridors. The chamber had a slope to it. The higher side was where most of the action had occurred. The lower side featured large closed doors that looked to have burned.

The troll's eyes continued to follow the moving stick.

"Come on, Tonto," he said softly.

Hellard led and the troll followed as they descended the slope to the bottom of the chamber. The doors didn't budge. But a keyhole at foot level accepted one of the keys on the keyring. A lock clicked and the doors swung free. The troll, obedient and calm, shuffled along behind him, his full attention on the stick. A wall of bars confronted them. A guard opened a long sliding gate and stepped back. Perhaps he thought Hellard was the troll handler. The man's eyes went wide as Hellard came into view.

Hellard threw him the stick. The troll lunged and landed on top of the guard. The creature grabbed the stick and threw it in his mouth and happily munched as the guard groaned beneath the monster's weight.

Hellard relieved the man of a sword worn on his belt. The weapon was tiny in the ogre's hand. He smacked the guard a few times until he stopped squirming. Too many sounds carried from the several ramps and stairways beyond the sliding gate. There'd be no more hiding in the shadows going forward. And from behind began a muffled shout of alarm. Perhaps it was the game, but at any rate the castle would soon know the catacombs had been infiltrated.

One particularly wide ramp was lined with scattered hay. A large ring with a thick chain was set in the stone floor. A few chewed-up wads of pulped wood marked where the troll had been kept preceding the game.

He led the troll up the ramp. A pair of cellar doors led to the interior of what smelled like a stable. Four large stalls divided the room. A diminutive stable girl with ribbons in her hair stood frozen as Hellard waited for the troll. A closed door to one of the stalls creaked as a second troll pushed against the wood.

"Who are you?" the girl asked.

"Troll rescue. Stay put and don't make a sound. I'm not going to hurt you. You work here?"

She nodded. "Tonto's still alive! They said he wasn't coming back."

Hellard tossed the troll another stick. "Looks like they were wrong. Where in the castle are we?"

"The troll pen. Right next to the carriage house."

He didn't know where any of that was. "How do I get out of here?"

She looked confused. "Why?"

"This isn't a discussion. Is the outer wall close? Is there a side gate near this part of the castle that leads outside?"

"The closest is the main gate. And the wall would be difficult to climb even for someone...a person...a little less..."

"I know. I'm big. And I'm not going alone."

"You're taking Tonto?"

"I'm not leaving him to get chopped up in the catacombs."

Something in the girl's dull eyes shone. Before he could stop her, she ran for the second pen and began to undo several bolts holding the gate shut. When she swung it open a second troll emerged, this one with olive skin. The girl picked up another bag and threw the troll a stick from it, which the troll snapped out of the air. The new troll grunted with pleasure as he crunched on the treat.

She beckoned the new troll. "Come, Mudo."

"What's to stop these things from killing us besides fish-flavored sticks?"

"Keeping them fed. But the queen ordered them starved this week. I snuck Mudo food but wasn't able to give Tonto anything."

As if on cue, Tonto belched.

Hellard stepped back. "I think he ate. So if the wall can't be climbed..."

The girl took Hellard's bag of troll treats and went to the barn door. "There's another way."

They emerged between two large wooden buildings with the castle on one side of them and the high stone wall on the other. The sounds of the catacomb party swirled around them. But Hellard also heard a commotion from the ramp below the troll pen. The castle also kept plenty of guards on the walls. Soon an alarm would be raised and they would be surrounded. Killed.

The girl ran around the corner of the neighboring wood building. Hellard followed but stepped aside as both trolls lumbered after her. Twin doors stood open. The queen's resplendent carriage waited inside. But the girl continued along to a square drain cover. The metal grate led down to a dark hole.

He almost laughed. "I can't fit down that. And if I can't, they can't."

"It's our only chance. I've cared for them for months and don't want to see either of them hurt."

The trolls were completely incurious about the sky or world around them. Both had their attention fixed on the bags with sticks, even as both chewed noisily. They stank of sweat and rancid fish.

"Then why didn't you take them out of here before today?"

She kicked at the grate. "Because I was scared. And I'm not strong enough to move that out of the way."

Hellard took a moment to consider the wall. Perhaps climbing was still an option. But even as he considered the possibility he saw there were no fingerholds to accommodate his supersized digits. He crouched and lifted the grate. It resisted him for a moment, then gave. Clumps of dirt fell away.

He stepped aside.

Without hesitating, the girl scrambled down the hole. "Tonto! Mudo!"

Amazingly, the giant green creatures followed. Seeing the monsters squeeze down the hole made him realize that if trolls ever set their tiny minds to infiltrating a place, there would be little anyone could do to stop them. He didn't know what twists and turns the tight space beneath his feet might hold. He took a final look at the castle.

He wished his new friends a good fight before their inevitable deaths. Hoped they'd take many a pureblood nobleman with them. Then he jammed himself into the hole, pausing long enough to draw the grate over him before plunging into darkness.

Chapter Forty-Three

DIGGER TRIED TO TUNE out the rising wail coming from ahead of him, but it only got louder as he ran down the hall. He pushed the sight of Paulus dying from his mind. The wound in his side ached and felt damp. He must have popped stitches sometime during the last fight.

A door before him swung open and he paused at the doorway.

The wail ceased. The unseen audience above stirred as the room lit up.

Four bluish-green globes threw light across an ornate bedchamber of ridiculous proportions. Water poured from the mouth of a stone serpent mounted on the wall. Sheer drapery dangled from the ceiling, creating the illusion that the room resided beneath the waves. The "bed" occupying the center of the room was a raised platform of bright, polished pebbles with a headboard and footboard of driftwood. The walls featured colored carvings of fish and a rising forest of kelp.

Isabel reclined on the bed, propped up by a mountain of pillows. She still wore the seashell gown and octopus mask she had been wearing earlier. She held a silver scepter in her hand but appeared to be struggling just to sit up.

Standing by the bed's headboard were four fel wearing fancy armor and helmets. They had swords in their hands. A thin chain attached each of them to the stone floor. All four of them were muttering and breathing hard. One of them was of slight build. He wavered on his feet.

Digger hurried towards him. "Monty?"

Bootsteps and voices were approaching. Angel and his fellow contestants would be there any moment. But as Digger reached for Monty, his brother snarled and swiped his blade. Reeling backward, Digger almost dropped his club as he retreated. Monty reached the end of his chain and was gasping while slashing the air wildly. The other three bed guardians perked up, spewing a mad, meaningless string of words. One laughed. Another started to moan.

As he looked at Monty and the chains holding him, the door to the hall swung shut. He could hear the contestants shouting and banging on the door.

"As the gallery fills, witness the spectacle of the nymph's bedchamber!" the game caller announced.

The crowd sounded like it was settling in. A curtain obscuring the gallery opened, revealing an array of spectators. There were oohs and whispers.

"Move so I can see!" the heckler said.

Another moment of rustling and scraping followed before the game caller spoke again.

"Here the undersea goddess plies her lust on her slaves! Their minds have turned to madness as their bodies are hers to command. But as our surviving adventurers will discover, her slaves aren't her only defense. Tread lightly, brave warriors!"

The door to the hall opened. Angel and the other contestants entered cautiously with Marisol in the lead.

The light globes shifted from green to red. The seaweed paintings now revealed illustrations of fanged monsters hiding among them. Something clinked behind the headboard. One of the other bed defenders who had been tugging at his chain suddenly came at Digger as the chain length extended. Digger circled around one of the light globes but the mad fel kept pursuing him.

The booming voice of whatever actor was playing the nymph resounded from above. "You dare come here to my sacred home and disturb me?"

"They dare," said the heckler, snickering. "Otherwise we wouldn't be here."

"Face my magics! Face my wrath!"

A thundering wave effect rolled through the lights. Game attendants must have been pounding sheets of metal or using other noisemakers. Even the mad fel paused to look around him in fear and confusion.

"Ignore everything but him," Angel said to Marisol.

The two began to march towards Digger.

One of the other adventurers motioned to his fellows and pointed at Digger. "He's the one with all the tokens." They were all coming for him now.

Digger maneuvered around the outside of the room. The fel chasing him hurried to follow but the extended leash reached its limits and stopped him short.

He searched for any advantage as he looked behind him. "Monty? Isabel? Snap out of it!"

Monty and the other two chained fel remained in place. They seemed wary of the contestants moving past. But Isabel managed to kneel on the bed. She pointed her scepter towards the group of adventurers.

"Thorn!" she shouted.

The last adventurer in the group fell to the floor, clutching an arrow in his side.

What had just happened?

Isabel also looked surprised. She wavered and looked as if she was struggling not to collapse.

But Digger had little time to think as Marisol was closing in on him. The fel who had chased him rushed her. Marisol parried and stabbed the fel in his arm, causing him to drop his blade. With a thrust, she slipped her offhand weapon between segments of the armor and into him before shoving him aside.

"Isabel! Whatever you're doing, do it again!" Digger said.

She held the scepter out. "Thorn!"

An arrow flew. Another adventurer went down. This caused the others to take cover. Isabel pointed towards Marisol.

"Thorn!"

Marisol was struck in the back and fell, squirming as she tried to dislodge the arrow.

Isabel was grinning now. Glaring at Angel. "I hope this hurts. Thorn!"

Nothing happened. She shouted the word again. Waved the scepter about with no results.

The game caller announced, "The nymph's magic is spent."

Angel let out a laugh as he rose. But as he began towards Digger, the adventurer with the locks of black hair smacked Angel across the back of the head with the flat of his short sword and kicked his rapier away. He seized Angel by the arm and shoved him towards Monty and the two chained fel. The two didn't hesitate. They grabbed Angel and proceeded to pound on him, dropping their swords and using their fists. Each blow was a meaty smack. One of them began laughing wildly.

The contestant with the fancy hair turned to face his companions. "Lord Angel deserves none of the spoils. They're ours. Let's finish this."

Monty threw down his sword and tried to pull his chain further, but it wasn't extending. The other two were tearing through Angel's shirt, perhaps believing he held the means to escape. Angel slapped feebly at them.

Digger stepped around one of the lights as three adventurers moved to hem him in. He swung his whale bone and shattered the globe. The purebloods flinched as glass flew. Digger ran across the room to the next one and smashed it too. A rapier-wielding man charged, but Isabel hurled the scepter and caught him across the legs, causing him to stumble.

"Kill the lights!" Digger called.

He ran for the third globe and brought his whale bone down. Isabel leaped off the bed and scooped up a dropped short sword. She dashed the final light to pieces. The illumination above the walls wasn't enough to keep the room lit beyond a milky gloom.

"We can't see!" the heckler cried.

Digger's keen eyes adjusted quickly. Isabel made it to Digger's side. She had thrown off the mask and headdress and had the hem of her gown bunched up in one arm. He pulled her along towards the gurgling fountain. That corner of the room held the deepest shadows.

The contestants had paused to regroup. They exchanged whispers. Digger could easily make out their shadows as they began moving slowly towards Digger and Isabel. They swished and probed with their weapons.

With his club, Digger busted the ceramic edge of the fountain's pool and stepped away. Water poured out onto the floor and more kept flowing, gushing from the serpent's mouth.

The contestants continued to advance. Soon their footsteps sloshed as they stepped into the growing puddle. They stopped.

"Where are they?" one of them whispered.

The shapes edged closer. One kept thrusting his rapier while the second kept his head low as he walked, palm forward and rapier back and ready to strike.

Digger tapped the bone in the water.

"Right here," he purred. "We're right here."

The man with the mane of black hair was in the lead. "Darkness and a little water won't save you. Give up your tokens and I let you live."

"It's us or them, boys," Digger said. "Us or them. Use your nose. Smell the perfumed soap. And listen for their steps."

"What are you talking about?"

But Digger hadn't been speaking to the pureblood. Just a moment before, Isabel had whispered, "I pulled the chain pins. The other fel are loose."

The two who had been savaging Angel charged, crashing into a pair of adventurers. The contestants screamed as the fel dragged them to the floor. But two were still armed and closing in on him.

Digger sprang forward and delivered a pair of sweeping blows. The first knocked the dark-haired contestant's sword back. The second took him across the head and dropped him. But Digger's bone was now cracked in half. The last standing contestant sidestepped, stabbed upward, and caught Digger in the left shoulder. Digger pivoted and used what remained of his club, bringing it down on the steel blade, ignoring the searing pain exploding down his arm. The rapier slipped from his opponent's grip. Digger dropped the bone and leaped onto the remaining adventurer. Even with one arm dangling uselessly, Digger clamped a hand on the man's throat. He slammed the contestant's head onto the wet floor until the man stopped moving.

"Isabel?" he called.

The collared fel were still busy savagely pounding on their victims. Past them, Isabel was making her way around the bed.

Digger picked up a rapier. His brother was cowering by the entrance door. Digger pulled him to his feet and walked him to the bed and had him sit. Looked him in the eye.

"Are you hurt?"

Monty shook his head.

"Don't move."

Digger found Isabel crouched over Lord Angel. She held the tip of the short sword under his chin. He appeared unable to move. His face had been beaten to a pulp.

His words bubbled and sounded thick. "You can buy your freedom, little Sprite."

"That's not my name," Isabel said. "Not to you, anyway."

"Isabel then. I won't use your pet name ever again. There's enough tokens to pay for all of you to get out of this cursed place. And I can give you...as much as you need. Set you up like Jamie wanted to do. I guess you'll be free to run off with him. My father doesn't even need to find out. You'll be together."

Her tone was frosty. "You'd do that for me?"

"Yes. Anything. Please."

Lights were coming up from the gallery above and from unseen lanterns behind the walls. The etchings vanished. The water stopped flowing. The *tick-tick-tick* of the clock yielded to the gonging of a bell.

"Round is over," the game caller said. "The game...is over!"

The crowd murmured softly. Isabel was pressing the tip of the blade against Angel's neck. Another ounce of pressure and they'd be done with the nobleman.

Digger placed a hand on her shoulder. "I'll do it if you can't. But the round is over. Killing him will be a new crime."

She shook her head. Withdrew the blade. Angel had his hand up to ward off a blow, but she cast the weapon aside.

The queen clapped her hands. "Why aren't we congratulating the victors of this round of catacombs?"

A round of tepid applause began but died out quickly.

The game caller cleared his throat. "The nymph's champions have prevailed! Her magic and her slaves have overpowered the squabbling adventurers. If any of them survive, it will be as her new thralls."

He kept talking but Digger stopped listening. He watched Lord Angel for a while until he was sure he wasn't going to get up. Once Isabel moved, he could finish him with a quick thrust of the rapier.

"Weapons down," a game attendant hissed.

Digger turned to see several hidden doors had opened. The previously invisible archers stepped in holding short bows loaded with arrows.

The brightly dressed fel attendant was marching ahead of the archers. "Put the sword down."

Digger hesitated for a moment. But he set the rapier on the bed.

The two chained fel squinted at the new lights and scrambled behind the headboard. Monty looked dazed. Even Isabel was wobbling on her feet. Were all of them drugged?

Digger rose to face the attendant. "We're pardoned? All of us?"

"Yes. By the rules of Queen Claudia's games, your infractions have been erased. The monsters have won the day. Bravo. This can be inscribed upon your skin for all to see, if you wish."

He gestured to Angel. "What about him?"

The queen appeared above them at a section of the gallery where the bars had been removed. "The round is over. The game is over. You had your chance."

Crouching, Digger picked Angel up. The nobleman began to struggle. Digger got him into a headlock.

"What if your game is over but mine isn't?" Digger asked.

The queen's steady smile never wavered. "Kill him and see what happens, dearie. Murder is illegal on my island. You know that."

"But he can kill my kind?"

"You've won. You have your freedom. You have wealth, if you take your prizes. But you better move fast if you want anything for yourself."

It would be so easy. So quick. Angel would never hurt anyone again. Digger would lose his life but Paulus would be avenged. But surely Monty and Isabel both would pay for his act.

Digger turned in time to see Isabel pocketing tokens from each of the fallen adventurers. The archers remained focused on him. He tugged the token from Angel's lapel and let him drop to the floor. He flipped the token to Isabel. Handed her the rest of them from his pocket. She looked at him with a blank stare before moving to the last of the contestants.

He got Monty up. But the guards still had their bows trained on him. A murmur rose from the crowd.

The queen clapped her hands. "My guests! To the banquet hall for refreshments and the awarding of prizes."

While they filtered out, leaving her alone in the gallery, Digger and the rest of the fel were kept in place. He tensed up, expecting the worst as he steadied his brother.

He fought to keep his voice calm. "We'd like to leave now."

"Aren't you forgetting something?" the queen asked. "Before you walk free from here, you have something which belongs to me. A piece of paper. A trifling thing you should never have had."

Digger fished the crumpled page out. The attendant moved to take it but at the last second Digger held it back.

"Lord Angel wanted this so badly, enough that he'd try to kill for it. Your plans—I know what they are."

"Do you?" the queen asked.

"I know what lies to the east of your walls. If your catacombs expand that way, I know what will happen."

"What is it you think you know?"

"There's a lot of fel in this city who have buried loved ones in East Hill cemetery. The oldest of the crypts run this way towards the castle. What do you think will happen when the population finds out what your expansion will mean?"

"My subjects will do as their told."

"You can push us only so far." He wadded up the page and tossed it over. The attendant grabbed it, unfolded it, and nodded to the queen.

Digger tried to get past the guards. At any moment he expected them to either seize him or attack. But he had little strength left to do anything about it. Monty was breathing hard and had his eyes clamped shut.

"It's okay. It's almost over."

The guards stepped aside.

"Oh, champion?" the queen called. "You're welcome back here anytime."

Chapter Forty-Four

DIGGER AND THE OTHER monsters were escorted through a series of narrow hallways and several sets of stairs until they returned to the original waiting room. More food was there and a few waiting servants immediately moved to help them. Monty and the others appeared groggy, their earlier madness evaporated.

The attendants assisted in removing costumes and makeup.

Monty was unhurt but continued to shiver uncontrollably. Digger sat with him as his own bleeding shoulder was sutured and bound. Isabel was returned to the room, having been changed out of her gown and into a simple dress with an apron and bonnet. She eyed the servants with suspicion before checking on Monty and Digger.

"He's okay," Digger said. "We're okay."

She nodded and sat next to them. She didn't seem to want to speak in front of the castle staff. A moment later she began counting her tokens.

The other fel were tearing at the buffet. It was as if they hadn't eaten in days.

A servant began wiping thick makeup from Isabel's face with a white handkerchief and some kind of cream. Isabel placed the tokens into the pouch of her apron and allowed herself to be tended to.

"Is that enough to buy you what you want?" Digger asked.

"And what is it you think I want?"

"You want your Jamie to live. He survived. You want Lord Angel to land in trouble with those gangsters. But using the tokens to buy that thing will make you a target. It'll also justify this place in the eyes of the entire city."

She pushed the servant away and proceeded to wipe the makeup from her eyes. "I don't like your tone. We nearly died today. What's wrong with wanting to salvage something out of this?"

"Taking a prize validates the games. Think about every pureblood who watched us fight. In their minds we earned our reward. If we take it, it means we agree to play by their rules."

"From what I've heard, more of them died this season than any other. Thanks to you."

"So what do you think claiming the queen's prizes gets you?"

"Security. A place of my own in Diregloom."

He scoffed. "You think you and Jamie will be safe here?"

"No. Jamie will have to go home. He was stupid to come. This place is too dangerous. And if you think I'm being selfish, I do support the Black Rock Mission. They saved me once. I'll keep doing what I can for them so they help others like us. My question for you is, why don't you want any of those things?"

"Because there's no such thing as security here. Not for me or my brother. What's going to stop Lord Angel from coming after you?"

"Angel's days are numbered."

"So you say. But if you haven't noticed, these nobles have a way of making sure they wind up on top. You're going to want to vanish with your winnings. Get as far away from here as possible. Maybe Hellard can help. We can't take the chance Angel is just going to get taken out by this gangster."

She nodded but appeared to be in thought. She scooted over to look at Monty. Took his hands. Digger was surprised to see his brother manage a slight smile.

"He'll be fine." Digger got up and tested his shoulder. The ache was fierce, the pain sharp. Each motion sent jolts up his neck and down to his wrist. He paced impatiently for whatever was to come next.

The attendant in the clown costume appeared at the cell door and invited them to follow. They took a hallway to the base of the ramp that would lead them up out of the maw of the catacombs. From the sound of things, the party above was well underway.

Digger stopped the clown. "We're released, right? Isn't there another way out?"

"It's part of the show," the attendant said. "Act fierce, if you could."

The clamor died when they emerged out of the demon's mouth and faced the throng of spectators. A few people cheered, including a man who sounded like the heckler. But most jeered and all too quickly there came a hail of canapés, fruit, and wine glasses.

Digger did his best to shield his brother as they walked through the mob. Isabel tried to face the crowd defiantly but had to duck more than a few wine flutes that shattered around them. The other two fel followed closely. The initial barrage petered out and stopped entirely when a waiting group of palace servants wearing long brass-buttoned orange coats stepped forward, providing them a corridor that led to the front of the castle.

The queen and several other nobles waited. The queen's smile had been replaced with regal coolness. Angel's brother Jamie stood at her side. A balding man dressed in a white ruffled shirt and waistcoat spoke up. Digger instantly recognized the voice. He was the game caller.

"The victors of the games may now choose their prizes. Please follow me."

The queen and her entourage preceded them towards the castle doors. Most of the nobles in the crowd bowed.

Isabel began to climb the stairs after her. "Aren't you coming?"

Digger remained where he was. He had Monty by the arm. The exit gate was a stone's throw away. He had one last token in his pocket. He tossed it to her.

"Wait for me," she said.

Digger made no promises.

IT FELT UNREAL WALKING out the castle. It was as if any moment a guard would stop them and they'd be rearrested. Some new rule would be added, or their charges would be reinstated at the whim of Angel, the queen, the sheriff, or some other random noble.

The mass of partygoers outside were clapping wildly and no one threw anything. Most were fel, but there were also many pureblood rank-and-file citizens of Diregloom surrounding them. None of the faces gawking at Digger and Monty had been in the gallery. They had heard the details of the game's outcome secondhand. Perhaps some had made money off the long odds of a monster winning the games. It didn't matter, not to Digger. He had to get his brother out of there, find a new way to keep their heads down, and hope by the end of the next week their faces would be forgotten.

They were jostled. More than a few backslaps followed, and then some buffoon spilled a mug of beer all over Digger. Digger shoved several people aside and hurried Monty past the worst of it. The crowds thinned by the time they made the first fountain.

Monty looked greener than normal. "Where are you taking me?"

"I'll figure it out. We're almost out of here. We'll find someplace safe to hide."

His brother shook his arm free. But he was instantly unsteady, and he leaned against an olive tree growing at the side of the cobblestone street.

Digger steadied him. "Just throw up. You'll feel better."

Monty was breathing deeply. "I don't need to..."

He threw up.

Digger waited until Monty was done and guided him to the spraying statue where six cherubs spouted water from bugles. Monty rinsed his mouth. There were still too many eyes on them.

"Hurry up."

But where to hide Monty? Certainly neither of their apartments. The decision came to him as he helped his brother down the length of Fountain Street towards Stockade Square. He'd take him to the last place anyone would look.

The graveyard.

THE WEIRD TWINS REFUSED his offer of coins. This was good, because he didn't have any left. They wore identical smiles and their frog eyes were wide and impossible to read.

The sister with the eyepatch draped an arm around Monty. "One as handsome as he? I'll watch him close and keep him safe."

The second sister took Monty's hand. "So smooth. So soft." She peered into his eyes. "Yet troubled."

"Keep him out of sight, even from the other gravediggers. Will your father be okay with this?"

"He's at the games," the sister with the eyepatch said. "Left us to care for the yard. Besides the other diggers, no one comes on a day like today. Yet you're here."

The second sister's tongue flickered from her lips like a snake. "With company."

"Digger?" Monty asked as he was led towards the cottage.

"They won't hurt you. I'll be back. Say, I need to borrow a cart. I've lost mine. Some tools as well."

The sister with the eyepatch raised her eyebrow. "A cart *and* tools? This will cost you, Digger. And how do you propose to pay?"

Digger sighed and waited for her terms.

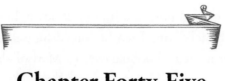

Chapter Forty-Five

ANGEL WOKE TO THE SOFT beat of a distant drum. The sound only grew as his mind tried to focus on where he was. He had been fighting in the catacombs. Overwhelmed. The gravedigger and Isabel had been making threats. Demands. But then he had passed out.

Judging by the soft linen and the bed, he guessed he was somewhere in the castle. The bed was smaller. This definitely wasn't his room.

His face itched. And still the drum kept beating, and it only got louder. He groaned as he sat up. Gauze and bandages wrapped his face. There was a wad of gauze inside his lower lip. As he pulled it out, he felt loose teeth.

Four other beds filled the room. Each had a patient in it wearing bandages. Splinted arms and legs were elevated by wires on harnesses attached to the beds. Two white-clad women tended to one of the patients. Orange light spilled in through a window.

It took Angel a moment to realize the patient the nurses were caring for was his cousin Marisol.

He swung his legs out from under the sheets. White pain shot up through his side. He felt something shifting. Broken ribs, no doubt. He gritted his teeth and prepared to stand.

A third nurse came rushing over and placed her hands on his shoulders. "You're in no condition to get up."

The nurse was a fel.

"Get away from me."

Bang-bang-bang.

A wave of dizziness almost sent him back down, but he thrust his hand out and gripped the fel's arm. Then he forced himself to stand. The nurse assisted him. He managed to hobble over to Marisol's bed. Her pallid face looked like that of a corpse. Her mouth was agape. At first he thought she wasn't breathing, until finally she drew in air and let it out in a ragged gasp.

"It's a wound to her spine," the nurse said. "One of her kidneys has failed. We will have to operate. The surgeon is coming but he's working on another wounded contestant. Lord Clement."

"Get him here now."

Bang-bang-bang. The drum kept pounding.

"He's performing an operation."

"I don't care. Tell him the queen's nephew has ordered him here."

Bang-bang-bang.

Angel winced. He had to lean on the footboard of Marisol's bed. The reek of something astringent threatened to make him gag. But the hammering wouldn't stop. The incessant pounding made his ears ring and his molars ache. He began to peel away the bandages from around his face. The noise...it wasn't coming from the window but was beating inside his skull.

"I wouldn't do that, sir!"

"Where's...my aunt? Send for her."

"I'm afraid that won't be possible," Rochus said. The steward entered the convalescents' room through a pair of double doors. He still wore the clown outfit but the cap was off and some of his makeup had streaked. The buzz of a distant party and violin music followed him.

"Don't provoke me, Rochus. Send for Aunt Claudia."

"She won't see you. You're to take your rest. And then, you're to return home."

"What do you mean?"

Rochus barely contained a smile. "The queen thought it best you go back to Bahia and your family. Loom Island isn't good for your health."

"Let me talk to her." He fought to get out the word. "Please."

"She was most insistent."

"I got her what she asked for. Everything that was taken has been returned. She can't reject me now. If I could just see her for a minute."

"She has her guests from the games and is quite busy. Perhaps I can dictate a note."

The throbbing in Angel's head felt like it was going to split his brain in two. The thought of dictating anything to his aunt's pet fel made him sick. Judging by the look on the steward's face, he wasn't going to gain an audience with his aunt anytime soon.

But then another, darker thought brought clarity to his clouded head.

"The games are over?"

"Two of the victors left before the ceremony. Quite rude. But it seems the girl Isabel held more tokens than any catacomb contestant has ever won. She purchased quite a few of the queen's prizes, to the reluctant accolades of the nobility. If I'm to be honest, several of your peers were shocked at the outcome. An upset, truly. The monsters' winning has created a buzz. Strange, though. You'd think more of them would be scared off by such an unforeseen outcome. But we've had more contestant candidates immediately apply to fight in our next season than ever before in the game's history. We'll be able to select the best nobles. The queen is very excited."

"I don't care about any of that. My aunt...her assassins...they're no longer out to kill me?"

"I'm sure I have no idea what you're talking about."

"Where's my brother? I need to see him."

"He was at Lady Claudia's side for the duration of the awards. He seems to have recovered from the blow he suffered. She's quite taken with him. Now won't you go back to bed? Your aunt has given me a bottle of her best medicine she says will make you feel...what were her words? Right as rain."

"Stay away from me, Rochus."

Angel pushed past him. Despite wearing only a nightshirt, he ran out the door of the castle ward in search of the exit.

THE SWIG OF FORTIFIED wine he took only made him feel queasier. Yet he clung to the bottle he'd taken from one of the revelers as he hobbled out the castle stable and tried to mount his horse. Even with the stable boy helping him, Angel kept hopping around in circles until he finally pulled himself to the saddle on his belly. He managed to swing his leg over, the bottle slipping and shattering at the horse's feet.

It took another moment of gripping the reins as the animal jerked in surprise before he could take control of the horse.

Bang-bang-bang went his head.

Too many green faces stared at him as he urged his horse through the crowd at the front gate. Lanterns illuminated the evening, lighting the way down to the waterfront. He shivered. He felt clammy with sweat. It wasn't very cold out, although Diregloom's fog was coming in. Yet the touch of the air felt like ice as he clutched his nightshirt and directed his horse to his townhouse.

He didn't need much. Clothes, certainly. While most of his luggage was at the castle, he had brought a couple of satchels of party clothes to the rental house along with toiletries and his best shoes. And if he didn't want to wait for the morning ferry, he'd need money to pay a fisherman to climb out of bed and get him away from Diregloom. He had a small stash of silver, his emergency stash. It would be enough.

He needed time to regroup. Heal. Find new allies who would return to the island with him. Then he could confront Jamie, find Sprite, and take the treasure that belonged to him. His injuries and the embarrassment he had suffered were all temporary setbacks.

Returning to the townhouse was a risk he'd have to take. Red Eye would still be looking for him. But Angel would gamble that the gangster had heard he had been in the games. Angel's departure would fool everyone.

As he tied the horse off at the hitching post, he thought of whom among his cousins he might borrow money from. Red Eye would settle for a partial payment with the promise of more to come. Address the vig, worry about the principal later. Perhaps Sprite had done him a favor by winning. With his brother in the city, she'd be easy to catch.

Next he could figure out what to do to return to his aunt's favor. He managed to smile. He knew he'd think of something. Let her see he was willing to play by her rules and be a part of her games. Whether Marisol would recover was anyone's guess. He'd miss her, but a rising star like him would gather more moths.

He realized he didn't have a key. The townhouse was locked. He went around the side, trampling the flowerbed so he could get to the backyard. The small yard in the rear of the townhouse was little more than a gazebo with a pair of benches. But the back window was the easiest to reach.

He paused for a moment to press on his forehead. The throbbing felt like it might be abating. Once he got his stash, he'd be on a boat within an hour.

He didn't remember a handcart in the yard. Perhaps the owner had been by. It smelled of dirt. The flowerbed had been recently planted. No doubt the owner had been busy sprucing up the place. Angel would have to avoid him too in order to skip out on the month's rent.

The window slid open with ease. Philip or one of the others must have been careless and left it unlocked. Small blessings. It was only after he climbed inside that he saw the latch lying on the floor of the dark back bedroom. It was as if someone had forced it open, causing the latch to pop out of the window frame.

He hadn't seen any of his other companions recuperating in the ward. Had Hector died in the catacombs? Perhaps Cy or Philip had escaped from the ogre and had needed to break in through the window. But then again, maybe Red Eye had sent a leg breaker to lie in wait.

Leaving would be the best option. With his pounding head and other injuries, he was slow. But then he saw he was in Gavin's room. Gavin had brought a pair of rapiers with him. He'd worn the nicer of the two into the catacombs. But the second one still leaned on the wall behind the bedroom door.

Whatever thug was waiting for him was in for a surprise. The thought of sending Red Eye a reminder that Angel wasn't so easily pushed around almost made the banging in his head bearable.

He drew the blade and kept the stiff scabbard in his left hand. It would prove useful for parrying.

He opened the door to the front room. A set of stairs went up to the main bedrooms. Here was a small kitchen, dining nook, and what had been his companions' party room. It smelled of spilled wine and beer. More than a few bottles littered the floor along with food wrappers. A table was covered with cards and scraps of partially eaten apples, a dish of bean dip, popcorn, and half of a cake on a broken plate.

Someone was sitting on one of the couches.

Angel had been quiet but not that quiet. But the figure appeared not to notice.

He raised his rapier. "Hey. Philip, is that you?"

The person didn't answer.

"Who's there? Speak up or get hurt!"

When he got no response, he jabbed the tip of the sword into the person's arm. The figure leaned and toppled over. Stepping cautiously forward, Angel looked down and saw a scarred-face thug he thought he recognized from Red Eye's bar. But a chill ran through him as he realized the thug had fallen forward and yet his half-open, dull eyes were looking at the ceiling. His head had been twisted.

Angel's breath caught. He began to back up. Heard a floorboard creak. Turned, his instincts screaming. He raised the scabbard, but not in time. He was too slow to stop the flat blade of the shovel from smashing him in his already broken face and sending him to unconsciousness.

Chapter Forty-Six

DIGGER'S SHOULDER AND side were hurting too much to try and get Lord Angel out the back window. He wheeled the cart around to the front door. In went Lord Angel, and after a moment's deliberation he also brought out the mystery goon and lifted him into the cart. Using a bedsheet, he draped both men.

Lord Angel was tied with a curtain cord and had a rag stuffed into his mouth.

What had seemed so obvious when he had left Monty at the cemetery was now gnawing at him.

Lord Angel was the main driver behind the attempts to reclaim the lost watch. With him out of the way, the nobleman's companions were all who remained who knew their faces. And the sheriff. He didn't know what Hellard had done with two of the companions. At least one had died in the catacombs. Perhaps all of them were dead, but he thought Marisol had still been breathing. Taking out their leader might distract them long enough for him and Monty to slip out of the city.

It still left the queen's wrath. His current course would place him squarely as a target of her vengeance, if he wasn't already there by spoiling her games. He didn't believe for a moment that he, Isabel, and Monty would be forgotten.

But Digger wasn't the only one after Angel. Digger had been surprised by the man inside the townhouse and they had fought briefly. Isabel had been right. Angel had someone out to collect from him or kill him for skipping out on a debt.

Leaving Lord Angel alive would make the situation worse, he decided. He had seen in the nobleman the kind of resolve he knew too well. This kind didn't forgive or forget.

The evening streets remained busy. Another night without curfew brought the citizens out. Yet with his newly acquired black hood taken from the assassin and his wagon and its repellent cargo, he moved through Diregloom like a specter.

By the time he made the graveyard gate and East Hill, his body cried for sleep. His limbs ached. He paused to look through the quilt of fog at the crescent moon. He decided not to get a lantern. Best the sisters and Monty didn't know he had returned. He made his way to the top of the cemetery. Found his spot.

Luana – Died in Winter – Beloved Daughter of Ellen and Pablo.

Did this poor girl, whoever she was, deserve such company? But what was Diregloom but a city of strange bedfellows?

He thought little as he dug. His body was an automaton, doing what it did even as the fires within him had burned down to embers. To think was to allow the pain in. He'd rest when his brother was safe.

In the cart, Lord Angel began writhing. His boots banged on wood. Digger climbed from the pit. He dragged the nobleman off the cart and dropped him on the ground. The man landed hard. His eyes were wide and pleading. Digger was about to go back to his work when he paused and crouched.

"I have nothing for you. You have nothing you can offer me."

Angel screamed through his gag. Digger could make out the word "please."

"This isn't what you expected," Digger said softly. "But I won't waste a lesson on you in your last moments. Think on who you are. Pray, if it helps. But damn you and your kind for bringing us here."

He gave Angel a minute of quiet before finishing him off with the knife taken from the gangster. Digger then stepped back into the grave and dug the last of the dirt out before pulling Angel's body in. When he was done filling the pit he sat on the packed earth. Thought of his parents and how he had been too late to save them.

He took a moment to walk to their grave. In the silence broken only by the steady crash of distant waves, he plucked the few weeds sprouting next to the wooden grave marker.

Time for tears later. His work here finished, he headed down the hill to collect his brother.

The moon was gone but so was the fog. The wash of stars above him was a million eyes that looked past him and his world to some unseen place he would never know. He gathered the pick and his shovel and threw them onto the cart.

Lanterns were making their way among the white grave markers and headstones. At first he thought someone was looking for him, but then he saw a pair of gravediggers he knew bringing a cart to the communal grave. Another laborer was already at work, clearing the ground for the latest additions.

The dead from the catacombs, no doubt.

He avoided them as he returned his borrowed tools. He knocked on the cottage door. The sisters opened the door but said nothing. Their father, Xavier, was visible in the main room. Digger handed over a coin purse taken from the assassin. The one-eyed sister took the time to count each coin and then pocketed it without comment. Digger knew he had overpaid. Perhaps it would buy sealed lips for another day.

Monty came out of the cottage. He wore a thin blanket that he bundled around himself. He appeared cold but walked steadily as Digger led him away from the cemetery.

They were passing through the slums. By now the streets were empty. They had made the fel market and Violet Avenue when Monty stopped.

Digger frowned. "Keep up." When his brother didn't move, he held a hand out.

Monty took a step back. "No. Not until you tell me where we're heading."

"We're stealing a boat down at the waterfront and getting out of here before dawn."

"I'm not going."

Digger let out a sigh. He tried to take his brother by the wrist but Monty slapped his hand away.

"I said I'm not going."

Looking around to see if anyone was nearby, Digger saw they were mercifully still alone. But voices carried in the small hours.

"This isn't a discussion. If you want to live, you do what I say."

"No. You want to find some hole to hide in, go ahead. But that's not what I'm going to do."

Digger tried to sound calm but it was impossible. "And what are you going to do? We wouldn't have gotten into this trouble if you hadn't decided to flex your cooking chops and announce a poker game with gourmet catering."

"Don't pin this all on me. Lord Angel trying to kill Isabel started all this. But we've been pardoned. Queen Claudia said so."

"Don't believe for a second that's going to save us."

His brother crossed his arms. "I'm going back to the Dragon. And to Sofia."

"Don't you think that's the first place they'll look? Don't be an idiot."

"I love her. And I have a life I want to live. It's not enough just to hide. What's the point? How many more years are you going to live alone in your little apartment?"

"You don't even know where I live."

"Yes I do. I asked around. It took months. You're up on the fifth floor in the slums. You leave your cart where anyone can find it. Not as smart as you think."

Digger felt his face grow hot. He had done everything in his power to watch over his little brother, and now this? His voice trembled with irritation. "Go on then."

Monty hesitated. "Are you still leaving?"

"What does it matter?"

"Maybe it doesn't, at least not to you. But why couldn't you have visited? You tell me to hide and stay hidden and leave me a few coins to live on, but can't be bothered to spend an hour with me? Don't say it was to avoid being caught. I know there's a sheriff looking for you, maybe both of us. But it's been two years."

"There's a new sheriff in Diregloom. The duke of Bahia hasn't forgotten about what we did."

How could his brother not remember? The image was still burned in Digger's mind. He had returned to Loom Island after running for weeks from whatever provosts the Duke had sent after him and any others of his ranger unit who had fled instead of submitting to arrest. Digger had been too late to stop his parents from losing their lives to the gallows. He had found Monty standing over the blood-soaked corpse of the restaurant buyer. He'd had to pry the chef's knife from Monty's hand. Digger had taken his brother from there and hidden him away. Then Digger had gone after the magister who had colluded with the pureblood restaurateur in obtaining the property and business for a pittance.

His brother had always been fragile. But that night his spirit had shattered. Now hearing Monty stand up to him was both infuriating and a matter of bad timing.

"They're after you as much as me," Digger said, fighting to keep his voice even. "And after hundreds of spectators got a good look at us, we can't remain anonymous in this city. This sheriff isn't stupid."

"But you don't know if he knows. Maybe we'll get lucky. I became someone different. It's time for you to do the same. You know where you can find me."

As if that settled the matter, Monty marched past him, taking a street that would lead to the Temperance District and the Dragon and Rose.

Chapter Forty-Seven

✕

DIGGER DIDN'T THINK he'd miss the infernal curfew bells. At least they told him how much time he had before dawn but now he could only guess.

He had trailed his brother through the early morning streets and down the back alley towards the bar. Monty left the back door open when he entered. Digger remained outside.

He could hear Lady Sofia shouting and then laughing and crying. He shut the door softly and paced the alley, considering his options.

How long before the queen's guards, another cousin of Lord Angel, or the sheriff showed up? Did Monty have the night or a week before his fantasy life came crashing down? He'd give his brother until dawn. Then he'd get him to the waterfront, dragging him kicking and screaming if he had to. They hadn't survived this long just so Monty could cook a last meal with their parents' recipes.

The laughter inside only got louder. Deeper, too. Someone was inside the bar that wasn't Lady Sofia or Monty.

Digger entered, storming through the storeroom. He snatched an empty wine bottle by the neck and stepped into the bar ready to pounce.

Hellard was sitting at a table with Lady Sofia and Monty. The ogre appeared naked at first, but then Digger realized he was wearing underpants. Each held a frothing cup. A mostly empty bottle of brown liquor sat between them. They paused to look at Digger and burst out laughing.

Digger felt the stomach acid building. "What is going on?"

Monty gestured vaguely across the table at the ogre. His green cheeks were flushed a reddish brown. "Sprat's here."

"I can see that. Hellard, why are you here and why aren't you wearing pants?"

Lady Sofia tried to make a serious face but couldn't stop smirking. "Because he stinks to high heaven."

Hellard set his cup down. "I slipped through the sewers to get out of the castle."

"Why were you in the castle?"

"I was trying to get you guys out of there. I made it as far as the catacombs but there were too many guards."

Hellard grabbed a few walnuts from a bowl and cracked them open with his hands.

The ogre ate noisily. Digger waited for him to stop, which took a moment. "So why did you come back here?"

"Because we never finished our discussion. Maybe we can do that tomorrow morning. Which is almost now, isn't it? Sofia, honey, you need a clock in this place."

Lady Sofia shook her head. "Nope. Seeing the time spoils the mood."

"Hellard, there's nothing to discuss," Digger said. "Monty and I have to go into hiding. Lady Sofia, I know you and Monty love each other. Come with us. It's not safe for any of us in Diregloom."

Sofia took a swig. "This is my bar. I'm not abandoning it."

"We're staying," Monty said. "We talked about it while you were outside sulking."

Digger raised his arms in frustration. "So what are you going to do when the sheriff comes in here with a dozen men to arrest us all?"

"Why would that even happen?" Monty asked. "He came here looking for Lord Angel's companion. Lord Angel isn't around anymore. You made sure of that, didn't you?"

The table grew somber, with the three looking down into their cups.

Digger couldn't believe what he had heard. "You told them?"

"I'm right, aren't I? You didn't say you had anything to do with the magister and his guards, either. But I know you. You had the same look in your eyes then that you did when you dropped me off at the graveyard. But Sofia and Hellard are involved. We all are. Together."

A thumping came from somewhere beneath the floor. Hellard raised a finger to his lips. The thumping stopped.

"What was that?" Digger asked.

Hellard grunted. Sipped, but there was nothing left in his mug but a residue of suds. "I wasn't alone when I left the castle."

Digger went behind the bar to the trapdoor. A young girl was curled up asleep on a blanket. On top of the door was a bag with sticks that reeked of fish. He started to raise the trapdoor.

"I wouldn't do that," Hellard said.

"What's down there?"

"A surprise for anyone looking for us."

"Two surprises," Monty added. "Trolls." Then he started laughing.

Sofia's face soured. "You still haven't explained how it is that those things aren't going to climb up here and kill us."

Hellard refilled her cup from a pitcher and then his own. "Simple. We keep them fed."

"And you're okay with this?" Digger asked Sofia.

"No. But right now I'm drunk. At noontime if the lot of you are still here, we're going to have a conversation. I'll probably do some yelling."

The front door flew open.

"I thought you locked that," Sofia said.

Monty gave her a guilty look. "I thought I did too."

A gray-cloaked figure stepped inside and slid the deadbolt closed. Digger was preparing to hurl the bottle when he saw Isabel remove her hood.

"You're here?" was all he could think to ask.

"And you didn't wait for me in the castle."

"We got out of there as quickly as we could."

"I noticed. I had to face the queen alone. Things got a bit crazy. Apparently both of Queen Claudia's trolls went missing. It didn't stop her from continuing with her party. There was a ceremony for the winners. She asked about you."

"And what does she know?"

"That you're a laborer who assaulted the sheriff. She doesn't know what you do, exactly. But she was hoping to talk to you."

"About what?"

"Coming back. Fighting in her games. She said she would offer you more money than you could hope to make in a lifetime of toil."

Digger set the bottle down on the bar.

"So she has no idea I'm a gravedigger? What about Monty?"

"She didn't ask about him. As far as I can tell, she doesn't care about him or me. It's only Lord Angel who knows about us, and he's recovering in the castle ward. Once he's able to stand, he'll cause problems. With Jamie here, his father won't be pleased. Jamie was recognized by more than a few people at the awards ceremony. Word will make it back to the mainland. But Angel is the one we'll have to watch out for. He won't forget."

"About that. Lord Angel won't be looking for anyone."

Hellard let out a laugh.

"And how is that, exactly?" Isabel asked.

"It doesn't matter. He's gone and won't bother any of us. It's only the rest of his family we need to worry about. What about your Jamie? Won't he help you?"

She was silent for a moment. "I couldn't risk his life by showing we knew each other. He kept trying to make eye contact. I can only hope the queen and nobles didn't see. He tried to talk to me but I avoided him. The queen was keeping him close. She has something in mind with him, I can feel it. He's in danger. I still love him. I have to save him. But that castle—that woman—today wasn't the time. So I got out of there with my winnings. But now you tell me Angel is dead. When Jamie finds out about his brother..."

"Angel had an assassin waiting for him at his townhouse. No one will ever find either of them. No one will know what happened. But you knew he had gangsters chasing him. Others might too."

Hellard nudged a chair out with his foot. "Grab a chair."

She stood awkwardly and looked back at the door. "I didn't mean to get you all in so much trouble."

"You have your gold watch now," Digger said. "Congratulations. Be careful out there."

She hesitated. "I didn't buy the watch. At least not that one."

Digger noticed she had a large purse clutched under one arm.

Hellard snorted. "And you brought your loot here? With this gang of criminals?"

"Why are you here, Isabel?" Digger asked.

"I wanted to thank you. All of you. I would have died if Angel had caught me. But I was also thinking about what Hellard was saying earlier. There's nowhere to go but this island for our kind. We can do good if we work together. I bought as many pieces of gold jewelry from the queen's stash as I could. Those will be easier to sell. The money will help our kind."

"You said you worked at the Black Rock Mission. Why aren't you there instead of talking to me?"

"I'm not here to talk to you, Digger. I didn't even know you'd be here. I wanted to speak with Lady Sofia about her bar."

Hellard and Monty both started laughing. Digger wondered not only how drunk they were, but whether he was going to need to help his brother breathe.

Something under the floor thumped.

Isabel looked down at the floor. "What was that?"

Digger shook his head with disgust. "The queen's missing trolls."

"They're here? Those monsters are vicious."

"Hey!" Hellard said, grinning. "Watch who you're calling a monster. Those trolls are quite docile once you feed them."

"And what did you feed them?"

"You remember Angel's two companions who we grabbed?"

"You didn't."

The ogre's grin only got wider.

Lady Sofia cleared her throat and got up. "I've got a fresh basket of eggs in back, some peppers and onions. Monty, let's go make some omelets. That'll soak up some of the booze. After we eat, I'm taking Isabel up to my office where we can speak in private away from you clowns."

She took Monty back through the swinging door to the kitchen.

Hellard drained his beer and then did the same with Monty's abandoned, half-finished cup. "I don't know if that was a euphemism or not, but I hope they're actually making something to eat."

Isabel peered behind the bar where the stable girl slept.

"That's Vinca," Hellard said. "She's with me. Poor little thing is all tuckered out."

"I see. Actually I'm surprised to find both of you here. I thought perhaps Lady Sofia wouldn't like having you back in her place after everything that happened."

The ogre appeared to sober up. "Maybe it's time for a change of venue. We're doing a lot of talking with a pureblood listening in."

Digger sat between them. "My brother trusts Sofia. That's good enough for me."

Isabel joined them and leaned back on her chair. "Where does that leave you guys? Are both of you staying on the island?"

"It's a terrible idea," Digger said. "If what you say is true, you'll have a family of nobles who want to see you punished. Hellard here has the Karanog gang looking to kill him. My brother and I both barely escaped the catacombs. I don't believe the queen or the sheriff is going to forget about us and leave us alone. And now there's two trolls in the cellar."

Isabel shook her head. "How did they even get down there?"

"There's a reason you're sitting next to a half-naked ogre."

"I thought I smelled fish and maybe...something else. I just didn't want to comment. Why are you sticking around, Hellard? It doesn't sound like anyone wants to join your rebellion."

The ogre grinned. "I've got some things to think about. Maybe I just came here for the card game. Sit tight. I'll refill the pitcher and then we can solve all our problems."

Chapter Forty-Eight

DIGGER FELT LIKE HE had anvils attached to his legs as he trudged up the steps towards the fifth floor of his apartment building. The dirty nickel, indeed. He ached. The events stretching from when he had interrupted Monty's card game at the Dragon and Rose up to his early-morning sit-down with Monty, Hellard, and Isabel kept replaying in his mind.

"Fools. We're all fools."

He hadn't realized he had stopped until someone brushed past him heading downstairs. Two someones.

"Hi Digger!" one of the two boys said. It was one of his neighbor's sons, a dark-green youth with black eyes and a bright smile.

He offered a wave. Their mother wouldn't like them talking to him.

"Mama says you owe her two silver."

"And why is that?"

"She cleaned up your place, did your wash, and left you some beans and hominy. She also wanted me to tell you not to leave your cart by the stairs."

"Thank her for me, Adan."

But Adan was already gone, shouting after his brother. It was Sunday, so no work at the factory for either boy. As he approached his door he could see sunlight illuminating the tops of the nearest tenements.

Stumpy waited for him. The crow cawed once and stared intently.

Digger fished a pair of walnuts from his pocket. He cracked them and laid the nutmeat out for the crow to pick at. He watched the bird for a moment as it messily tore at the offering.

"You're going to have to learn to care for yourself."

The crow ignored him until it was finished eating. Then it took off and flew to the top of the closest building where it landed near several other crows.

People were moving in the courtyard below. Digger looked down, expecting to see more children out or neighbors on their way to Sunday worship, but instead saw Diregloom guards.

The bootsteps coming up the stairs weren't hurried and it only sounded like one person. Digger waited by the front door of his apartment. At least out in the hallway there'd be room to maneuver.

The sheriff appeared. He wore his signature green hat and cudgel and was alone. He spoke softly as if not to be overheard. "By the by, you did quite well for yourself yesterday."

"You were there?"

"I wasn't provided tickets. Besides, the games aren't my cup of tea."

Digger kept an eye on the sheriff's every movement. "It's your system of justice. Shouldn't you witness the outcome?"

"This island sees an interesting intersection of the duke's law and whatever Queen Claudia decrees."

"You handed me over to be executed in her games. Sounds like you're on board with it."

The sheriff raised an eyebrow. "You would have faced the rope for attacking me."

"And now I've been pardoned. What do you want?"

"Your pardon covers your assault on a pureblood. Not murder."

"What murder are you talking about?"

"Do you have more than one to confess to?"

Digger spread his arms wide. Gestured towards his apartment door. "If you have an accusation, you'd be arresting me. This is my place if you want to search it."

"Don't mind if I do."

The sheriff led the way inside. He made a cursory inspection of the apartment, which took only a minute. He lingered as he examined Digger's stringless mandolin.

Digger leaned in the doorway. "Maybe if you tell me what you're looking for, I can help."

"The magister that vanished two years ago—one of his last signatures was on a forfeiture order to a restaurant. Two owners, one fel, one pureblood, but the pureblood wouldn't sign off on the new title so the property was seized. There was an incident of not quitting the property and resisting arrest. The magister's notes were vague. Apparently there was a buyer who also went missing. The magister mentions two sons of tainted blood. Halfbloods. Like yourself."

The sheriff paused, perhaps expecting Digger to fill in any blanks. But Digger knew this game. He kept quiet.

"Stockade records show both the owners were executed for assaulting the city guards who served the eviction. I could only imagine how upsetting this would be to their sons, watching their parents hang, and then losing what sounds like a successful restaurant business because of the duke's edict on fel property ownership. Seems like it would have been simple for the fel party to sign over to the pureblood spouse, but the notes don't go into such detail."

Digger was clenching his jaw.

"Unfortunately the Loom Island guards aren't fond of record-keeping. For most of the guards it's hard to tell who is who among your kind. They view your people as one homogenized problem to be handled. The law, however, treats everyone as an individual."

"Is there a question here for me?"

The sheriff had the mandolin in his hands and was continuing to admire it. "These two boys would have motive to carry out an act of vengeance on the official who caused their parents' death. I seem to recall at the bar where we first met that someone there knew how to cook."

"Plenty of people do. You say this magister is missing. But then you say he was murdered."

"A court official who might or might not have been involved in suspicious activity disappearing along with his two guards, all preceded by the pureblood owner of a restaurant also vanishing? This smacks of foul play. Your pardon doesn't cover you for capital crimes you haven't yet been charged with."

"I'm but a humble citizen at your disposal. If I'm to be arrested, then I'm not resisting."

The sheriff studied him for a moment. "Of course. But if you were, I wonder if I would be able to do much about it. I also wonder, judging by your footwork displayed during our altercation, what would have happened if you had been armed with something more potent than a shovel. Would we even be having this conversation? But I digress. My investigation is ongoing. Now I know where to find you. And your brother? Did I hear right that he was one of the contestants and he also survived?"

"He and I don't see much of each other."

"Fair enough. I'm sure I'll turn him up." He produced a handkerchief and coughed. "The bad air does tend to cling to this level. Maybe if you had retained some of your winnings, you could afford better accommodations. I'm sure I'll be seeing you again, Mister...?"

"Digger. Call me Digger. Surely you already figured out where I work. And don't worry, I'll be around. Because everyone sees me eventually."

Epilogue

QUEEN CLAUDIA THE SECOND relieved her attendant of the makeup pad and tried her own hand at blending the foundation over the lines at the sides of her eyes. The dark marks beneath them were suitably covered, but bad sleep after a week's preparation for the games and two long days presiding over the festivities had taken their toll on her skin. She checked her face a final time and put the pad back in its gold case.

Sunday wasn't fun day.

She had guests to see off, mundane duties she had postponed. But first, church.

The bells tolled. These were her least favorite, brightly melodic but tinny. The tune the chimes in the Loom Island steeple played was set to a dreadful Third Scripture parable about a pair of birds which abandoned their fledgling baby that refused to learn to fly. Paying the clock keeper to change the song was on her to-do list.

But not today.

She hurried down the stairs. Her dutiful steward fell in behind her. Whether he ever slept, she didn't know.

"My queen..." he prompted.

"No time, Rochus. I managed to oversleep and I'm late."

"Viscount Ilario was hoping to speak with you before he departed."

She stopped at the bottom newel and cocked her head. "What? He's supposed to accompany me this morning to church. Where is he?"

"I persuaded him to wait in the tearoom. He almost left at dawn."

"Why didn't you wake me?"

Rochus dipped his head. "My apologies. Your orders."

Her Sunday gown wasn't made for hurrying. Her outfits from the previous days' activities had been surprisingly lightweight and able to handle the many stairs of the catacombs. But today she hadn't been expecting to do more than step in and out of her carriage.

"My dear viscount," she said as she glided into the tearoom.

Viscount Ilario was dressed in a stark black suit with a white shirt and dangling black bowtie. His face was ashen and stern. He offered her a slight bow, the kind of deference one shows an equal who happens to be sitting in a higher chair.

She grabbed his arm and led him to a couch. "What's this about you skipping out early? We were to go to church together this morning."

"I'm afraid I need to cancel our plans. I must return to the duke with my report."

"But that's too early. You haven't had the opportunity to experience everything Loom Island has to offer its visitors."

He sniffed. "I've experienced quite enough."

"What's changed? My dear Ilario, you can talk to me."

"The bloodshed yesterday. It was too much."

"You weren't at the games."

"I heard the reports in detail from those who were," he said sharply. "A lady of the House of Afonso told me about a pair of noblemen getting their brains battered in by a fel, others dying by sword or club. Something you could have put a hold to the first day of such madness. This is what you have to offer our duke?"

She dropped her voice. "I was clear with what I have to offer. Some come for the sport, others the story they'll tell their whispering circles at court, but most come for what they can't have in Duke Tito's land. And it's nothing he has to approve of. But he'll see a profit from this. I saw the books last night. And before you mourn any of those who lost their lives at the games' series of upsets, know that I was sure to vet all those who came through. None of them were anyone the duke would ever miss. He'll have to soothe the spirits of a few mothers and fathers who lost their errant boys to the iniquities of my island. He can rail about it, about the fel who drew the blood of the pure, about me. But Tito's no fool. Neither are you. Diregloom has a place in his kingdom. And, lest he believe we've completely lost our way, you can report that we pray for our souls and honor the sabbath. You can witness this firsthand."

He blushed. Had this pious man not heard the bells?

She continued. "I was hoping you could accompany me to church, my dear. We're already running late."

"I respectfully decline. I'll be returning to Bahia this morning."

"Oh, such a pity. I do enjoy your company. Tell your wife Trisha I send my greetings. She's a lamb, isn't she?"

"You know my wife?"

"I just finished writing her. Two letters, actually. You and I, we've had such a visit together. I'm sure Trisha will want to hear all about it. Which letter, I wonder, will be delivered?"

Ilario was completely flummoxed. He stammered. "You...you can't."

"I'll tell you what will help me decide which letter will be handed her. Seeing you in church."

The viscount didn't protest when she stood up and led him down the grand hallway to the front steps. The guest carriage awaited. Attendants helped him up and closed the door, and the carriage rode off. Her own carriage pulled up, drawn by a team of piebald horses. The mystery of the missing trolls had yet to be answered and the city watch was searching. But she had only used the trolls for her more dramatic events revolving around the games. Her horses wouldn't scare the devout, although the thought of it almost made her titter. The decorations had all been removed from the carriage. Wasn't the sabbath a day for humble reflection and modesty?

The windows to the carriage were drawn. She accepted Rochus's hand as she stepped up into the compartment. Across from her sat a red-haired young man in a peach-and-cream suit and polished buckled shoes. He closed his eyes and bowed his head. Claudia peered out the curtain as the carriage got underway.

"Not too fast," she called up to the driver.

The young man across from her appeared uncomfortable as she switched seats to join him.

"My nephew?" she prompted.

"Is still missing. One of our agents was waiting at his townhouse and vanished. There was some evidence of a fight. But our spies on the waterfront saw no signs of him or any of the other contestants you told us to watch out for who might be fleeing the city."

"The docks are a big place."

He nodded. "But Red Eye knew how important this was to you."

She patted his hand. "Did my Angel kill your agent?"

"It's possible. But if so he managed to hide the body."

"That doesn't sound like my sweet Angel."

"We also found a rapier on the floor that didn't belong to our agent. I believe Angel was disarmed."

"And then what?"

"There's no trace of him. We have men searching."

Claudia sat back to think. The clatter of the wheels faded, and even the occasional cheer from the streets didn't distract her. If Angel was fleeing from the island, as well he should, who else would be looking for him? Red Eye had bought up all his markers. Getting Angel to play her game had gone better than expected, deliciously even, as she never once thought he'd be foolish enough to steal from her to pay his debts.

"Keep looking," she said. "But be careful. This matter is, of course, sensitive. His brother is staying with me and would be most distraught if news arrived of something untoward having happened to Angel. If he's found, then let the game reach its natural conclusion. But when you discover anything about whoever might have taken him, come see me immediately."

The young man nodded. "My queen."

She opened one of the curtains and looked out at Fountain Street and the corner of Saint's Road. The church loomed. Sunday walkers on the street bowed and curtseyed as the carriage drove past. Claudia waved.

A mixed crowd waited in front of the church. They wore their best and brightest and held white and yellow peonies in hand. They raised their floral offerings and hailed her. Her steward swung down from the driver's seat and helped her down. She took him by the arm. Pureblood and fel together for all to see. For wasn't that what Loom Island stood for? Home and hearth for all of God's children.

The viscount was already entering the church. She paused to look at the sea of faces. Adoring. Loyal. Yet someone among them had taken her nephew, and most likely killed him. But she kept suspicion from her face and maintained her smile.

Angel's brother Jamie, the oldest of her own brother, Count Barca, was waiting at the church entrance. His presence would surely cause a stir. Barca would demand his return and would complain. The duke would hear about it. Yet Jamie had agreed when she had invited him to stay on the island, at least for a while as he recuperated from his concussion. Claudia had been so delighted he had decided to play in her games. And now she knew that he was smitten with the fel woman who had purchased up so many of the game rewards.

As if she'd miss the big eyes those two lovebirds were making with one another.

Claudia had made him promise to tell her the full story at supper this evening.

She felt flushed at the thought of how amazing everything had turned out. The game, the surprises, the thrills and shock the crowds had felt. It truly warmed her. She feared she would fidget throughout the sermon. She couldn't stop thinking about the catacombs.

How odd the winner was, and she didn't even know his name. How he had fought to save his own kind! And after his victory? He had given all his tokens away. The fel woman hadn't hesitated to snap up enough gold jewelry to set her up quite nicely. But the winner, this halfblood who had been convicted of assault on the sheriff, had hurried off, perhaps so overjoyed with freedom he didn't want to spend another minute in the castle.

Still, Claudia smiled.

She would need to speak with this fel. He had gotten his hands on her notes for expanding her catacombs and had even dared confront her at the game's conclusion. What would happen if word got out about her plans?

Trouble.

So much could be solved with a new round of games. If the winner could only be persuaded to return. Claudia would gain a veteran player and have the pleasure of seeing him silenced. Those nobles who had lost loved ones to the games and to the winner's brutal hands were angry, and that anger needed to be directed to the right place. If he didn't come back, he would have to be found. She didn't like losing. This fel was playing his own game where she didn't know the rules.

But Queen Claudia the Second was a quick learner.

He had been the sheriff's prisoner. Perhaps he could shed light on his identity.

With a regal smile, she held out her hand and collected Jamie. With him on one arm and Rochus on the other, she strode through the tall copper doors of the church with a thrill. Along with the next season of catacombs to plan, there was a new game to play. And Lady Claudia always played to win.

THANK YOU FOR READING. I hope you enjoyed *Midnight Monster Club*.

Please take a moment to leave a review. Even a short comment helps small press and independent authors find new readers. I look forward to reading your comments.

The Dragon and Rose **continues the adventure!**

A killer of purebloods stalks Diregloom...

But this time Digger has nothing to do with the crimes.

As the bodies start stacking up, he realizes there's a connection between him and the perpetrator which lies in Digger's recent past.

If the murders continue, the dark crimes will upend the fragile liberties enjoyed by the fel of the city. Siding with the sheriff will make enemies of friends and reveal his identity to Queen Claudia, who has been searching for her reclusive catacomb champion.

For Queen Claudia has new games in mind more deadly than any her subjects have ever seen. And Digger is the missing piece which will make her dreams a reality.

Part two of the Fallen Rogues series, *The Dragon and Rose* continues the dark fantasy adventure started in *Midnight Monster Club*. Grab your copy today![1]

Kind regards,

---

1.   https://books2read.com/dragonandrose

Gerhard Gehrke
https://www.gerhardgehrke.com/

Other novels by G. Gehrke

Goblin[2]

Goblin Apprentice[3]

Goblin Rogue[4]

Goblin War Chief[5]

Goblin Outcast[6]

Fallen Rogues

The Midnight Monster Club[7]

The Dragon and Rose[8]

The Chapel of the Wyrm[9]

The Minders' War

Refuge[10]

The Glass Heretic[11]

The Children of Magus[12]

Blood of the Masked God

Red Wrath[13]

Blue Mercy[14]

Yellow Envy[15]

---

2. https://books2read.com/goblin

3. https://books2read.com/goblinapprentice

4. https://books2read.com/goblinrogue

5. https://books2read.com/goblinwarchief

6. https://books2read.com/goblinoutcast

7. https://books2read.com/fallenrogues

8. https://books2read.com/dragonandrose

9. https://books2read.com/chapelofthewyrm

10. http://books2read.com/minderswar

11. http://books2read.com/TheGlassHeretic

12. http://books2read.com/thechildrenofmagus

13. http://books2read.com/redwrath

14. http://books2read.com/bluemercy

15. http://books2read.com/yellowenvy

Milton Keynes UK
Ingram Content Group UK Ltd.
UKHW040634310723
426074UK00001B/280